“If you
Dane’s
missing

Top Pick, nominated for
Urban Fantasy Novel for 2014

“In *Blade to the Keep*, Dane combined a variety of different themes, strong characters, vivid world, and high stakes to keep me enthralled. I am super excited that one of Dane’s many releases next year will be the third installment in this series because it has become one of my favorite UF series. I give *Blade to the Keep* an A.”

—*The Book Pushers*

“This book should be up any paranormal romance reader’s alley.”

—*RT Book Reviews* on *Goddess with a Blade*

“The thing I like the most about the book was probably the world building. I like the aspect of Rowan being the vessel for a goddess, and acting as the keeper of the treaty. It was a nice blend of mythology and vampires that was a fresh and new idea.”

—*The Book Pushers* on *Goddess with a Blade*

“An urban fantasy with vampires and a heroine who’s the vessel of an honest to god(-dess) goddess? Sounds pretty intriguing to me. But this novel offers so much more. The world Dane creates is detailed and vibrant. The way her characters lead us through the story shows how much love and work she’s put into this one.”

—*Book Lovers Inc.*

Also available from Lauren Dane and Carina Press

Second Chances
Believe

Goddess with a Blade series

Goddess with a Blade
Blade to the Keep
Blade on the Hunt

And from Lauren Dane and HQN Books

The Best Kind of Trouble
Broken Open
Back to You

And from Lauren Dane and Cosmopolitan Red-Hot Reads from Harlequin

Cake

Watch for the next book in the Goddess with a Blade series, coming soon!

LAUREN

DANE

BLADE ON THE HUNT

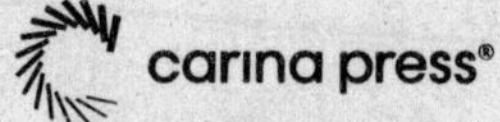

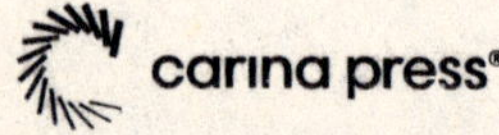

Recycling programs for this product may not exist in your area.

ISBN-13: 978-0-373-00286-3

Blade on the Hunt

This edition published by arrangement with Harlequin Books S.A.

www.CarinaPress.com

Printed in U.S.A.

Over most of 2014 I was dealing with some
pretty intense chronic health issues.
Along with every other part of my life, my writing
schedule was knocked hopelessly out of balance.

Though I'm finally recovering, I wanted to take a
moment to thank the entire Carina Press team,
most notably Angela James, for being so
amazingly supportive of me through it all.
It was one less thing to be freaked out about,
and that made a huge difference.

This one is for you.

BLADE ON THE HUNT

ONE

IT HAD BEEN a while since Rowan had seen so much blood. And considering what her last year or so had looked like, that said a lot.

She took a look at the male who was her father in all ways but genetic. Blood and gore stuck to his skin, matted in his waist-length hair. He had a faraway look on his face, what she could see of it.

Rowan had been dreading this. This inevitable decline into his personal darkness that would take steadfast and at times brutal dedication to see him through to the other side. The time when a few brief periods between the bouts of madness made you thank providence he was just run-of-the-mill insane and dangerous instead of supercharged *oh-yeah-those-fairytales-are-really-about-my-dad* hair-trigger slaughter-for-kicks sort of insane and dangerous.

Unpredictability in a creature as ancient as Theo was exactly what made him dangerous. There was no rule book. No comparison to be made. He was his own fearsome storm.

And Rowan, ill equipped as she was, still remained one of the very few who could coax him away from the song of his bloodlust.

It didn't matter whether she wanted it, or that he'd

nearly killed her more than once. Like being a Vessel to a goddess, this too was Rowan's path.

All the sounds in the night around them had cut off. No night birds, no insects. Fear and barely leashed power danced around one another in a way that gave an edge to the urgency of a solution.

There were others nearby. Theo's staff were far quieter than the two Scions who'd approached. Unable to take her attention away from Theo and risk being seen as prey, she had to hope no one did anything stupid.

But as people doing stupid things she had to risk her hide to save them from was a regular occurrence, Rowan figured she didn't have long before someone screwed up.

She took a step forward. The moon was nearly full and high overhead so it was easy enough to watch as Theo tipped his head to the side, the movement more birdlike than human.

Brigid, the goddess who inhabited Rowan's body from time to time, didn't rush to the surface, but rather filled her from the skin to her bones. Not anger as much as the need to soothe.

Goddess of the forge, yes. Ferocious in battle, absolutely. But Brigid's magic sought to heal and comfort as well. Theo wasn't well. It seeped from his pores as he stood in the middle of his fine garden, the oldest and First Vampire looking quite like an extra from a horror flick.

"Did you go out on a hunt tonight, *Vater*?" She called him father to bring him back from the brink, to underline who she was which would also hopefully keep her alive too.

Given the layers of blood and…gunk stiffening his

clothing, he'd hunted and *eaten* and then hunted some more. It said up close and personal revenge—he didn't kill them in a rage, or get superhungry and feed too long. He ingested his prey. He defeated them on every level and would hack bits up later.

Rowan wished really hard that she hadn't thought of that.

It wasn't his usual. Not even his usual slaughter in a rage. The way he killed the people he was wearing said holy mission. And there was only one reason for him to seek that sort of extreme justice—the attack that left Rowan barely clinging to life just two months before.

As for Theo's field trip? There'd be no evidence found unless Theo wanted it. *If* he had the presence of mind to remember to cover his tracks.

Things were tense enough within the Vampire Nation that if he made a mistake with this little homicidal breakdown he could be facing a big threat to his leadership.

Gooseflesh rose on her skin as she tuned her focus. Theo's pupils were enormous and his gaze unfocused. His energy was tense and unsettled instead of dreamy or drunk.

Rowan needed to exert iron will to get her heartbeat under control. If she got upset or he sensed she was scared, things could go sideways again instantly.

At least he'd be a little slower because he was digesting, but he was fast enough to kill every one of them without breaking a sweat.

Without turning around, Rowan spoke to those who were standing behind her. "Send for Nadir and Enzo. Immediately. Someone else get with Dina. She'll know what to do with the human staff."

More footsteps, this time retreating quickly, obeying her.

Good.

Theo still had his attention caught between Rowan and whatever movie was playing in his head.

"Rowan, what do you need?" Clive Stewart, the Vampire Scion of North America—and her boyfriend/lover—asked.

Clive was smooth. Elegant and classy in his custom-tailored Savile Row suits and hand-sewn Italian loafers. The Vampire had handkerchiefs on him at all times! But he could be vicious. Brutal. He was powerful. Strong. Possessive of late.

And for whatever reason, against the laws of nature, she found herself deeply in love with someone who by all rights should have been her enemy.

"We'll handle this." Warren Farrelly—yet *another* motherfucking Scion clogging up her shit when she was already standing in the middle of a minefield—spoke as he inched closer.

That unsettled energy began to sting as Theo made a sound, low in his belly, his gaze shifting from Rowan to Warren and then back to her. It took everything she had not to run and, before a breath or two, She coursed through Rowan's veins. Power at the ready.

From the corner of Rowan's eye, she caught sight of the household staff backing up slow, not attracting attention. She wished the two behind her would.

"If either of you gets any closer I will personally set you on fire. Please get the hell away from here until this is stable." Rowan kept her voice soothing and melodic as she put her body between Theo and the two master Vampires at her back.

Clive touched her shoulder and Theo *really* didn't like that. He stepped closer, the stench of death and pain seemed to come off him in waves. The glaze had gone from his eyes. This Theo stared at Warren and Clive, sizing them up. Idly thinking about ripping off arms and legs.

Yanking his attention back, Rowan went to one knee, wrist out. "*Vater.*" What she'd called him the whole of her childhood, even as he'd given her his lessons that sometimes gave her scars and always ended in blood.

What she'd called him until she'd found out her entire life had been a lie and the Vampire who'd raised her had been the one to order her birth parents killed.

Years after she'd run away and then trained to kill Vampires until she became the best at it, she found herself there on one knee, the mark of service on her wrist exposed to him. Father on her lips, ready to talk him off the ledge.

"I am here. I am well. Do you see?" She spoke in German at first. Taking more of his focus, getting him back to the present. He had to let go of whatever place he'd gone to. Whatever place the seductive song his bloodlust let free transported him to.

Until then, this imbalance would only increase until he erupted again.

The last time Rowan had thrown herself in front of Theo when he'd been overcome by madness and bloodlust, she'd been fourteen years old.

He'd been in a bad way for weeks. Had terrorized everyone, took it out on the staff. One night he'd lunged at someone and she'd stepped between. Begged him to remember them all.

He'd fed on her until she nearly died and left her crumpled on the floor of her room. She'd choked on her blood as he'd toed her to her side before walking away like she was nothing.

So *not* the time for this little stroll down memory lane.

Theo stepped closer and she tried to breathe through her mouth. He smelled of rot and death, and terror rolled off him in waves as she tried not to drown in the memories of her childhood.

Rowan switched to their old language, something close to Etruscan, she'd discovered recently. "Come inside and have some tea. I've returned from Las Vegas."

He got to his knees then, right in front of her. He took her wrist. "You were away for so very long. *They took you.* I went to find you." He spoke around a mouth full of teeth so sharp he could crunch through bone like it was nothing. The very old ones got like this in full bloodlust. It wasn't just a matter of the incisors lengthening, but of utter destruction via rows of jagged teeth that seemed to burst out. His voice was rusty and yet pointed and full of burrs.

Theo was in there and strong enough to get control again if she could just get him that last little bit. Rowan slowly raised her other hand to cup his cheek. "I am here," she repeated. "No one's taken me. You trained me too well for that. You saw me to the airfield when Clive and I left for Las Vegas. Do you remember that? I told you I'd return. I have."

He blinked several times. "You've come home, Petal." These words surer and in German. His use of her nickname was a good sign as well.

He frowned, so sad and lost. "For a very long time

you did not. You were the only sun I had and then you were gone. It tore a hole in me." His voice broke as he bent his head.

Rowan let herself love him, flaws and all. With a sigh, she hugged him briefly, pressing her lips to his temple. "I'll need to leave again. I have a life that's outside these ramparts. But part of my life is here too. I'll come back each time."

Theo shuddered for long moments as the emotions tumbled from him, over her, battering at her control. He let it all go and she had no choice but to reach out again, to touch and offer comfort.

Finally, with one long exhale, he straightened and she let go. When he looked to her again his teeth were back to normal but the darkness still lurked at the edge of his gaze.

The immediate danger had passed, but they were by no means safe, or out of the woods just yet.

A discreet cough to alert her that someone approached. It was her cousin Enzo, Theo's vassal—his companion, his servant, the person who took care of him and kept an eye on him to be sure he wasn't veering into coming back after two days covered in entrails territory.

He'd stepped into that place, a place that had been Rowan's until she'd escaped.

Enzo dropped to one knee next to Rowan, also showing his mark of service. "*Ovilius*, we've been concerned."

"I believe a cup of tea after a bath might be in order," Rowan said to Enzo. They needed Theo up and in control.

Enzo used that opportunity to be efficient, to exert

some control and said, "Yes. Just the thing. I'll have Cook make up a tray so you can have a meal and your tea with Rowan after you're settled."

The energy around Theo flexed and then unspooled with a graceful sort of menace. Rowan and Enzo remained on their knees until Theo had reached his full height.

Theo straightened the front of his jacket as if it were the finest thing in all the land. And then, as if he was impatient with how slow they were being, he raised his brows. "Well? Make that happen. I'll need my hair brushed afterward, Rowan. Then you can tell me about your trip."

She hoped he'd tell her about his. She wanted to be sure he was protected. That by some weird chance he hadn't left behind any evidence. A second pass over the scene by his Five would do that.

"I'll handle the kitchen," she said to her cousin. "You attend to him." Rowan stepped back and handed the reins over. It was *his* job now. She had one of her own to do.

"Don't tarry."

How Theo managed to flounce off with all that gunk on his clothing, Rowan didn't know, but flounce he did as he disappeared into the house with Enzo clearing the way and handling things.

She turned slowly to face Clive and Warren. "If you see him like that again, don't engage unless you're ready to be torn to pieces."

Warren looked up at the moon. "What if he left behind bodies? Witnesses? Survivors? We need to deal with whatever mess he—" Warren caught himself, corrected, "—with whatever may be at the scene."

Why Warren was making so many mistakes Rowan didn't know. He was old. He needed to never let his guard down. To have a rumor get to Theo that one of his Scions spoke ill of The First? When Theo was in this state? It could be disastrous with a dash of apocalyptic to keep it fresh.

"He wouldn't have left any bodies."

Warren had the nerve to sigh at her and give her a pity face. Like she was too naïve to know what was going on. "Rowan, you can't just—"

She cut him off with an impatient snap of her hand. "*Think*. He'd *ingest* his prey or leave it in the light. Given the state of him, he ate."

Rowan started back toward the house. Dina, the cook and kitchen manager waited for her at the doorway.

Dina had been with Theo her entire life. She, more than just about anyone, understood what was at stake here. Rowan was so relieved to have her around.

"I'm putting together a meal myself right now."

Rowan got very close, taking Dina's hands. "He's in a bad way. I'm going to need you to cut the household staff here in the evenings. No humans but for his approved skeleton crew. Send them on a vacation or whatever."

"He's been teetering on the edge for a while now. Thank goodness you got back today."

"I can't save him from this." Occasional bouts of full-on crazy seemed to come with over nine hundred years or so of existence, and Theo had hit that one multiple times. "But I can help. Hopefully. When was the last time? Was there an episode in the years I was gone?"

"He was…difficult for about two years after you left. But he righted himself. Nothing like the last time. When you…"

Rowan waved it away. The past was past. She could not dwell there and live her life fully.

Rowan focused on Dina's gaze. "All right. Thank you. Please keep David in the loop so I'm up to speed. He'll remain in contact with me as I travel." David was Rowan's valet. He'd been assigned to her several years ago and pretty much did everything she needed him to. Sometimes—okay a lot of the time—things she didn't even know she'd needed until he'd provided them.

He was bright. Loyal. Strong. Brave. Resourceful and smart. Rowan had long since given up trying to pretend she didn't think of him like a younger brother, or even a child. He'd wanted to come on the upcoming hunt. But Rowan had instructed him to remain in Las Vegas to keep things going on that end.

He'd been pouty. Had argued and got really mad. But in the end, Rowan had remained firm. There was no way she was going to lose him. She'd rather have him alive to be pissy than dead.

"Thank you, Dina. I'm going to speak with a few people, change my clothes and then head to him so give me about twenty minutes if you can."

Dina wanted to hug her, Rowan could tell. But she nodded instead, patting Rowan's shoulder and then headed off to deal with the food.

Nadir was waiting at the base of the stairs leading to Rowan's rooms and Theo's personal wing. Nadir was the official Voice of Theo's personal security force, the Five. None spoke in public but Nadir.

She inclined her chin slightly—an indication of

rank and respect—at Rowan's approach. Rowan did the same.

"Recht is with him now," Nadir began to report as they headed to the ready room the Five used as an operations center for the entire Keep. It was safer to speak there, warded against spying.

The long hallway had the sunshades up so the night sky, clear and full of stars, seemed to surround them. Rowan had loved this part of the Keep as a child. Had loved the onyx on the doorknobs, the veins of malachite in the floors. The antique furniture was lovely and intimate without being fussy. The art on the walls had changed since she was last there.

"Is that a Rothko?"

Nadir smiled. Or she thought about it and it might have shown for just a moment. But Rowan was sure of it just the same.

"It is. Do you like it? I see it more out here than I would in my rooms. It was a gift from a gentleman who seems to have more swagger than sense. But sometimes those are the ones I find hardest to resist."

Oh she wanted to know more about that story, but it wasn't the time, and given the long, handsome outline Clive made, leaning in the doorway of the ready room, Rowan wagered there was some sort of Scion business to attend to. She was happily busy which worked in her favor as she wanted absolutely no part of Nation shit. Hunter politics were bad enough. Rowan didn't need to go borrowing trouble from the Vampire Nation.

When she halted at his side, Clive searched her features for a moment before speaking. Making sure she was all right. She was working on accepting it when he did stuff like that.

"Hunter." He tipped his chin. "I'm going to talk with Warren and Paola. We're all squarely in his service." Clive'd just underlined his loyalty to The First, which she appreciated. He'd done it in the hearing of Nadir as well. Just knowing he was behind Theo made Rowan feel better, even when she knew crazy times were coming. "Come to me when you finish. We'll both have a meal with him."

Rowan shook her head, knowing that wasn't possible. "He's not going to tolerate sharing my attention with anyone else right now. I'll come to you after."

He wanted to argue. She saw it in the set of his mouth. Naturally he did because he was a master Vampire with a great deal of power and money and he was surrounded by *yes*. His staff. The Vampires in his territory—which, by the way, was an entire continent. Vampires and humans alike took one look at that face, at the clothes, the cars, the way the man so obviously knew how to treat someone in the sack, and they fell over themselves.

Rowan was a whole lot of *no* in Clive Stewart's life. He needed more *no* to combat his fussy, uptight control freakish nature. Normally it was amusing to see him struggle to accept that she'd just said no. But given the situation, she'd think it was amusing later.

In the end, he didn't argue. Which was one of the reasons she usually found herself far more enamored of kissing him rather than staking him. "All right. If you need anything."

If she needed anything he couldn't help, but she had no doubt he'd die trying. Which was more than she ever thought she'd have.

"Thanks."

He left after one quick look at her, and Rowan blew out a breath as she turned back to Nadir. "Okay so you share with me what you think I should know. This is urgent enough we're just going to have to trust one another."

"When it comes to him, to his best interests, I do trust you, Rowan." A pause before Nadir continued. "As you know, we've been investigating who assisted Enyo after she left here." The Five had been on the trail of Enyo, the badass bitch Vampire who ambushed Rowan nearly two months before.

Theo had come upon them near the end of the battle Rowan had been on the losing end of. She'd been barely alive and Theo had made the choice to save Rowan instead of continuing his pursuit of Enyo.

The depth of his rage that his rules—Vampire Nation rules—had been violated and the infraction had left his daughter clinging to life was bottomless. Rowan hated Enyo for her own reasons, but from what she'd witnessed and felt, Theo's feelings must have been more like volcanic revenge-filled hate. He'd banged her way back in the early days. Like of the world and stuff since they were both old as dirt. Enyo'd put a geas—a magical choke chain—on him so he couldn't discuss details of her origins. But Rowan knew her foster father and *he* knew those details and would simply see that geas as a way to handle Enyo on his own before she got another crack at anyone under his protection.

"Last week we located some Blood Front Vampires who had helped Enyo the night she attacked you and escaped the Keep. When we showed up to handle our breach of security, several of them had left and though we vigorously interrogated those remaining, none seemed to know where the traitors had gone to."

"Did you report this to him?" Rowan asked Nadir.

"Yes of course. You understand how our command works. And when I awoke the evening he eventually disappeared it was to find we had a few leads. I briefed him on that. We split up the leads but I'm guessing he decided to aid us."

Goddess.

Nadir continued, "Once we knew he was gone for sure, we began to head to each location we had a lead on. There were two left so I've sent out operatives to each. I'm going to assume that's where The First has been."

"You'll clean things up when you do figure it out?" Rowan asked.

Nadir only barely resisted rolling her eyes at Rowan's question, which made Rowan feel better. At least Vampires being arrogant was normal. Normal was good.

"I apologize for my impertinence." Rowan didn't hide her smirk and Nadir gave her one right back. "I'm on my way to change and then go to him now."

A quick touch at Rowan's wrist to pause her exit. "You did well," Nadir said quietly. "With him I mean. He might have been a lot worse off, and so all of us would have been too."

It meant a great deal to hear that. But it wasn't something Rowan could afford to dwell on for a while. She nodded, brisk. "I've instructed Dina to adjust the staffing. No humans here but for a well-trained skeleton crew, only in the daytime and escorted home before twilight. I think the Vampires need to do the same, but that's your stuff, not mine, so I leave it to you."

Nadir agreed. "We all feel this would be the safest option. Recht will accompany you when you leave in two days. I will remain here with the others and keep watch."

They couldn't stop Theo, not really. But every one of the Five had been with Theo for several centuries so they knew how to handle him best.

"He's going to want to come. He's made that clear over and over. He can't." Nadir meant Theo. She didn't have to give all the reasons why. She and Rowan both knew them.

"No, he can't. Not like this. I have enough to handle. I can't keep tabs on him or prevent some sort of incident. And he's absolutely veering into *I do what I want because I'm old and superpowerful* territory. I'm working on a way to bring it up and present it." She'd been working on it for the last six weeks but finding him like this only underlined it. And made it a million times more difficult.

"You know him better than most anyone else," Nadir said, letting the subject drop.

After receiving one last promise that she'd be informed of any new information, Rowan jogged back to her suite of rooms to change.

TWO

CATALINE, THE MAIN housekeeper and the overall manager of all household staff at the Keep, waited in Rowan's rooms.

"I've come to help you dress." At the Keep, Rowan found herself torn five different ways between who and what she was the years she lived within those stone walls and who she'd become after escaping. The girl she once was had been born to service. One in a very long and esteemed line that had served The First. And, she'd been special because he'd made her his. She'd been his daughter for all the good—and scarring—that came with it.

Many of the residents of the Keep still viewed her in that sense. The wardrobe full of gowns in expensive and sumptuous fabrics she'd never wear anywhere else was an exception she made. A thing she knew pleased not only those in the household, but her foster father as well.

As the dresses were complicated and tailored just for her, they required help getting in and out of. Rowan nodded. "Thank you."

Cataline strode to the wardrobes Rowan hadn't been using at all. "He purchased some new gowns for you while you were in Las Vegas." She opened the doors with a flourish.

"Some?" Rowan blinked at the wardrobe, overflowing with beautiful dresses in blues, greens and other tones that worked well with her hair color.

"You know how he can get. He discovered the internet."

So the oldest and probably one of the most powerful and dangerous creatures walking the planet stayed up late and bought shit he didn't need from eBay just like everyone else.

She'd let that be funny after she brought him back from the edge of murderous insanity.

"I was only gone two weeks."

"Time is different for him. He had trouble finding his way. Thinking of things to please you seemed to help."

Rowan shucked her travel clothes—she and Clive had learned of Theo's disappearance upon their arrival. They'd only been back an hour or so before the panicked screams had led them to the garden where they'd found Theo looking ready to go trick-or-treating.

Cataline held out the royal blue dress for Rowan to step into. While laces were done and hooks hooked, Rowan worked quickly to braid her hair and pin it at the base of her head as Theo preferred.

It would be easier to deal with him if she didn't have to hear a thousand little complaints about stupid shit like her hair.

One last look in the mirror before heading to the door. She paused at the hall. "Thanks, Cataline."

Cataline pressed a kiss on Rowan's forehead and stepped away quickly, like she sensed Rowan might pop her one.

"Please go to your rooms for the rest of the night. I'll seek you and Dina out after the sun rises."

The firming of Cataline's bottom lip told Rowan she didn't think much of that request. "You're going to need someone who knows what to do."

"He's fine for now. I promise we'll talk after sunrise. I need to know everyone is out of the way. I won't be able to really figure out what this problem looks like, much less think about a solution, if I'm worrying about how I'd begin to get you all out of harm's way should things go wrong."

"We were here when you weren't, Rowan."

Rowan's brows inched up before she could stop them. Did she detect some judgment there? After what happened to drive her away to start with?

The slap of it, the hurt wasn't something she much liked. "Yes, well, if I hadn't been here for him to drain and leave to die on the floor of his rooms, you might have been his victim. I'll have you sent for when I finish."

Rowan headed past.

"Wait."

"I need to get to him. He'll be done bathing by now." And Rowan needed to get her head back on straight. All this memory bullshit was slowing her down. This was no time to lose it over being misunderstood.

"I didn't mean to make light of what you experienced growing up here." Cataline's features were full of remorse.

A year before Rowan would have let the stabbing, snarling part of herself take over. Instead, Rowan let Her take over, filling Rowan's body with gentle, warm waves. She held Cataline's hands and looked into her eyes. It was there that Rowan was reminded that *everyone* had their own struggles. Easier to let yourself get harder to protect yourself, but at some point, it got difficult to connect with empathy. Empathy was the difference between you and the monsters you had to kill.

Cataline's life had not been easy. Her choices had been few. Far less so than Rowan. But she loved Theo with a nearly religious zeal. She wanted to protect him and Rowan too. But she was scared. Like they all were. Like Rowan was.

"We'll get through this." Just four words, but they were enough to erase some of the lines on Cataline's forehead.

"Go to him."

Rowan turned on her heel, but let Her stay, needing that comfort herself as she headed to Theo.

RECHT WAITED OUTSIDE Theo's doors. He gave her a look—assuring himself, Rowan wagered—that her appearance wasn't going to upset an already unstable First.

Also, Rowan figured, he was making sure she was strong enough to deal with Theo in his current state.

If she wasn't they were all fucked. No pressure.

There in the quiet of the antechamber to Theo's suites, Recht spoke. "He's just gotten out of the bath. Cook sent a tray. I took it in. She wasn't pleased when I made her leave."

Rowan shook her head. "We need to talk about that later. I'll go to him now."

"Don't think this means I won't make you work twice as hard on the practice floor later."

"Never dream of it. Not like I believed you'd give up any excuse you can get to cause me pain."

His usually serious features bloomed with handsome promise when he smiled like he did just then. He'd been her trainer for most of her life, ever since she could walk. When she got a workout from Recht she usually bled and left the space covered in bruises from being whacked with the practice swords.

She brushed hands down the front of her gown, smoothing the material and soothing herself in the bargain.

"Ready?"

Rowan nodded once and Recht opened the doors and she went inside.

His rooms were warmer than the hall she'd just been in. The drapes at all the windows had been drawn back and though it was cool outside, many of the doors leading to balconies and parapets had been opened.

The cart had been left in the small butler's pantry, so Rowan wheeled it into the main room where Theo had just entered with Enzo at his side.

He'd cleaned up and changed into something less murdery. A lovely pair of soft pants that were clearly made just for him. Probably a hundred years ago. And a long-sleeved shirt. He wore his favorite, hand-sewn slippers and if his eyes hadn't been port instead of their normal brown she might have thought him an eccentric professor who probably had loads of students with crushes on him.

The color meant he still struggled with his bloodlust so she knew to be extra careful.

"Come," Theo said.

She'd already shown him her mark. Once was

enough. Hopefully. Instead she took her place next to the cart and began to pour out his tea.

"You're angry with me, Rowan." Theo sat and took his cup and saucer with murmured thanks.

She was angry with just about everyone, nearly all the time. It was her basic setting. But this made her more protective than angry. More worried for him than afraid of him. As twisted as it was, she loved him.

She focused on his eyebrows for a moment and then continued to peek under lids and domes to see what Dina had sent up.

"I'm not angry with you. Did you do something I'll be mad about?"

His smile sent a rush of emotion and memory through her and she shut it all away because the last thing she needed was to be soft or distracted by that impish thing he could do sometimes.

"Okay. Would you like to tell me what happened?" she asked.

"*I'd* like some of those dumplings." He indicated the covered dishes on the cart.

How he could fit in a dumpling after he may have eaten a whole village of Vampires or humans was unclear. But maybe he didn't eat a whole village. She hoped he hadn't.

Not so much because she felt bad for whoever he'd um, eaten. Because if he had, that Vampire deserved it. Probably. And they would have been part of whatever happened to Rowan so she wasn't losing any sleep over it.

But.

"Sometimes when you're gone I forget you'll be back." His voice was sad and lost.

He didn't need to go getting mired down in the past either. "I live in Las Vegas. I work in Las Vegas. I'd been gone from there six weeks so there were several messes to clean up. You know how Vampires get the minute anyone in charge's back is turned."

His grin was nearly boyish. "Did you rough up any of Clive's people?"

"Why do you grin?"

He laughed then. "It amuses me to imagine him ruffled and agitated with you. Heaven knows you don't care when the men in your life are vexed. I'm pleased you're focused on him instead of me for a change."

"To be completely honest, he's quite capable of roughing his own people up when they step out of line. That classy exterior doesn't fool anyone who's seen him in action." Rowan wasn't too worried about Theo that she didn't warm a little when she thought of how Clive looked when he got worked up.

She needed to stop that line of thought.

Rowan reached for her old friend sarcasm. "If Vampires kept their teeth where they belonged I could retire. Sit on a beach somewhere and have cocktails."

"Petal, there are other creatures on this planet to make trouble who aren't Vampires. And you would hate the sand after a few hours. Think about how many cheerful humans you'd have to deal with."

She harrumphed but held her tongue. Rowan normally only made very careful jokes when he was in a good mood, she certainly wasn't going to make things worse when he was so clearly on the edge of losing his shit. His little tee-hee jokes were fine, but they also showed some fraying at the edge of his control. He usually kept his delight that she tortured people to himself.

He sniffed, vexed as he'd claimed earlier. "You left. And then my Five found some information about a group of Vampires who'd helped Enyo that night. I lent my assistance. I'd hoped to have this finished by the time you'd returned."

He paused to finish off a dumpling and she did the same and then had two more.

"I suppose you're angry with me. But Enyo nearly killed my child. And then these Vampires, an established house in my Nation gave her succor? They gave her a place to hide from me. From my vengeance. From my discipline. Obviously that is not…acceptable. It won't happen again. But I won't apologize."

Ha. Like she'd ever expect him to. Plus she didn't feel bad that he killed someone who broke their laws and helped a murderer like Enyo. Lastly because he worded that last bit so carefully it wasn't actually clear whether he was saying what he'd done was unacceptable or what they had done was. Theo was so sneaky.

And then she knew it was the latter when he kept talking. "I took care of some loose ends. As is my *right and responsibility.* I lead them. *I. Do.* Do you see what happens when they're not corrected regularly when they misbehave? I have to take stern measures."

Having been on the receiving end of his *stern measures* more than once, Rowan was glad he never did to her whatever he did to those Vamps. "Can you share the details with me? Who? Where? Then I can work with Nadir to add it to the database we've built for our upcoming hunt."

"I'll tell you when I'm along, naturally. I can remember a great many things."

Rowan avoided looking over at Enzo or letting her

expression change in any way from her calm, slightly blank mask. He could he genuine, he could be testing her. Whatever was going on, she had to step carefully.

"I think perhaps it might be wise if you stay here. If you're away, there are those who could use that to move on your position. This is the seat of your power. Your Vampires need to know you're here and firmly in charge."

He narrowed his gaze at her and deep inside she began to conjugate in French to keep her countenance free of any signs of agitation. Of course Brigid didn't like that at all and the warmth of Her rush of power seeped into Rowan's bones.

She didn't push, but when you had a Goddess for a boss, you paid attention when She did something.

Theo made a sound, a near growl. Clearly he'd sensed Brigid's magic. "She is so often inside you, Petal. Can I not be spared tonight?"

Brigid didn't much like Theo and he didn't much like her back. But not only was She part of Rowan, she *protected* Rowan. Seems like the two had radically different ideas of what protecting one's charge meant and the Goddess disapproved of what the younger Rowan dealt with.

"I'm going to be arranging a meeting between all the parties with a stake in this hunt. Mainly the Nation and Hunter Corp." Rowan hoped to interrupt what could be a twenty-minute-long complaint session about the Goddess. She and Clive had been traveling since the day before and Rowan lacked the stamina to dance around to keep people from getting maimed.

Enzo handed her a brush. The walnut handle was warm in Rowan's palm. Smooth from centuries of use, this had been the same brush Rowan's father and her grandfather before that had used to brush Theo's hair.

A brush she'd used from the age of three or so, when she began to attend him. "Would you like me to brush your hair now?"

"Do you think me so easily swayed?"

Goddess, if only.

"I can quite honestly say I do not think you easily swayed on any issue."

His brows rose and then he smiled like a toddler who'd been caught sneaking a cookie.

"All right then." She stood and held the brush aloft. "You know you can't come. You're going to extract something from me as a bargain to stay here so let's get negotiating."

Theo clapped his hands and moved so she could settle in behind him and begin long strokes through hair as pale as moonlight. Soft. The cool silk of it on her arms and hands as she brushed it was a good memory. Brushing his hair had soothed them both many, many times.

"You know you're the only one I allow to do this. Enzo is very good but he doesn't massage my scalp like you do."

Rowan met her cousin's gaze over Theo's head. He didn't react when she rolled her eyes, but she knew he was amused.

But it was still dangerous. The air in the room was unsettled. Theo gave off angry waves of energy from time to time. He wasn't under control. He tried though, and that had to be enough until she could figure out another away or until this madness passed and he returned to red alert homicidal and cranky instead of melting the crust of the earth going to destroy everyone crazy.

"You're very spoiled." She brushed and brushed, feeling the tension in his muscles release little by little as she kept up.

"I am."

"Where did you go, *Vater*? Your Five need to know."

"Do you think me so careless as to leave evidence?"

She kept her tone soothing. "No. I think you're very powerful and sometimes you forget the human world is different now. They can find so much with one strand of hair."

He waved a lazy hand.

"Don't underestimate them. I work with humans daily. They're not as strong as Vampires, but they're curious and inventive. They already have so much fascination with Vampires that if they knew you really existed you might find armed troops on your doorstep while you are resting."

"I still know how to pour boiling oil on anyone attempting to breach my lair."

True. He kept giant cast-iron cauldrons at the spouts and there was always enough tinder to start a fire and get that oil—already waiting in the cauldrons—boiling hot and ready to kill invaders.

Some kids had earthquake drills at their houses growing up. Rowan had learned that and laughed and laughed.

"You think me weak?" He was cranky again, though it wasn't aimed at her. Not yet.

"I think you very powerful. A shark sometimes forgets it's not the only creature with teeth in the ocean, yes? I do not want you to get kidnapped by shadowy government agencies." Not that they could hold him very long, but it would be quite the mess.

"Bah, shadowy!"

"Bah? I *work* for a shadowy agency. I would be one of the type of people sent to take you. And your household staff. And your Vampires all over the planet. You take this far too lightly."

"You said you weren't angry, Petal, but I think you are."

She realized she was. Worried about him too. Fuck it all twice sideways. She wasn't supposed to be back here wanting to protect him again. Seems old habits died hard and damn if she didn't love this whackadoodle old weirdo.

"I'm angry you're being careless with your safety. I'm not questioning your ability to protect yourself when attacked. But there are elements—human elements—who'd stop at nothing to have you. And there are Vampires who would use this to take over the Nation."

"You worry for me?"

"Of course I do. Where did you go? Let us help or I shall be very cross with you."

He stilled and she continued to brush and hoped she masked her fear.

"I will tell you and I will stay here."

She waited, brushing, knowing there was more.

"I would probably feel far better if I was able to see my daughter more often. You're very stingy with your time."

Stingy? He was so dramatic. "Did I not recover here for six weeks before I went back to Las Vegas? I'm here now and will be for a few more days. Hardly stingy."

"You were nearly dead during part of that time and would not do well to remind me of it."

Anyone else on the entire planet and she'd have hit him on the back of the head with that brush hard enough to render him unconscious for being so annoying.

Instead she made herself not yank the brush too hard and waited him out. He'd spill it eventually. After he pouted and complained some more. She needed to have Carey add a few terms to his search list so she'd think on that while mentally scouring Theo's complaints until she got to the heart of it and finally worded her offer however he needed to hear it so they could be done.

"I would rather like to see you. And Clive, he's permanent is he?"

"He's not dying anytime soon. Unless he annoys me too much."

Theo made a sound and waved a hand. "Don't avoid the question, Petal."

"Yes, he's permanent. He's in the family business so to speak. He's nice to look at. He doesn't burst into tears when I have to kill something."

Theo laughed this time. "Bring him then. I'll need to invite Warren for another time or he'll be petulant."

"Warren?" *Petulant?* Really? She wasn't sure she'd ever seen Warren petulant.

Theo looked over his shoulder at her, chiding. "While the Keep is akin to Vatican City, Germany is in Warren's territory. Another Scion comes to visit and it only makes all the rest of my children petty and childish about what is fair. Fair. Beings who span into the millennia and they still mewl at me about who gets more love from poppa."

Oh that. Vampire politics were so dumb. She'd make a crack, but again, scary old Vampire on the edge and also, Hunter politics were just as dumb so she couldn't really cast stones. Though maybe she should cast them at people's heads so they'd be unconscious and she could get on with her business.

"I know you come to Ireland for your goddess' holy day and your birthday at that time. I won't get in the way of that part of your life. I know you belong to Her then. Afterward, I'll expect you for a week."

As Brigid's Vessel, Rowan returned to Kildaire every year at Imbolc, Her holy day in February. Which also happened to be Rowan's birthday. She always spent a week or so in Ireland, visiting with the women who revered Brigid. Many of whom had a part in educating Rowan in what it was to be who she was as a Vessel. They were her elders, much like aunts.

"I can do that. He...well I don't think Clive will be in Ireland with me, but I can meet him here a week after Imbolc." Clive tread carefully when it came to the side of her life belonging to Brigid. He seemed in awe and maybe a little scared of it. Which sort of was how Rowan felt about it too so she wasn't offended.

He held up three fingers. "One visit agreed on. And the other three times? It's been far too long since my Keep has celebrated the winter holidays. Come then. We will have trees like the Christians and Druids. Cook will make croquembouche. You will allow me to give you presents and not complain about how much they cost. *Not once.* I want presents in return. A framed picture or something of that sort. Not a painting. I have paintings of you. No silver, no matter how funny you think that is."

She gave in to the smile at the memory of giving him a silver-handled mirror after reading *Dracula*. She must have been ten or so. He might be old and out of touch in a lot of ways, but all Vampires, no matter how long they'd been around before Stoker's novel, knew the reference.

Vampires weren't bothered by mirrors, but silver did harm them. They were all pretty insulted to be considered bug eaters and crypt sleepers when most Vamps liked high-thread-count sheets and tended to be snobs about food.

But he'd laughed when he unwrapped her gift. A good memory.

Still, there was no way she could just freaking put her life on hold and make the trip from Vegas to high in the Wetterstein four times a year.

But it didn't matter. He wanted it and she knew, in the end, she'd agree because she needed him at the Keep instead of marauding across Europe where she'd have to watch him every minute so he didn't start snacking on passersby who looked at him sideways.

Plus Clive would be getting more face time with The First, which would be good for his career within the Nation. Not that she'd admit to either male that she cared, but it mattered to Clive so it mattered to her.

And just maybe it was nice that Theo cared enough to use his power with her to demand not concessions to the Treaty, but time with her.

"I can't just fly like you and Clive can. The trip takes me way longer."

"I'll send my private jet for you and Clive. That'll

keep him safe for travel as well and you'll be brought right here to our airfield down the mountain."

"I can agree to do my best. Things are chaotic right now so I can't say yes. I will do my utmost to make it happen."

He reached up and patted her hand. And then he gave her the names of the Vampires he'd executed and agreed to stay at the Keep as long as Recht went with her on the hunt.

THREE

CLIVE STALKED BACK down the stairs after ending his meeting with the other Scions. He needed some distance from Warren Farrelly. Being in Germany meant it was Clive on the defensive in the power dynamic. He wasn't a fan.

Clive was smarter. Certainly far better looking and more charming. If pressed, Clive believed he would prevail in a physical challenge. But Farrelly had been a soldier in the middle ages and had battled alongside Clive's father and uncle during the war that brought the Treaty into being. He held Europe ably and, despite his annoying ego, had been a solid ally along with Clive to back The First.

Warren was a pompous prat who looked at Rowan far too often and for far too long. Made Clive want to rip the other Vampire's head off.

Rowan was *his.* Yes, yes, no one truly owned Rowan but Rowan. But she'd given herself to him. She was his in ways she'd never be with anyone else. Clive found that immensely satisfying.

When Clive rounded the corner he came upon Nadir.

"I was just looking for you. Do you have a moment to update me on the situation?" Technically he outranked the Five, but it did no good to antagonize or disrespect them. They were powerful. Feared for a reason. In truth, they were far more powerful than anyone other than Rowan when it came to dealing with The First.

She nodded back, paying him the same respect. "Yes, now is appropriate. With Rowan's help we've been able to identify those who've been disciplined by The First." Nadir handed a piece of paper over to Clive.

Shock skittered along his spine as Clive read the same last name over and over. Lacoste. A line long powerful within the Nation. They'd held their territory without any trouble as far as Clive knew. If they'd done what The First had alleged—and Clive trusted his master on that—they wouldn't have died easily. Or quickly.

"We'll need to get with Rowan and Hunter Corp. on this new development." Which would also give him a reason to speak with her quietly and privately. And hopefully without clothes.

"She's going to train with our weapons master for a bit." Recht's voice was smooth and quiet, but held a whip of command as he approached. Recht was the weapons master and had taught Rowan most of what she knew, so Clive could only cheer on the idea that she'd be able to take her aggressions out on Recht. By the time she came to Clive, they could get one another relaxed in other, less antagonistic ways.

Still, Clive didn't miss the other nuances of the situation. Recht made a claim on Rowan's time. And issued a little bit of warning. It said they all needed to take care of Rowan and help her get through the end of what had been a really rough day.

Rowan would never accept anything she considered pity or coddling. But in her own way, she'd understand this workout with her mentor and teacher was affection she could accept. Clive had no plans to miss taking in that spectacle.

Clive loved to watch Rowan fight. Single-minded and bloodthirsty, she was more Vampire than most Vampires he knew.

Fierce. Sexy. God above she was devastatingly alluring to him. Strong. Vicious. Intelligent. She understood strategy in ways it had taken him several hundred years of Scion training and an education at Oxford to gain.

Before her, he'd always taken on lovers who were calm and elegant. Cultured. Women who loved the opera and had closetsful of expensive clothing. Manicured, plucked, well-coiffed women.

And then there'd been Rowan. Foul-mouthed. Moody. Aggressive. Angry and resentful. And even then he'd wanted her. As he'd come to know her, he could add wary. At times totally unaware of her appeal. At other times, quite aware and she used it with such precision it made him hard just watching it.

Loyal. Righteous. Beautiful. Singular.

There was quite simply no one and nothing on earth like her.

Rowan. This woman he started off hating and now adored more than anything he'd ever dreamed he was capable of. And there she was, just a few feet away. She'd changed into her workout clothing and still looked as if she could kill with a fingertip. Magnificently vicious.

Nadir's amused expression told Clive he'd been woolgathering a little too long and had been obvious about his affections for Rowan. But here and with these Vampires it was safe. They wanted to protect Rowan too. They loved her and accepted her nature, appreciated it.

"I'll head to my rooms to change and clean up. I'll see you both shortly, then."

They nodded crisply as he excused himself. He'd elected to fly with her from the States. He'd rested during part of it but he knew Rowan. She would not have rested. She'd have used the time to work. Think. Plan.

He smiled as he entered his suites.

Rowan would never, ever let go until she'd handled this business with Enyo. It wasn't just the pain and recovery. It was that Enyo had bested Rowan. She'd attacked, would have killed Rowan had she not been interrupted. And escaped.

Since that night Clive had nearly lost her, she'd been sidelined as she regained her strength. His prickly Rowan couldn't let the imbalance between her and Enyo remain uncorrected.

He fed quickly, checked in with Alice, his assistant, who assured him all was well and then headed to the practice space where Rowan was already stretching.

Her hair had been pulled back from her face and the braided rope of crimson hung to her waist. She'd tuck it in to her collar once she started with Recht but for the moment it swung slightly as she moved in body hugging workout gear that showcased a powerful and toned form.

He kept out of her vision but she would know every person in that room. Would know their footfalls, if they moved in anger or fear.

Rowan was a sharp-edged weapon. He'd yet to have met any being more aware of her surroundings than she.

Recht came out, his hair similarly pulled back from his face and wrapped into a neat bundle at the base of his skull. Smart, Rowan had no problem fighting hard and vicious. She'd pull hair out, poke an eye from a skull, kick the balls up into the lower intestine. Whatever she had to.

A series of chimes sounded and Rowan and Recht squared off across from one another in the practice ring. Each bowed to the other, keeping gazes locked on one another.

Clive heard her jaw click closed in his head when Recht announced broadswords. Given her overall mood and the day she'd already endured, Clive figured Recht wanted to get her tired, sweaty and sore enough that she could exorcise some of that mountain of emotion she buried so deeply within.

"As you're aware, you need my approval to sign off on this hunt. In order to do so, I need to be sure you're fully recovered," Recht said as he sauntered past, handing her a very fine replica of a broadsword Clive knew the other Vampire had used in the original war against the Hunter Corporation troops.

For just a moment she let her defenses down. Rowan was tired. Exhaustion emanated from her in waves. She'd never have exposed that vulnerability to anyone else. Not even for a second. But she trusted everyone in that room knew she was the strongest, baddest bitch around.

Clive smiled at that, having heard it in her voice as he thought it.

A smile that faltered when he caught sight of Rowan's valet, David, as he entered quietly. The young hunter clearly tried not to catch Rowan's attention. But he was hers to protect and as he'd been there when Rowan had told David to remain in Las Vegas during this hunt, she would be doubly aware of his presence just then.

She tucked her hair into her shirt and rolled her shoulders, loosening up. Her features had hardened into an utterly blank mask. The Rowan he'd first met.

Clive knew she was already planning her next several moves. Recht had chosen a heavy weapon. To tire her while also reminding her she was more powerful then than she had been her entire life.

When she'd been barely clinging to life after Enyo had attacked, Rowan had been given not only The First's blood, but the blood of the other Scions and two of the Five. She hummed with a force-field-like energy now. More powerful than he'd ever seen her.

More than that, Clive had noted how much faster Rowan could call on Brigid. And how fast Brigid manifested herself if She felt the need. The loop between Vessel and Goddess seemed to have strengthened by leaps and bounds.

He and the being of power who shared Rowan's body had come to a wary truce and Clive was all right with that. If Brigid was on alert, it only served to keep Rowan safer.

A hush brought total stillness over the area. Recht inclined his chin slightly and stepped into the practice space. Rowan echoed his movements and stepped in.

"Has being back in your city of luxuries made you soft, little goddess?" Recht taunted.

Rowan's mask remained in place and suddenly she moved, faster than Clive had ever seen. Recht, startled, met her slices and her stabs.

Clive couldn't take his gaze from them. A master Vampire, one everyone he knew feared and respected, The First's weapons master, locked in hammer and tongs battle with a human.

A human who moved like a Vampire. Who moved as fast as an *ancient.* The light shone from her as she spun and had to lean back to avoid a strike that would have dislocated her jaw had Recht landed it.

A bell sounded and they moved apart, never taking attention from the other. Neither looked more than moderately winded.

There was no teasing when they went at it again. Rowan, instead of flagging after so much intense physical exertion, seemed to brighten and flex, grow more confident and steady.

He loved to see her prowl around Recht, her gaze roving over him, assessing constantly. There was no fear there. Not that Recht would truly hurt her. But it was more than that, it was *confidence.*

Rowan, with a snarl, chasing Recht across that floor, the thud, clank and clatter of the practice swords and the grunts and snarls of exertion as they went at one another without holding anything back was quite truly the most alluring thing he'd ever seen.

His woman.

His warrior.

He wanted to make her his queen. Wanted to shower her in every pretty bauble and expensive fabric. But she was skittish and defensive, so he found her far more receptive to gems and couture if they came with a weapon.

Sometimes she wore both—recently it had been a bladed sheath at her thigh and a long rope of rubies and diamonds around her neck—and nothing else. His favorite. And his alone. Because she gave herself to him. Because she made the choice to be with him.

Pride roared through his system. She loved him. This creature like no other came to him, revealed herself, let herself be soft—*just for him.*

Rowan filled him with greed. With pleasure and vexation. With respect and awe at her abilities. Rage too. No one could make him angry like she did. On purpose. To toy with him. But also, because to Vampires, that sort of snarling back and forth was foreplay.

She incited him as another Vampire would and yet, she did it in a way no one else could have. And she did it knowing it made him even hotter for her. It was her way of preening for his attention. Which she always had.

Whatever it was, he'd given up questioning why he liked it and loved it instead.

After two more timed matches, Recht finally called things as finished before taking a long look from the tips of Rowan's toes—which were bare because she preferred to work out that way—to her face.

"Little goddess, look at you. Not soft at all. And very ready to get out on this hunt."

Her impassive mask broke away as she grinned, grabbing the towel Recht tossed her way and wiping her face with it.

It buoyed Clive's heart to see that expression. She'd needed the exertion definitely, but it was the job well done from her mentor and teacher that had been the salve she'd be healed by most.

Warren pushed from the doorway where he'd been

taking the whole scene in. Clive narrowed his gaze at the other Vampire.

Clive knew Rowan. This moment she was sharing with Recht was important. Intimate. And she would see it as no one's business but hers and Recht's.

Clive simply waited for Rowan to smack Warren's nose. Which would be sexy and satisfying on many levels.

"YOU'VE RECOVERED MORE than well." Recht looked at her again, taking inventory, and there was something satisfying with that. With the expression he wore, which was proud.

"I'd already gotten faster, but the effects of the blood don't seem to be wearing off. It's been six weeks now and it feels more like…" Rowan paused trying to figure out how to say it, "…as if I'm becoming more adept at managing it." Like her new abilities were permanent and had been absorbed, just waiting for her to figure out how to use it all.

Still, she'd been faster than she'd ever been before as they'd sparred. Rowan had let it happen. Maybe it was due to her exhaustion and dealing with Theo. She'd turned off everything but instinct. And the power had simply leapt to her will. She'd been overthinking and slowing herself down as a result.

Warmth pooled in her belly. Brigid was pleased with that deduction.

Rowan would talk to Clive about it once they were alone. About all of it. Theo, this power, the hunt. She'd gotten used to that. Bouncing ideas off him. He was brilliant and had plenty of life experience so it usually helped her out. And it was…nice.

It would never be anything approaching normal. But she was a human, raised by The First Vampire, honed into a weapon by Hunter Corp. and fueled by the power and magic of the Goddess who lived within her. It wasn't like Rowan ever expected normal.

"Nicely done, Rowan." Warren eased over the line and into the practice space and into her thoughts.

"Is there a problem somewhere?" There had to be or he wouldn't have interrupted like they were all down at their local gym having a wheatgrass juice or whatever after they did their workout.

"No. For now it seems quiet enough. I just happened by and stopped in to watch you work."

"Why would you do that?"

He appeared confused by her question and then looked around the large room, lingering to her left for a few extra seconds.

She knew Clive was there. He hadn't moved from his place. Knowing she'd want this moment alone with Recht. Rowan bet he wore her favorite version of what she called his Lord of the Manor face. Arrogant and impassive. But he'd be thinking of fucking her. Which was next on her to-do list, not dicking around with Warren and his compliments.

"You're impressive. Who wouldn't want to watch?"

Rowan only watched other people spar if she was trying to learn something from them, usually to find their weaknesses and strengths. Though she did watch Clive because he was ripply and sweaty and so vicious when he fought and it was such a contradiction to his normal calm demeanor.

Hot as hell.

Impatience rode her. "Okay then. Thanks." She

tamped down her normal impulse to be blunt enough to chase an annoyance away. Warren had been part of her life for as long as she could remember and he'd been an ally during the Treaty negotiations and had backed Theo solidly.

He bowed and she managed not to blink at him again at how much deference he'd shown her. "Please keep me apprised of the situation with Hunter Corp. and this operation."

Rowan nodded, all business. "I'm preparing a report with recommendations. I'll get it to you and yours by the time you wake this evening."

"Will Clive be seeing it first?"

"You presume too much, Scion." She stood taller, letting some of her power unfurl between them. "You'll see it when I want you to. If someone sees it before you, I have a reason for it and I may or may not feel compelled to explain myself."

He smiled and she found him pretty hot for yet another arrogant, bossy old Vampire who led with his years instead of his brain. Dark hair, a lot of it, made an artful tousle around his face, only highlighting blue eyes.

Still, Vampires tended to be attractive so it wasn't as if a pretty face was rare when surrounded by them.

Plus, she already had an arrogant old Vampire who was magic in bed and she didn't have to hide who she was with him. She'd put in so much time training him already that she really had zero interest in anyone else.

And the not really small detail of being in love with said arrogant Vampire. Before she'd come back to the Keep her plans had been several hours of hot sex after consuming dumplings and pork products Dina would spoil her with.

And yet, since the moment they'd arrived it had been one thing after the next getting between her and those plans. She hated that most of all.

"Of course. My apologies if I offended. I'll speak with you again this evening." He stepped back and turned, leaving the room.

Recht rolled his eyes and after he critiqued her form awhile, took pity on her and dismissed her to get cleaned up and rest.

"When I wake later today, we'll speak." Recht had her shoulders in his hands. He meant about Theo and she could only be relieved that she could rest a while before that conversation. "Until then, be assured things are as under control as we can possibly make it."

"Thank you."

"Go on. He's been there waiting patiently. Even through all that with Farrelly."

Vampires.

FOUR

She approached Clive, trying to pretend it was no big deal that he seemed to draw her to him. It was the only way to hold it all together because this thing between her and Clive was deep and scary and wonderful and she really liked it even though she knew she shouldn't.

"Someone must be tired." One corner of his mouth slid up just a tiny bit.

"Yes, well. Some people play video games where they have sword battles with Vampires. I live it. It's better for my ass."

He looked around her body. "I certainly have no complaints about your arse. It's a part of you I never tire of seeing."

"Unlike my mouth?"

He stepped just a little bit closer, enough to send her body chemicals into a tizzy she wanted to blame on plane travel and physical exertion.

"Hunter, I quite like your mouth. It's so delightful it's not hard to overlook your appalling vulgarity and inability to recognize authority."

She swallowed hard, that slow pulse of sexual chemistry filling her up. "You don't overlook my vulgarity. You get off on it." And he did. The breath she sucked in turned out to be full of him so it made her want him even more.

"I never claimed it didn't also add to your appeal. My cock loves a mouthy woman entirely capable, and frequently more than willing, of scuffling and brawling and really filthy talk during sex."

It was the step he took away—for just a moment—from the smooth and elegant Clive to be dirty because he liked it as much as she did, that got to her more than anything else. "I really can't keep up with nearly five centuries of the game you bring."

He laughed and sent a little of his power to caress her skin. Even six months back she'd have been nervous about it. But by this point, she'd stopped lying to herself and let herself enjoy it.

Her voice was just the barest breath of sound. "I need to take a shower and I can't see wasting water or nakedness without you there."

He smoothed a hand down the front of his shirt. "I'm always available to scrub your back. Remember it gives me a great view of your arse. As we've established I quite enjoy that."

"I'll be in your bathroom, naked in twenty minutes. I need to deal with one last thing."

They both looked over to where David stood, waiting.

"He is your valet. And so much more than a boy you need to shield from harm," Clive murmured in her ear. "Let him be here with you. You have your path, he has his."

She huffed her annoyance but he kissed her forehead and stepped back. "I'll expect you in twenty minutes, Rowan. If I have to come find you it won't be like a fun game."

"Really? I'm sort of disappointed by that." A fun

game of Clive finding Rowan and having his way with her would be a super way to spend a few hours.

"Cheek." He shook his head. "*Twenty minutes*. I'll stop by the kitchen and request a meal sent up for you."

He really was so much better at this relationship thing.

"Thanks."

He smiled one last time and headed out of the room.

She turned to face the person she'd told to stay home in Las Vegas. "So here's a thing. You're not supposed to be here."

His normally earnest and mellow expression hardened with the passion in his voice. "I know you're angry, *Deese*, but I can't be set aside. You leave me at the apartment in Las Vegas when you go out to work, which is fine. But I'm your valet. It is my sworn duty to be here with you on a hunt."

He was human; he'd die of old age when she still looked about thirty years old. But she wanted, very much, for him to die a very old man and not at the hands of a murderous Vampire. Especially when David had so much left to do and experience in his life. If something happened to him she didn't know if she could bounce back from the loss and her own failure to protect him.

"You are my valet, yes. And you do a very good job."

He interrupted, which was generally not something he did—which was why she tolerated it. "If I did a good job why send me away? Other Hunters don't. Their valets accompany them on fieldwork. I give you my word I won't fail you."

Rowan withheld a sigh. She'd fucked this one up so

badly. "Of course you won't fail me. You haven't yet and as you've noticed my life is sort of full of danger and drama. This isn't about *you* not being good enough. And I don't care what other Hunters do! Is this the place where I say, *Young man, if other valets jump off a bridge would you do that too?*"

He nearly smiled.

"You're important to me. I don't want you in danger. I need you to deal with people so I don't have to. I need you to always find the onion bagel with the best-toasted onion on it. I need you to keep me from making people cry when I don't actually want to make them cry."

He harrumphed at her. "You're going on a hunt with several master Vampires. Do you know how agitated you're going to be by day three if I'm not there to keep you diverted and from killing creatures you may need later? Not only that, but I've been training. I carry weapons. I know how to handle myself."

Rowan sighed. "It's not a matter of any of that." She waved a hand. "Go to bed. But before you do that, can you please set up a video conference with Hunter Corp. for about two hours after sunset tonight?"

"Of course." He bowed and then hurried off to handle things.

She hadn't agreed to let him go on the hunt. She wasn't convinced it was wise to have this be his first official hunt. She needed to think on it more and also bone her boyfriend. The sun would make him pretty useless in the boning department for at least five or six hours so she really needed to be about time management right then.

With a growl, she put her practice sword back and headed to Clive.

CLIVE SPED HIS PACE, wanting to get back to his rooms after getting the food arranged. He'd fed before going to see her, and he *never* fed where she'd be spending time so he wasn't concerned she'd see something upsetting if she got there first. But he wanted to be sure the flowers he'd asked to be put in his bedchamber had been set up. Red peonies, her favorite. There'd be some bloodwine, which he planned to enjoy, and some cider for her.

And if he was fortunate, the robe he'd ordered for her would have arrived as well.

Most of his people had left the Keep at least a month before and the rest had gone home when he and Rowan had returned to Las Vegas two weeks ago. So it was fairly quiet as he entered the wing that held the personal apartments of the Scion of North America and his associates. An approaching footfall told him Alice, his assistant and closest advisor, was on her way to him.

She reached his room first and opened the double doors ahead of him. Sweeping through with a critical eye. He never had to worry about it once he'd told her to handle something.

She had her ever-present clipboard and notes clutched in her left arm. "I've handled all your donors for feeding while we're here at the Keep. You'll meet them twenty minutes after sunset in the same little library down at the end of the wing you fed in tonight."

Clive let the efficient cadence of each thing she felt needed his attention center his thoughts. She would have taken care of every detail, never wasting his time with anything unnecessary.

Alice had been with him since the very start. She'd been assigned to him the first month he'd been inducted into the Scion training program. She'd received her own sort of training on how to serve a Scion at the same time.

It was Alice who'd helped him build who he was as the Scion of North America. She traveled with him everywhere he went and generally made his life easier. Her connections were vast, varied and impeccable. Not only did she have a mighty brain, she was a passionate fighter. Trained to be deadly in his service.

And yet he really didn't want her coming on this hunt.

Originally he'd planned on having her stay at the Keep and run things from there and coordinate with David back in Las Vegas. But with The First being in the state he'd been in earlier and David now in Germany, it might be safer to bring them both along. He needed to speak to Rowan about it as well.

"All staff is under strict order not to disturb you—either of you—without my or David's express permission. I put the boxes you had sent from Paris on the couch in your sitting room. I made sure to put some human pain reliever in the cabinet in your bathroom. If she's feeling any discomfort, the medication the doctor left for her is in there as well. David brought it. You can tell her that if she's uncomfortable."

He hid a smile. "Thank you."

She paused at his door. "Is there anything else I can do to help?"

Alice had a soft spot for Rowan, seeing right through her bullshit and to the ferociously loyal heart beneath.

"She's a survivor." In truth how could Rowan be anything but distressed? The First out there on the grass earlier that night was a Vampire teetering on the edge. And she understood more than most anyone just what that could mean.

"Sometimes you should do more than just survive."

Clive agreed. And the truth was, Rowan *did* far more than just survive. She lived her life to the fullest, always keeping her path central, but she wasn't *just* anything.

Rowan had risen from her the ashes of her childhood and become something else. Something more.

But he also had a job to do so he'd do it and give Rowan all his focus when she showed up.

"Please coordinate with Farrelly's assistant and set up a meeting with the Scions about an hour after sunset." He'd already had a detailed conversation with Warren and Paola about the Hunt and who they wanted to send along with Rowan. He knew Rowan would be speaking to Hunter Corp. that evening as well to fill them in on her recommendations so he wanted to keep everyone in the loop enough to get them off his back.

And they'd need to deal with this situation with The First. After everyone woke that night they'd know more and would have to update the other Scions.

Rowan knew who she wanted to go with her on the hunt. She also knew who she *didn't* want along. Clive wasn't sure how successful she'd be on the latter, but he understood Rowan enough to be convinced that team would have every single member she recommended.

He trusted her on this, though certainly he and Farrelly as well as a number of others were quite good at hunting and tracking. He looked forward to showing Rowan he was more than a Scion in a suit.

He thanked Alice after she assured him she'd handle all the details for the call the following sunset. As he'd entered his suites, Cataline, the house manager, rolled a cart laden with food his way. A rather beefy Vampire stood with her and followed her instructions as they set up for a meal in his sitting room.

Cataline, once finished, pointed at a pot of tea she'd put a cozy on to keep warm. "Cook says to make sure Rowan drinks it. She'll complain. Sweet-talk her into finishing."

Clive withheld his opinion of sweet-taking Rowan into anything she didn't want to do to. Guilt might work better and he planned to use that and sex and some presents to get her to comply. Or to attempt it.

"I'll do my best. Thank you." He bowed.

"It's rather chilly in here. She's still recovering." Cataline gave Clive a look, as if he'd personally been the one to attack Rowan.

He wasn't going to explain anything to her, even though she certainly said all that in Rowan's best interest. But Rowan didn't like to sleep when it was too warm and she rarely slept in his bed until he woke anyway.

"Thank you for thinking of her comfort."

They left and he'd only taken two steps back from the door when Rowan rounded the opposite corner.

"Three minutes to spare."

"Come on in here. I'll give you something to do with that one hundred and eighty seconds."

FIVE

"I've been ordered to make you drink tea and to warm my rooms up for you because you're still recovering. So do eat and drink all that tea and then we'll shower."

She walked past him into his rooms, comfortable in his space in a way he hadn't thought possible six months before.

"You're adorable when you try to give me orders." Her tone was loose. Easy and warm. Teasing. A test to his resolve.

"You're *not* adorable when you don't just do what I ask because it's the best thing for you and you know it."

One of her shoulders rose and fell. "I'm contrary and fickle. You say so yourself."

He gave in and smiled. "You are. And I do say so. I'll make you a deal. I'll make you come for every cup of tea you drink."

"You're going to do that anyway so I don't need to make a deal with you. And you like it when I make you work for it." To underline that, Rowan pulled her tank up over her head and tossed it to the side.

Contrary. Though absolutely correct. He did love this little push and pull game of theirs. "Tea!" He pointed and raised his brow. "Dina and Cataline both made me promise. Otherwise I'd let you get sick just to teach you a lesson."

"You're such a liar." Still shirtless and now, as she tossed her bra to the side, bare from the waist up, she poured the tea into a cup and sipped it, challenge in her gaze.

"A liar? Darling Hunter, why would I do such a thing?" He made himself stay where he was, across the small space. Close enough to smell her, sweat and skin, power and magic. But not close enough to touch. Which was good because he wanted to touch her but they were playing a game he planned to win.

He kept his patience, knowing they'd both be naked and touching shortly.

"You'd let me get sick to teach me a lesson?" She sipped her tea, topless, like the spawn of hell she was to tempt him so. "You would not. You like me, Scion."

During the first days after her attack, when her life had been so very thin and tattered, he hadn't wanted to leave her side. The First had to order Clive to leave and rest as the sun came up each day she'd been unconscious. Even once she'd gotten past the danger point and had begun to recover in earnest, he'd hated to leave her each morning. Worried something would happen while he wasn't awake.

No, he wouldn't let her get sick to teach her a lesson. Not for a few years. He needed the time between himself and nearly losing her to ever consider being cavalier that way.

"Granted, I do feel rather fond of you so to let you get sick would be counter to my goals of sex as often as I can get it."

"You're the one who's making me drink tea instead of putting your cock inside me." She shrugged.

"For now."

She finished her tea and raised a brow his way. "I've got an empty teacup here."

"You're spoiled."

Her smile promised all sorts of things he'd like.

"You're the one who spoils me. I was just a gal with a valet who made her bagels and brought her coffee. You're the one who buys me gemstones and makes me drink whateverthefuck is in this tea. Going to guess healing mojo. Probably make me sleepy really soon. I may not even be able to have sex at this rate."

He laughed, despite his best intentions. "What a terrible outcome to have to wait eight hours until the sun went down to have you. Again."

Rowan sighed. "I may be too busy for that. Once the sun sets I have to yell at people and coordinate a schedule to keep everyone in this hemisphere safe. Probably too busy to fuck."

"Now who's lying?"

Her laugh, low and sexy, stroked over his skin as she used her power to get his attention.

Which she already had.

Rowan shuddered as she downed the last of the stinky liquid. "Two cups of tea down."

"If you promise to eat after the shower, I'll make you come three times anyway."

She stood in the same graceful, boneless way Vampires did and his incisors pressed against his gums. She made him want like nothing before.

A smile of carnal promise curved her mouth. She made an X motion over her heart. "Done. After those orgasms I'll need the calories to keep my strength up."

"I do so admire your thinking," Clive said, following her through to the bedroom where he'd laid the robe out on his bed.

She gave him a look over her shoulder.

"I saw the color and thought of your skin."

ONLY THIS MAN could move her this way. Rowan brought the deep blue silk to her cheek. She was too tired to pretend she wasn't pleased by the way he sought to take care of her.

"Not that seeing you in my shirts isn't ridiculously attractive, but I thought you might like something to keep here, in my rooms."

He reached out, cupping her face, and she told herself the way she leaned into his touch was for him when she knew she'd allowed herself to need it.

"I know you aren't always comfortable sleeping with me during daylight hours. I know you need your own space. I don't want to own you. I want you to come to me when you need me. I want you to know you're welcome at my side, in my bedchamber and in my life."

The words seemed to soak into her. Damn him and his ability to know exactly what she needed to hear right when she needed it.

He wasn't a responsibility. Didn't need protecting or saving. Being with him was easy in so many ways, even though he was a Vampire and bossy and one of her dad's employees so to speak.

"Thank you. It's beautiful. I'm going to spill something on it in five minutes. You know that right?"

He pushed her to the en suite bathroom and turned the water on to get it hot.

"It can be cleaned."

"You're so patient with all this. Where's my uptight British asshole?"

His features softened. "I love you, Rowan. You've had quite a day. I'm always pleased to poke you into a state of agitation and you're so surly it's not very difficult. But there are times when I'm content to let you be because you need someone in your goddamned life who's your safe place. Selfishly, I like you better when you're bitchy over something not me and easily punched into obedience."

She finished getting out of her sparring clothes, tossing them to the side. Not wanting to do something horrifying like cry at his kindness, Rowan busied herself undoing her hair.

She did, in fact, really dislike being around Vampires when they day slept. It wasn't so much like he was dead or anything, but they rested very deeply and their bodily functions slowed down drastically so they got very cold and very still. He wasn't going to cuddle with her while he was out—not that she was much for cuddling anyway. He wouldn't even know she was there.

And she needed a moat around herself sometimes. Needed to be alone in a place no one would bother her. And the miracle of it was that Clive accepted her nature.

She got into the shower and he followed, not crowding her physically, but taking up all her attention anyway.

The water was blessedly hot and did great things to her muscles as she grabbed his soap and ran it all over his skin.

"You should let me take care of you."

"Be quiet." She continued, letting herself find comfort as well as titillation at the feel of him, steady and toned against her palms.

His mouth quirked but he didn't argue. His cock liked what she was doing in any case, so it wasn't like there was a problem.

She stretched, going to her tiptoes to kiss his neck, licking over the sensitive skin at his jaw, letting herself delight in his groan when she grazed her teeth against his jugular. Pushing right to the edge of breaking the skin. She didn't have teeth made for such things but when she bit down he arched into her and spun, backing her against the tile at her back.

His eyes were lit, reflecting the light back at her. She drew a breath through a gasp as sensation ripped it from her.

"I'd say you were playing with fire, but you know that." He gripped her easily, leaning his weight against her to hold her in place as he kissed across her brow and down her cheeks.

"I like fire." Some might say it was a flaw, but Rowan understood it brought this man to her, so she was good with that.

"Of course you do. Why not? It's dangerous and could easily harm you."

She laughed, her fingers sliding into his hair as he nibbled down her throat and over the upper curves of her breasts.

"You'd be bored otherwise."

His hands, slick with soap, roamed all over her body, paying particular attention to her nipples until she writhed against him. And then…he went south, dropping to his knees before her.

She closed her eyes as the water rushed over her

skin and sighed happily when he spread her open and took a lick and then another, nudging her thighs a little wider to get more of her with his mouth.

He didn't waste any time, instead driving her hard and fast until she came in a sharp rush of pleasure.

He didn't stop there. A man of his word, he pushed her into another climax that felt so good it nearly hurt.

He surged to his feet and kissed her. She held on as he devastated her lips and tongue, his taste filling her.

It hadn't even been a full day since they'd had sex last, but this was different and they both knew it. He knew more about her now. Had seen enough to render her vulnerable to him. And she hadn't worried. It meant he knew her more. That knowledge was achingly intimate. Raw.

She hadn't hidden her reaction to it. Had let him see her vulnerability and that had deepened their connection. Especially when he hadn't rejected her or walked out.

He broke away, pulling her from the shower and wrapped her in a warm towel the size of five people, picked her up and deposited her on the edge of the counter, stepping between her thighs.

"Here you are again, between my legs."

"My favorite."

It was a tease, but she loved the lazy confidence in his tone.

The counter put him at the perfect height to slide right inside her with one hard stroke. Hard enough she grunted and then adjusted her position to wrap her legs around his waist while she leaned back and braced her hands on the edge of the counter, just inside where his rested.

"Yes, just as delightful as the last time I was here." He kissed her neck, teasing them both with a graze of his incisors against her skin. Always walking that edge and never crossing it. Never showing any resentment that she'd never given over to him and let him take her blood.

She'd never told him why. He'd never pushed when she hadn't shared the details, though he did manage to leave her feeling like he wasn't angry or insulted and that if she ever did want to tell him he was there.

She shoved that from her mind and rolled her hips to meet his thrusts.

Between them *this* was always perfect. She never had to think about sex with him, they just went at it and it worked. The rest of the relationship stuff filled her with various emotions and she already had a lot of emotions and was generally cranky and mean and yet he loved her anyway.

She opened her eyes to find him looking at her as if she was the most beautiful thing he'd ever seen.

She had no defense against this wonder he filled her with. She couldn't hold him back or wall him out. There was nothing to do but take that leap and be vulnerable.

"I love you," she murmured and his gaze sharpened, lips curving up as he continued to fuck her.

"I find myself rather pleased by hearing you say it." He leaned in to kiss her as she stretched up to meet him, their mouths colliding in a tangle.

There never seemed to be a point where she got enough of him. Never enough of this rutting and petting, of the sweat-slicked crush of his hips against her inner thighs. He filled her with fire.

"You are mine." He said this and took her bottom lip between his teeth. Harder and harder until he balanced on the very edge of drawing blood.

Her heart sped. Adrenaline spiked. He brought this out in her in a way no one else ever had. It was by turns exciting and deeply exhausting. She didn't know what to do with the tenderness so she just sort of pretended it wasn't there until she tripped over it or figured it out.

He let go slowly and licked over the sting. His strokes had slowed, but they'd gone harder and deeper.

"Nothing to say, Hunter?"

"Your cock feels really good."

He snarled but then laughed.

He nipped her bottom lip again. "You. Are. Mine."

That little snarly possessive thing was recent and it totally made her tingle. He was so all buttoned-up and well mannered that when he got a little tousled it was so unbelievably hot.

"Do you want me to agree? Right here with your cock in me? With my scent all over you and my toothbrush on your counter? Am I yours, Scion?"

"It wasn't a question, Rowan. It was a statement."

He added a swivel on each thrust so he ground himself against her clit and orgasm slowly began to build. Again.

"And are you mine then?" She regretting saying it aloud. It sounded…like someone else.

But his response, that widening of his eyes and the emotion on his features erased most of her embarrassment at needing reassurance. "Most assuredly. You're a pain in the ass. You kill my Vampires and scare the ones you leave alive. You're rude and ill-mannered. You do have very good taste in wine, I give you that."

She laughed. "Thank you, Scion. I'm glad to know my surly ways were what hooked you."

He kissed her slowly as he ground himself against her again and again. "You're so wet and hot. Drives me crazy. So close. You're tightening up around me. Give me number three then."

Rowan let it all go and came so hard she cracked her head on the mirror as she arched to take him deeper.

He put a hand between her skull and the mirror and sped his pace, making that hot little fuck-mumble only she got to hear, and came, closing that loop between them.

SIX

HE'D SET HER on her feet and she'd looked up, her affection plain on her features. "I'm yours, Clive."

He thought about it still, even as he made sure she ate and had some wine. The sun would be up soon. He felt it drawing power and his own waning. But he wanted every moment with her he could get before he went in to rest.

"The tea is working. I'm sleepy and warm and sort of lazy."

She hadn't said much and he wanted her to be relaxed so she could rest even more than he wanted to talk with her about The First.

"Come with me." He stood and she followed, taking his hand. The robe looked fantastic on her, as he knew it would. He liked seeing her in something he'd chosen. Growing up as she had in Vampire culture, she'd know wearing it was a sign of their intimate connection.

She hadn't just told him she was his, she'd *shown* him. He had another item, not necessarily a gift, but something he wanted to give her. But it wasn't time yet. Soon, he figured.

"You don't have to stay." He pulled the comforter back. He liked warm bedding, with some weight. Since their body temperature lowered so much as they rested, most Vampires tended to choose bedding that would keep them as warm as possible.

"It's not that I don't want to sleep with you." She got in and he watched the beguiling sway of her ass as she did.

He slid beside her and pulled her close.

"But you don't know if I'm here or not. You're unconscious and your room is so perfect and pristine and I'm not pristine. I like to work when I need to and sometimes that's before you wake or after you go to rest. I have to make calls and yell at people. That's a big job and it can jump time zones." She paused. Most likely reveling in the memories of the last call she made to yell at someone.

Rowan continued. "I eat in my bed and you hate that. I have snacks in my room and your eye tic comes back every time you open one of my drawers and find jerky. I leave coffee cups on my bedside table and you're obsessively and unnaturally neat."

He shuddered at the memory.

"I'm not hurt or offended. And I am glad you don't leave dried meat products in my dresser drawers."

She laughed. "Goddess you're so fucking uptight. You get faint when you see pillowcases that don't match."

"I knew it was love when my revulsion at your slovenly ways didn't stop me from wanting to be around you. You also forgot to mention you use a top sheet instead of the fitted ones. It makes no sense. You're supposed to use the sheets the way they're intended."

The look she gave him amused him greatly.

"I'm a rebel that way I guess. I hear using the wrong sheet is like a gateway to dogs marrying cats and buffalo roaming the streets smoking weed."

He had no idea what she was talking about, but it

was most likely one of her pop culture references to humans he'd prefer to avoid anyway.

"When we move in together we'll work around it." He hadn't meant to say it to spook her, but once the words were out he was glad he had.

She didn't even stiffen. "We'll need a place with two bedrooms on either side of a shared sitting room. I can eat crackers in bed and you can iron your underpants and have a stick up your butt about lint or the pinstripe on your pajamas being too wide in yours."

He groaned. "You're never going to let that go. A man has to have some style, Rowan."

"Pajamas don't need style. You're not even conscious when you're resting! It's not like you're out at a nightclub. Just who are you trying to impress? I'd rather see you naked and no one is in your bedroom to see your PJs but me. You could sleep in a T-shirt and your boxers or sweats even."

He curled his lip. "And while I'm at it I'll microwave a frozen dinner and watch a reality show too, shall I?"

She guffawed. "You make me laugh, you fucking weirdo. As I was saying, the problem isn't a solution between Rowan and Clive. We're both freakishly odd and for whatever reason that works. But your people would be in my house, especially if we live at Vampire HQ instead of away from that madness."

He wasn't opposed to finding a place outside the main part of town. Once they chose the next location for the Scion to live, he could get plans started there for a custom home. But contact with his people would definitely come with being his partner. "You're growing on them."

"I'd like to run them over with a tank. Except Alice.

You can keep her because she's like a badass Vampire Mary Poppins."

He'd have to tell Alice that. She'd love it.

"You're not arguing about moving in with me?"

"We have some killing to do first. But I'm not deluded about who you are. You're not just any old Vampire, you're a master Vampire. Which means you're super spoiled and haughty and used to getting your way in all things. You'll just mope and sniff and be British until I relent. David needs his own suites and your people aren't allowed there. I need a place to work, which will be a no Vampire zone. And a secure place to park my car."

He should be suspicious of how easily she was taking this. Maybe her tea had been drugged. He wouldn't put it past Dina to dope Rowan up to get her to actually sleep. But Brigid didn't usually allow such nonsense and quite often burned anything intoxicating from her system.

But he'd take it. Because he did want her with him. Wanted her in his home where he knew she was protected. And, where everyone knew she was his.

He also knew David was part of the package. "Of course." Along with Hunter Corp. and its endless politics and machinations—which he was less enamored of. But he'd take this as the victory it was and get started on the plans. Once they dealt with the hunt and whatever was going on with The First, he'd lock this living-together thing in

She sighed, content for the moment, and he breathed her in. He wanted this to be what he experienced before going to sleep and her scent on the pillow when he awoke was acceptable since he knew she wouldn't be staying. It was enough that she'd been there.

"He'll get better," she said very quietly, finally speaking of her father. "I think the adventure he went on eased some of the pent-up stuff that led him to this place. But he can't come with us. It would be total anarchy and I have too much to do already."

"All right." She didn't need answers from him. Rowan had more experience with The First than anyone else he knew. She understood him and while she had fear, she also had love. Complicated and twisty, but that came with what they all were.

"He's well enough to wrest a promise to visit more from me in exchange for staying here. You're coming too."

This pleased him immensely.

"I am?"

"Really? Now you want to be coy? After you nailed me on your bathroom counter you're going to expect me to pretend you aren't giddy and doing a jig in your head at more access to the boss?"

She snorted. "Well probably not a jig. Not even in your imagination. Though I might recall that image to keep from popping you in the junk the next time you get uppity. Which we both know will be very soon because you like being uppity. It's your prime directive. That was a *Star Trek* reference, in case you're so stunted you don't know what I meant."

He smiled against her hair, still a little damp from the shower, her scent now mixed with his shampoo.

"I find the return of your vulgarity and lack of manners reassuring now instead of horrifying. You've gone and done it, Hunter. I'm broken."

"Next think you'll be eating McNuggets and drinking diet soda."

"Let's not be hasty."

She laughed, tipping her head back to look into his face. "Go to sleep, old Vampire. Maybe I'll order you some Crocs while you're sleeping."

"Where would we put a crocodile?"

"In a moat we have around our new house. Which is a great idea, actually. But I meant shoes. Plastic shoes. People garden in them and chefs seem to like them too. They sort of look like orange rubber wooden shoes. With holes."

"*Plastic shoes?*" Horror spun through his system at the idea.

"You could go wild and not wear socks."

She was laughing so hard it was difficult to understand this last bit, but he knew she was teasing and quite honestly the mere thought of plastic on his feet was enough to turn his stomach.

"It's easy to mock when some people have standards."

She laughed more, hugging him. "I'm going now. Rest. Goddess, I feel better now. Orgasms and mockery overruled the stress. You're handy that way, Scion." She rolled from his bed.

"Leave the robe here."

She paused at the door, looking back at him over a shoulder. "And walk naked back to my rooms? All right then. It's late enough that I probably won't see anyone."

He frowned. "You do have a point."

"I'll return it here after sunset." She turned as she shook her head, moving back to the bed to kiss him one last time. "So spoiled."

"It's rather a nice situation for me, I do say."

She flipped him off as she left the room, calling out a goodbye as she left. She shut the door to his bedchamber and then he heard the locks engage. It would keep the room dark and free of sunlight and anyone not possessing the code out while he was more vulnerable.

He waited there as the sun rose and made his lids heavy. Thinking of her walking through the halls, going up stairs and around corners. He'd made the trip to her suites, housed in the same high security wing as The First, enough times to know how long it took to get there.

When he'd gone through the trip enough to be assured she'd be back, he let himself fall away and rest, knowing she'd be there when he awoke.

SEVEN

"WE'VE COMPILED A LIST of candidates for you to choose from, Rowan."

Rowan looked at the screen, glad the people on the other side couldn't see the tightening of the muscles in her back.

"That's not necessary. I don't require any personnel from Hunter Corp. with me on this mission. I'll need the resources I already make use of—archives, records, data, safe houses—that sort of thing."

Roth Wesslyian, king-sized asshole and a human she'd had the great pleasure of punching, cleared his throat. Sadly, he hadn't gotten fired after his little freak-out at the Keep. To be fair, he and several others had been influenced by magic. But he was still an asshole. And he still got up her nose. And he was still plotting to fuck with the balance between Vampires and humans.

"This isn't some personal vendetta, Ms. Summerwaite."

She loathed him nearly as much as she loathed having her time wasted. "Really? Thanks for telling me. I'd never have known that. In any case, I have my team chosen and don't require your opinion on staffing issues."

"Your valet has sent a formal request to accompany

you on this hunt." Susan Espy, mentor, stand-in mother figure and fantastic assassin, also ignored Roth's comments, but the David thing annoyed Rowan greatly. Having to deal with it then was a surprise and that showed and *that* weakened her.

He wouldn't have meant any harm of course. And that niggled, too, because if he couldn't have seen it coming it was an indicator he lacked the subtlety and political smarts to survive out there in the field.

He'd get his trial by fire either way, as she'd decided to let him come before she'd gone to sleep earlier that day. But she'd spank his ass for this bullshit later on.

"He's my valet. I'll decide where he should go."

"It's time for you to let him out in the field with you. That's his job, Rowan. I know you worry," Susan spoke before Rowan could interrupt. "We all worry those first few times a valet begins to accompany us on missions. Truth be told I never stop worrying." She shrugged. "But nonetheless, for us, it's another foundational support source out in the world. You need him and so I'm sure you realize this and already were planning on letting him go with you, but I wanted to bring it up."

This was all true and something she needed to hear. But not in that setting. Still, it was a warning. Damn politics.

"He and I spoke about this issue and it's resolved. I appreciate your bringing it up, but it's handled."

"You won't be allowed to showboat out there." Each time Roth spoke she hated him a little more.

Ice cold spread through her belly as Rowan turned her attention to Celesse. "Why do you invite non essential personnel to these meetings?"

"Someone has to hold you accountable," Roth shot back.

"By getting spelled up and nearly starting a war?" Rowan responded, baiting him with his behavior at the Joint Tribunal.

"By Vampires! You keep saying they're not a threat. I'm proof they are." He smiled like he'd made some sort of point.

"And I saved you. Along with some Vampires. And you're still fucking useless or worse, getting in my way. You serve absolutely no purpose."

A few partners muttered, angry that she'd spoken out the way she had. Of course none of them had been nearly killed because of something Roth had been part of.

"What? Oooh, upset because someone has a spine enough to speak the truth about the deadweight Hunter Corporation carries? All of you who ride desks, you know nothing of risk and you most assuredly don't know a thing about how to do the dirty work you and your little cabal rely on to stay alive."

Rex, Susan's husband and another partner at the Hunter Corp., put a hand in front of his mouth to hide his expression. Susan smirked, and Celesse, from her office in Paris, made that French wordless noise that sounded like approval and rebuke all at once.

Roth sputtered some more. "You're out of line!"

"There's not much worse than a man who thinks he's smarter than he is."

Before she could get truly warmed up and insult him and possibly make him cry, a knock sounded and David peeked in. "The Vampires are here. Are you ready?"

Rowan had planned to have this handled by the

time the Vampires showed up but there was nothing to be done about it and the outcome would be the same no matter what. Repeated bullshit like this call with Hunter Corp. or not, she had a mission and she would complete it with or without them.

This would be her team and if the Vampires and Hunter Corp. didn't like it, they could all go fuck themselves. Rowan was going to run Enyo to ground and kill her extra hard. If she had to quit a job that needed her more than she needed it, so be it. In fact, now that she'd allowed herself to even consider that idea, it didn't seem like an altogether bad one.

"Send them in." Rowan looked back to the screen.

Clive and Warren came in, sitting down on either side so they could see the screen with the London and Paris motherhouse staff.

"As I was saying, my team will be me, David, the Scions of North America and Europe and one of The First's Five. We will leave in two days' time."

Clive didn't say anything but it didn't matter, arguing started in London and Warren groaned.

She spoke to Warren in an undertone. "Shut up. I have to deal with you guys all the time and you're just as bad."

He grinned at her. "Is this one of those things where it's only okay to make fun if they're your family?"

"Yes. Which means I get to make fun of everyone and you get to make fun of no one."

Clive sniffed, but it was nearly a snort. She was such a bad influence on him.

Cheered up by that thought, she brought two fingers to her lips and whistled loud enough to shut down the arguing on the other side of the call.

"I'm going to go ahead and keep this call moving. You can listen or you can argue with one another. I had a meeting an hour ago with one of The First's people. There have been three possible sightings so *after* this call ends I can get working. David will be in touch with support needs."

"This isn't over. You can't just do whatever you want. This is Hunter Corp. business." Roth's tone made her want to punch something.

"This is *my* business. She nearly killed me. After Roth and his dumbass stepdaughter stirred the pot and made things worse. I'm cleaning this mess up because I can't trust it to happen correctly otherwise. I've been recuperating for some time and I didn't see any of you getting in the saddle to take out a Vampire barely made much less one who is older than most languages spoken on earth today. So do me a favor and quit yapping."

"Rowan, please." Celesse held up a hand.

"Please what? Come on. This piece of shit is attempting to hamper my investigation for what? What possible benefit is there in me letting you sandbag me with someone I'll have to protect and watch out for? All to run back to this garbage human to tattle? If you want to know what I do, ask. Otherwise I'm not an employee. I'm a full partner and this is what I'm doing."

"You're not the only partner though! This is not only your decision to make."

Truly angry now, she leaned close enough to the monitor, wanting him to see it on her face. "Listen here, you. I don't give even the tiniest hint of a memory of a fuck about how you think or what you feel. You've proven yourself to be petty, unreliable and a coward. You have nothing to offer me and I'm not pretending otherwise. You're not my boss, or my dad, or even anyone I'd cross the street to save."

She sat back, ready to burn something down. Constantly hindered and hampered by small-dicked assholes who didn't care about the balance the Treaty kept. Didn't care about keeping the peace and humans out of the cross fire.

"This sort of vulgar display is why you need to be reined in."

"You think you're the man to do it, Roth? I have to admit I'd love that. So please do come at me and I'll happily throttle you once more and toss you out like trash."

"This isn't useful," Celesse said with a sigh.

"You're right. It's not useful. It's waste of my time. It's a waste of my time as a Hunter. People like him are far too casual about tossing others into the way to take a bullet for them. I go out there and get between everyone else and the monsters they can't fight off if they tried. If that's vulgar, I'd rather be that than a fucking bootlicking coward. Now. I'm at the end of my patience here with this whole process. This is what is happening. If Hunter Corp. has a problem with that or thinks it can send someone else to do this, you better speak up right now and a hearty good luck to you."

"Are you threatening us?" Roth's voice had an edge of fear in it. Good. He should be afraid.

Rather than raising her voice, she leaned back in her chair and kept her tone smooth and patient. The Goddess let herself shine through Rowan's gaze briefly. "This is why you don't understand me. I'm not playing power games or trying to be cutting. You're not worth my energy. I'm telling you how this will go." But the voice was Brigid's as the Goddess filled Rowan up so fast it hurt.

Susan, hearing the tone of Rowan's voice, knowing the Goddess stirred and that meant trouble—leaned over, shifting her body to be between the screen and Roth, shutting him out. "This silly game has gone on long enough. Rowan is right. This entire charade is a waste of time. None of the rest of the partners has to deal with this level of interference."

"Everyone else has manners!" Roth proved himself totally inferior at understanding a threat to his existence.

Rowan rolled her eyes. "I don't need manners. I have a sword."

Susan gave her an exasperated, if not amused, expression and Rowan huffed a breath, but shut up.

Susan continued, "That's neither here nor there. Moreover, none of us is capable of handling this and we know it. I have appointments shortly. Rex and I have already submitted our feelings on this particular situation. We cast our votes in Rowan's favor."

"As do I and the rest of the partners here in Paris," Celesse broke in.

"I'll keep you updated via David." Rowan leaned forward and turned the screen off, cutting the call. There'd be fallout probably. But she didn't care.

"What a bunch of assholes."

She turned to Warren, a finger held up. "I already warned you about that."

"Just stating the obvious."

Rowan rolled her eyes. "No entourage either. You can have one support person for the three of you."

"That'll be Alice then," Clive cut in smoothly.

"Perfect. She knows David and they can work together. And she's good at everything without being too smug."

"Why not *my* assistant?" Warren asked.

"Because."

"Because?"

Because it would only make him more insufferable and it would make Clive unhappy too.

Europe was Warren's territory. He'd be handy for that reason, but also the power balance would be off and that would lead to Vampire antics because they were all babies. All sorts of feather displays and dick measuring and it was boring.

Alice was a perfect choice. Competent. Unflappable and a rather capable fighter when she needed to be. Clive would ease back and Warren would still be on his territory and Recht would only care if anyone got in his way or fucked something up.

"Because I said so. I don't want to trip over two dozen Vampires all there for the sole purpose of fluffing your ego and fetching you things. You're Scion so I'm sure giving Clive and Recht feeding privileges in the area will suffice for the duration of this thing." She snapped her fingers twice for emphasis. "This is a job. We go in, we find her and I cut her fucking head off. After that if you want to have a bunch of sycophants around to butter your toast and yank your wiener I don't care because I'll be gone."

"*You* could always fluff my ego."

She rolled her eyes. "Ew. Try it on a human who doesn't know what a bunch of weirdo control freaks you all are."

Clive actually growled but he didn't move so she

continued her work. There were complicated things going on between him and the other Vampires and probably something romantic she should be paying attention to. But she had no time for it. He'd tell her eventually if she missed something long enough.

Rowan pointed to the map she'd just unrolled. "I'm sure Recht already told you about the sightings." She then pointed to a rather thick file folder. "He's provided all the Five have gathered. I've sent a copy to Las Vegas where my staff will combine what we have and then get it all back to me with notes." Carey, her office manager and chief smart guy, would organize all the information just how she liked it.

"I plan to get started right away. I'm having dinner sent in so if you two need to handle your feeding business, now's the time."

Clive stood. "I'll let Alice know she's coming along."

Rowan saw the relief in his gaze. He'd been worried about leaving her there with Theo. She worried about the same. In the end, David and Alice would help and they'd keep one another safe and be out of Theo's reach in case he got cranky over something like eye color and ripped someone's head off over it.

"Be back shortly. I've already fed but I'm not going to miss whatever Cook sends as well." He left, as did Warren, who also said he'd return in a few minutes.

"With me," she said to David, who followed her out into the hall. "Please inform Recht that we're ready for him."

"You're mad at me."

Rowan sighed. "You went around me, behind my back when I'm already having trouble with them. You weakened me by filing an official request."

He went pale, shock on his face. "A report? No. No, I didn't! I would *never* do that to you. I know Ms. Espy's valet. I called her two days ago, not as your co-worker but as your friend and someone who has gone through the process of having a valet out in the field with her. She gave me a lot of wonderful advice but that's all it was. She said I filed an official request? Why would she do that?"

Rowan had no idea. "I don't entirely know. But what I do know for certain is that Susan Espy does nothing without a reason. She's the most calculating human being I've ever met. I thought it was a warning to get you under control, but that's obviously not it. I'll need to think on it more." If it was a warning of some type as Rowan suspected, the way it had been delivered indicated Susan felt she might be monitored in some way.

Rowan focused back on David. "I don't want you out there but you're my valet and you're supposed to be, so, okay. If you get killed I'm going to be so pissed off. So don't because I know people. I'll have you brought back so I can kick your ass myself. Alice is coming and she's an utter badass so that's good. Since we're flying private carrier you can bring your weapons. As you're going out in the field with me I will expect you to be at a constant state of readiness. My word is your law. This is not a democracy. I'm in charge. You obey me. That's how it works. Do you understand?"

He nodded. "Yes."

He had no idea. But everyone had to learn to survive and the world continued to get more and more dangerous. He needed to be his own best weapon. "Guns need ammunition. You have to remember to bring a knife, keep it clean, sharp, well oiled and loved. Your body and your brain is something you always have. Your training has only begun. Be careful what you wish for, David."

"Thank you for giving me a chance. And for believing me. I wouldn't harm you. Not ever. I never would have expected her to do this. I'm so sorry."

"We'll figure it out. She has a reason for it and it wasn't to embarrass me or dress me down. Go on and get Recht."

He bowed and was gone.

Rowan leaned against the doorway and stared up at the soaring arches above her. It was full dark by that point and though it was far quieter with the staff at skeleton crew numbers, the place still hummed with Vampire energy and power.

Even after being away for fifteen years, that sound seemed to automatically register as comforting background noise.

She'd need to go to Theo and take tea with him but this business needed to get in motion first.

Enyo hadn't just nearly killed Rowan. Hadn't just ambushed her when she was weaponless like a coward. For either of those things alone, Rowan would have hunted her down and ended her.

Enyo had done those things on ground that was *Rowan's.*

This Keep—with all the best and worst moments of Rowan's life in the stones at her feet—wasn't always a place she wanted to be, but it was home. This place was *hers.* Enyo had violated that and in doing so, the final thing had settled Rowan into a place she rarely went, but knew very well.

Oh, they all thought she was badass when she

was having a normal day. It was a point of pride, she couldn't deny it. But this?

This hunt was an exorcism. There was no mercy inside Rowan when it came to Enyo. There was nothing that would move or sway her from her path.

Enyo thought she had an enemy, a pawn in her game to take control of the Vampires and go to war with humanity.

That was small potatoes compared to what Enyo had truly done.

Rowan was on a righteous path. She waged a holy war with Enyo as her target. The master Vampire was dangerous on every level. There'd be no Vampire whisperer to get her calm enough to crate her for a while and set about *reeducating* the ancient.

Rowan would not truly rest until Enyo no longer existed.

And the Goddess within agreed with a flash of heat.

Before Rowan there hadn't been a Vessel for Brigid in centuries. It turned out Enyo had killed the last one and Brigid was pissed the fuck off and definitely on board with taking care of this problem.

She pushed out of her lean and stalked back into the conference room. She had a dangerous enemy to track down and kill.

Whistling, she got to work.

"I DON'T KNOW why it has to be your assistant who comes along. You're getting special treatment." Warren's tone was dangerously close to a whinge.

"I'm quite certain no one complains as much as you do, Warren." The Vampire had been alive during the dark ages. Why hadn't that made him appreciative of his life now?

Rowan. Rowan who seemed to glow from all the magic and power she stored inside her skin like a nuclear reactor.

Vampires were avaricious. Greedy. There was no one in all the world like Rowan. Warren wanted that for himself.

And Rowan was Clive's.

Clive pushed his annoyance away. It would be beneath him to alert this other male that he'd allowed himself to be rattled.

He'd keep it locked down until he had the proper chance to make his point.

They were predators after all. Clive was very good at patience. With the exception of one red-haired Hunter.

They were also leaders in the Vampire Nation and he needed to remember this hunt was about more than finding the perfect opportunity to use violence to make his point about who Rowan belonged to.

He smiled, thinking of her as she'd agreed she was his. Dark Ages warrior or not, Warren couldn't handle Rowan. Clive barely could but it was a glorious, frightening, vexing, exhilarating thing to belong to a being like that.

"This is my territory. It makes sense that it be my assistant."

"Pardon? I stopped paying attention to this conversation some time ago."

"I'm rightly calling attention to you getting special favors because you're seeing Rowan."

Clive gave him a steady look. "Seeing is a human word. A watery, weak term for what is true. Rowan is my woman. But I don't need my cock to get special favors. Alice is more than qualified for the job. She knows Rowan already, which is a plus. She's worked with Rowan's valet, which is also a plus."

"But it leaves me being the one person on the team without a backup. Which is damned convenient."

Clive stared at the Vampire for long moments. Normally things were not like this between him and Warren. They got along well enough and generally found themselves on the same side of issues and had developed a working relationship and tended to team up during negotiations and the like.

Both were loyal to The First. And always made up two of the opponents to any crazy notions about not renewing the treaty and the like.

But this was different because it was two Scions at odds over the presence of another, powerful predator tossed into the mix. Warren, seeing a powerful, desirable female with excellent connections, was doing what a Vampire of his age and class did. He wanted to make her his.

Which was of course impossible as Rowan was already taken.

While Rowan recovered, she and Clive had spent a great deal of time with one another. They'd grown comfortable, their intimacy sharpening, deepening. She let him in. Not all the time. He wasn't sure she'd ever be totally open with anyone.

She gifted him with glimpses. Sometimes nearly shy moments when tenderness rushed through him for her. Sometimes resentfully with her brows drawn together and a frown on her lips. He accepted like the gifts they were, no matter how they came to him.

He'd wondered how they'd do once they'd returned to Las Vegas and real life intruded again. They'd worked, yes, but spent those four or five hours before sunrise together every day. She let him be part of her life and though she was hesitant about his world, he knew she made an effort because of him.

So, the other Scion could just piss right off because Rowan Summerwaite was taken.

He gave one last look at Warren. "You're right. It's a conspiracy of massive proportions. Do go ahead and bring up your concerns with Rowan."

Warren shuddered a moment, and pride roared through Clive at the sight. So ferocious she scared ancients and she, barely into her thirties.

"Either way I win. You see if you agitate her, she'll only come to me and want to work off her anger. I'm sure you can imagine how that goes. *She comes to me either way.* I'm sure you understand that. I'll see you shortly." Clive turned at the short hallway leading to the office space he knew Alice was using.

Alice had been wrapping up a call when he walked in and once she rang off she looked to him. "Is everything all right?"

He staved off a growl. That reference to sex with Rowan had been more vulgar than he normally would have liked. And yet, it was a point that needed to be underlined.

"Not at all. But in this particular case I'm here to let you know you'll be accompanying us on this hunt. You'll serve as backup to me, Recht and Warren. David will also be coming along."

Alice's concern changed to delight. "Good. I'll coordinate with Warren's assistant. I must admit I'm not sure how I can best serve Recht, but we can work that out." She turned her attention back to him after she'd jotted some notes down. "Would you like to tell me about your meeting with the other Scions?"

He and Warren had decided it was best to be businesslike about The First's state.

It had been Rowan then who'd brought him back from the brink the last time and rumor had it he'd left her nearly dead as a result.

That kept the Vampires scared of both father and daughter and, as far as Clive was concerned, that was a good thing. Fear and power were tradeable goods to Vampires. Rowan had plenty of both. Enough to keep the Nation off her back when she sought to kill an ancient.

Clive set that aside. "Rowan already put some failsafes in place. The staffing here has shifted according to protocol. I spoke with The First earlier today and he was in good spirits." Though there was madness in his eyes, at the edges, and it left Clive unsettled.

And very glad to be leaving and taking all the people he needed to protect far away from this Keep.

"I'm heading back now. We'll be down in the main conference room if you need anything."

She stood. "I'm coming along. If I'm to be part of this I should understand it better."

"Good idea." And it would irritate Warren, which was an added bonus.

EIGHT

ROWAN POURED THEO'S TEA, listening to Chopin as it played through speakers in the background.

"You do know how I love Chopin. A long time ago I met him. Have I ever told you that?"

She turned the handle of the cup as he preferred and then put a few cookies on a plate she placed next to his tea.

He had told her the story. A long time ago when she played piano. She'd been learning but not fast enough for him.

"Ah. I did tell you. You were eight. Learning to play piano. You were awful at it. I felt your discipline was lacking. I was unkind. I wanted to push you into using all that drive you see." His vision sharpened as she sipped her tea. "There is much I regret."

She blinked back tears at this unexpected apology. There was too much to wade through as it was. All this emotion overwhelmed her.

Still, she knew a few things for sure. "It's too late for regret. For any of us. We need to go forward. You've been alive a very long time. So long I know it's easy to let go and listen to the music in your head and tune out all the filters and rules you normally hold yourself to. You're so rarely free. I imagine that's difficult."

He was so powerful and always had to be under

control. The farther away she got from her childhood, the more she could see. The more she was beginning to understand about Theo.

"But you can't let go, *Vater.* I need you to hold on and get yourself back under control. Like you wanted me to use my drive back when I was eight? I want you to use your control. Your Vampires need you. I need you. Right now more than ever. I can't do my job out there if I'm worried about you."

"You're worried about me?" His features softened.

"Of course I'm worried about you. You kept saying I had gone away. But it was you, Theo. You who went away this time. Like you did before. Do you remember before?"

She needed him to face it, even though she knew it made him sad and filled him with regret. He had to get it together or he'd lose everything and the whole world could easily go to shit when one apex predator suddenly disappeared from the ecosystem.

And damn it, despite it all, she loved him and she wanted him to be all right. She didn't want anyone trying to make a move on him because they thought he was weak. He'd kill everything within a hundred miles if he put his mind to it. She needed to be sure that didn't happen for everyone's sake. Including his.

"I need to go and hunt Enyo down. I'm taking Recht, Clive and Warren. Alice will be there to assist, along with David. We think Enyo might be in Prague and we'll be leaving in a few hours."

"I need to crush her. She nearly killed my child." He frowned. "Here in my home. In a garden space you played in growing up. Your father tended the trees in the greenhouse there. She ruined it. I can't go there to think about your father anymore. I only think about you, so close to being gone from me." His features hardened, went very ferocious. "I want to tear her to pieces and salt the earth. I want every single being that ever gave her respite of any kind to suffer a terrible, horrible death." He focused on Rowan again and she went very still at the raw emotion in his gaze. "I could not protect you. Not in your own home. I cannot stand it. I breaks my heart into a thousand pieces each day."

She was up, moving to him, kneeling so her head was resting at his knee. She couldn't look at him, it was too much. Too much emotion and she couldn't deal with it. She had to stay together, not fall apart, and if she continued to look at him with such devastation on his face at failing his child, she'd burst into tears and then he'd never agree to stay.

"You told me once that my path was one beset with challenge and rich with struggle. This is a challenge for the both of us. I need to go do this. I have your best at my side. I have the resources of your Nation and of Hunter Corporation at my back. We'll find her. I'll end her and then we'll move on."

He sipped his tea, relaxed as she sat, her back against the couch he was on, the fire crackling merrily in the fireplace to her left. Even in the summer, being so high up in the mountains meant it was chilly after sunset. And it was nice to have that to focus on and let go of her distress. The calmer she remained, the calmer he'd be.

She stayed a while longer, cleaned up the tea cart and turned to say her goodbyes.

"If you need me you will call. Immediately. I can be there. I will be there."

"Okay."

"Promise me. If you need me you will call. I will promise you in return that I will push back the icy cold song of vengeance. And only because you do this in my name with my Scions and one of my Five at your side. You promise. I promise. And then we are ready for you to leave."

She nodded. "I promise to call if I need you."

"I promise to keep myself together. But I would very much like to hug you."

She went into his arms and returned the hug he gave her.

And then she headed out to the main hall where Clive would be waiting for their trip to Prague.

ROWAN HAD SUGGESTED the Vampires fly ahead and she and David would follow by private plane.

Clive had just looked at her, appalled by how easily she put herself out front to attract trouble every time.

Recht had only given her a face, shaking his head.

"I think it would be a wise use of time if we worked." Clive simply walked onto the waiting plane instead of arguing with her. He wasn't going to Prague any other way but with her on this plane and she needed to understand that.

He saw the lines around her eyes. Not wrinkles, but worry and upset. She'd taken tea with her father and he knew a lot of that worry had to do with The First. But he wanted to fix it and knew she wouldn't allow it if she caught him at it.

Which was fine. Because she might be great with a sword, but he'd been alive far longer and knew a few things about manipulation. He'd do all he could and that was that.

David put an accordion file in front of her, along with a cup of coffee and backed off, sitting nearby but giving her space.

Clive didn't care about that. Space would allow her to keep a wall up. He didn't mind her walling the world out as long as he wasn't included. So he sat next to her and when she moved just enough to touch her thigh to his, he was glad he had.

They took off quickly and would be in Prague in less than two hours, but of course Rowan began to look over the map again.

The Five had come up with three possible Enyo sightings but they'd triangulated and they all had a strong feeling it was Prague.

Clive would come back with her to Prague after all this was handled. He loved the cobblestone streets, the bridges. Few cities loved art as much as Prague. They could stroll the city at night, just the two of them in a city teeming with magic.

He had places to show her. Restaurants he knew she'd enjoy. He'd coax her into art galleries under the pretext that he was looking for something and buy a present for her instead.

Smiling, he sat back and readied himself for landing.

Once deplaned, she heaved a sigh when she caught sight of the sleek limos waiting for them on the tarmac.

"Subtle. You really think with such long lives you guys would understand subtle."

"There's no need to ride in a jalopy. We're far from the only ones who will be picked up by private car at an airfield." Clive indicated she get in. First because he was a gentleman, second because he got a great look at her arse, and third because David had already slid inside, which meant she'd be effectively trapped between them and unable to escape easily in a fit of pique.

Clive sort of liked her fits of pique. Especially when they weren't aimed at him. But he wanted to get settled at this house the Nation had arranged and then she could be grumpy and he could tempt her away from a bad mood with sex.

They glided down narrow streets, through a series of gates, climbing until they reached a final set of wrought iron gates with the Nation's crest worked into the design where they met. The two limousines paused, waiting to be admitted.

Rowan's sigh was so fantastically laden with unspoken complaint and criticism he was truly impressed.

"I'm surprised there aren't any neon bits or inlaid gems. You guys are classy that way," she muttered.

David handed her a little wrapped square. "Caramel chocolate. Your favorite."

She unwrapped it and popped it into her mouth. "Is this your way of keeping me in a non-killing mood, David?"

Clive didn't say a word as her assistant blushed but wisely also said nothing.

"I sure hope there's enough room for us all," Rowan said—though less viciously—as they were cleared and the gates slid open.

"Your apartment is at least six thousand square feet. Hypocrite." Clive winked at her.

"So? You can't even compare this. Moreover, I do it better. And when Vampires come to call, I need the room for their giant egos."

"I figured you liked the giant other things," he said in her ear as he walked past her as they entered the home.

Servants quietly moved through the space, which was spotless and clearly ready for guests.

"I'm going to have to take a closer look at your friends, Scion. They're obviously a bad influence on you." One corner of Rowan's mouth tipped up.

He approved of her turn of emotion.

Until she rounded on a Vampire who'd been stalking David. She shoved him, hard, and he stumbled away. "You, back off or I'll rip your head off and shove it up your ass."

"I'd like to see you try," this obviously stupid Vampire tossed back at her.

Before Warren could complete three words of warning to his underling, Rowan had already punched him so hard—and unexpectedly for that Vampire—he wiped blood from his lip, blinking his confusion.

But the punch hadn't made him any wiser. The Vampire growled at Rowan, starting in her direction. "You think you're tough?"

"I think you're stupid." Rowan squared her shoulders and adjusted her stance. "I *know* I'm tough." She grinned and he came at her, as she'd planned.

Two quick moves and the Vampire ended up on his back, cupping his balls, blood freely running from a nose she'd broken.

The Rowan Summerwaite *break-the-nose-knee-the-balls* one-two.

"Golly, I'm feeling tough right now."

The Vampire roared and Rowan laughed, now clearly in the mood to bring the pain.

Warren sighed, stepping in between them. "My apologies, Hunter."

She frowned and waved him away. "I don't want those. I want to make my point to your sadly uneducated little buddy there." She said it in Czech and then laughed at their expressions. She addressed the bloody Vampire still on his back. "I know lots of things. Get up and I'll show you some more."

Bravely, Warren remained between them, and Clive had to admire the way he protected his staff. Though he knew it wouldn't last forever and regardless, the Vampire on the floor would get his punishment from Warren once this was cleared up.

Warren tipped his head toward Rowan as he addressed the Vampire on the floor. "This is Rowan Summerwaite. She's the Hunter and the foster daughter of The First. She's going to end up maiming you for your insolence before I can. And I need you to understand how much better for you it would be for me to do the upbraiding."

"I don't know why you're killing my fun." Rowan walked past, giving the Vampire on the ground her back to let him know just how insignificant he was to her.

Damn, Clive wanted to be inside her right that very moment. When she got this way there was no denying how much it turned him on.

"Let me show you to your rooms, Ms. Summerwaite." A human staff member bowed, hiding a smile, having watched Rowan school a Vampire Clive bet was a rude asshole to the humans in the house.

It wasn't as if Clive was that concerned for humans in general, but it simply wasn't done to be rude to one's staff and especially those humans who guarded them all at their weakest and most vulnerable.

It showed a lack of good breeding.

Clive followed Rowan but the human turned. "Scion Stewart, the Vampires have their own side of the house. It's light tight."

He frowned but Rowan strode back to him. "Come with me so you know where I am. I have something to speak with you about."

"Should we all be there for that, Hunter?" Warren asked.

Rowan, utterly clueless as to what he meant, turned and once that happened, Clive sent a look to Warren.

"Perhaps, Warren, you'd be more comfortable minding your own business." Clive raised a brow.

"I'm attempting to be kept in the loop."

Rowan, agitation clear in the way she held her shoulders, put a hand at her hip and glared Warren's way. "What is the deal here? Have I kept anything from you that's got you all pissy?"

"I'm not pissy. I'm just attempting to be sure we're all on the same page."

Recht growled and Warren stepped back, shutting up. Rowan rolled her eyes. "I'm not sure why this politics bullshit is rearing its ugly head but there's no need for it. I don't have the time or energy to fuck around with games and posturing. I want to find Enyo and put her down. You all want that too so stop being such a baby and obsessing over who I give the bigger slice of cake to. As far as this hunt is concerned, we're all on the same team."

"As far as this hunt is concerned?"

Rowan huffed. "Yes. As in, of course I'm giving

Clive more attention and spending time with him I'm not giving to you or anyone else. We all know why so I'm assuming it's not necessary for me to explain. But where it concerns something you're rightfully part of, I'll share information."

Warren frowned briefly and Clive merely smiled as Rowan turned his way again.

"See you all back here in half an hour," she called over her shoulder as they walked away.

It was amusing that Rowan seemed to not see—at all—the way Warren was preening all around her, trying to impress. Just another example why Clive was with her and a male like Farrelly was not.

Rowan wasn't immune to a pretty face, or to strength and power. None of them were. But what Farrelly missed was that Rowan looked, admired and went about her business. If she wanted you in her bed, you'd know it.

She'd be far too much for Farrelly to handle anyway. They'd find him rocking and weeping in some corner and that was enough to lighten Clive's steps.

Clive might be covered in fingerprint bruises, scratches down his back and sides and sporting a few love marks when he and Rowan were done fucking, but they were the best kind of sting.

It was primal. And no one had ever brought it out in him the way she did.

Once they'd gotten into her room and the door closed he backed her against it and she grinned up into his face.

"It's not like you won't know where I'll be," she murmured, her grin turning into something else. He heard the speed of her heartbeat, knew she *allowed* him to. Knew too—when she tilted her head ever so slightly, exposing the pale as moonlight skin of her throat—she'd done it to excite as well as soothe.

He had a boy's control around her when she did that. He knew the cost. The tracery of scars on her back were merely part of the ways growing up with an Ancient Vampire's idea of discipline scarred her. That she was as open and trusting with him was a testament not to him, but to her. Rowan was as ever, a phoenix. A being of fire and change. Death and rebirth.

He licked up her neck, pressing the tip of his tongue against the juicy, fat vein, his incisors grazing to either side.

Her breath came from her lips, shaky. Her skin pebbled against his mouth. He wanted to taste her so badly he nearly shook with it. Knew from one, accidental nick of her lip the first time he'd ever kissed her that she was rich and delicious.

"Are you thinking of it?" she asked, voice gone sultry.

Taunting. His skin heated and he groaned. Human women could be vicious at times. Some were quite good at mimicking that casual tease with a little bit of an edge. But he'd never met anyone but a Vampire who could do it without an effort.

Until she taunted him with the blood she'd not given him access to.

See this, Scion? Hmmm? Don't you want it on your tongue?

He knew that's what she meant when she'd asked him if he was thinking of it. And yes he was.

"Yes. You know I am." He squeezed her biceps and she shivered, stuttering a sigh. "You've had me on your tongue. Inside you. I'm in you still." He kissed to the hollow just below her ear.

"Y-yes."

He stilled for long moments. That admission…for her to give that to him after all she'd endured. For her to say it and the longing, the satisfaction that he gave her with that, with his lifeblood, drove at him.

"Shall I tell you what you taste like?" she whispered, her pulse hammering against his lips.

"Yes."

"Coppery. Sweet. There's a slight spice to you. Cardamom maybe. But you taste like London underneath all that. Like soot and smoke and black cabs and great pubs. You taste like expensive leather goods and private clubs with heavy snifters of top shelf brandy aged with blood. You taste like class and money and power. A lot of power."

He pressed her harder to the wall, nearly snarling as the breath whooshed from her lips. He rolled his hips, grinding himself against her. She slid one of her legs up his, meeting his thrust.

A groan stuttered from her lips as he knew he stroked over her clit.

She opened her eyes and met his gaze straight on. He nipped her bottom lip and she slid her fingers through his hair, tugging him back to look into his face again.

It hit her then, this game they'd played that got them both off so hard. Dancing on the edge of breaking her skin but never crossing the line. No matter how much she knew he wanted it.

He made her feel safe.

Struck still for long moments, she let that sink in.

No one had ever made her feel safe. And here, in

the unlikeliest of males, she found it and though she'd known it for some time, the acceptance of it, and the need to give back to him even a part of what he gave to her, drove her.

"You never ask."

"I know what it would cost. You don't need to pay that price with me."

Rowan swallowed hard. There had been a time in her life—mostly all of it until that moment—where a Vampire taking her blood didn't involve her consent. Or her pleasure. It had been about punishment or manipulation in some sense. It had always felt like a violation.

But it was integral to who Clive was and though he was a Vampire, he wasn't anything like those who'd used her like she meant nothing at all.

The way they teased had worked itself into foreplay and every time he tortured them both but never violated her trust allowed her to accept the deliciously carnal taboo of it.

Talking about how he tasted had only underlined for her this connection they shared. And that it was good and nothing like what had happened to her before. She wanted him to know her taste the way she knew his.

Wanted too, that increased, deeper connection she'd have with him once she closed that circle and let him drink from her.

Rowan brought his face to hers. "What if?" She grazed her teeth over his bottom lip and then slid her tongue all around each one of his incisors until his cock pressed against her so hard she ached. "We tried a baby step?"

She let go of her fear and slid her tongue against the sharpest part of his incisor and let it break the skin.

Her blood flowed and she let it. Let herself listen to him once her taste hit him. He gripped her tighter with a sound laced with so much desire it stole her breath.

Yes, this was what she should be doing.

SHE FLOWED INTO him and they went to their knees right there in her room, not breaking the kiss he'd been longing for ever since he'd allowed himself to admit he was in love with her.

So.

Fucking.

Good.

Caramel. Burnt sugar and salt. And power too. Goddess yes, the power from this small sip lit him up. Electric, she seemed to rush through him, filling each cell as though he'd been parched for something only she could provide.

And that was the truth of it.

She broke the kiss, blood on her bottom lip, her pupils swallowing all color in her eyes.

He leaned in and licked, taking that last bit of her.

Before he could speak, Rowan growled, her hands shoving between them until she reached the waistband of his trousers.

He leaned back to give her more access as she unbuckled and unzipped, pulling his cock free. She wrapped her hand around it, sliding up and down a few times until she flicked her gaze up to his.

"I want this. Now."

Arm banded around her waist, he hitched her up as she struggled one leg free from her jeans and panties before she was back, so hot and wet he nearly passed out as she sank down on his cock in one move.

He managed to get to his knees, keeping his arm around her waist to hold her where he liked, pressing her to the wall to balance as he thrust up into her body.

"Now that you have it, are you satisfied?" He licked up her neck again and she writhed all around him, yanking at his razor-thin control.

"Not yet, so don't forget that part."

Caught between a laugh and a moan, he kissed her, delighting in the way she tugged at his hair to get purchase enough to grind herself against him each time he slid deep inside her.

"I'll have you remember my impeccable reputation when it comes to making sure my lady always comes."

"I like to be reminded, Scion. I'm greedy that way."

"One of your finest qualities." He snarled a curse as she fluttered around him.

"I love it when you say bad words because of me."

"I'm sure you do. Impudent." He thrust harder, bouncing her and really enjoying the surprised pleasure on her face. "It's your own fault. Breeding, you see. You had good European stock and you had to go and reject that and turn yourself into an American."

He reached down between them to stroke a fingertip over her clit.

Rowan tried to soldier on, her words getting just a little slower at the ends. "And yet, it makes you come really hard. Fucking an American, I mean. You like it down here in the dirt." She swallowed, her gaze blurring for a moment, and Clive smiled.

"I like fucking *you*, who happens to be the most

American woman I've ever met and you're not even American."

"We both know I'm a rebel." Rowan always managed to find the energy to get the last word.

He laughed as he made her come so hard she lost all her words. Her head tipped back, her inner walls gripped him so tight he had no choice but to follow her into climax, fucking her harder and faster until they collapsed to the floor in a tangle of limbs.

NINE

Rowan strode into the room she'd chosen to be their operation hub for the time they were in Prague. "Let's get the maps up," she told David as they both set boxes of files, maps and other intelligence they'd gathered.

A human staff member came in and tipped her head. "Ms. Summerwaite, I'm Gemma, head of the household staff here. May I be of any assistance?"

The woman exposed her mark of service, a gryphon. Her family was nearly as old as Rowan's father's was.

She did regret losing that connection. Though she bore her mark, she was not of service. Not like Gemma was. Not like her father had been, her cousins. When Rowan had learned the devastating truth that Theo had been the one to order her parents killed, she'd broken that tie. Had stepped out of a noble tradition she'd been molded to be part of since before she was born.

She'd remained in contact with her father's family—though she'd never forgiven them for lying to her all those years just as Theo had. She'd let go of a lot of the threads holding them together. It made sense that as a result she was not as close to them as she had been.

But it still left her melancholy sometimes.

Rowan tipped her wrist out as she took the woman's hands in her own. "I'm pleased to meet you and yes, I would very much like your assistance here so we don't put tack marks into the walls or anything." As much as she grumbled about Vampires and their grandiose ways, she had a great deal of respect and admiration for the way they took care of their things and this remarkable home was no exception. She'd never purposely destroy something so beautiful.

Within five minutes, Gemma had a list and she left to procure the things on it with David at her side. Having people to handle details was awesome.

Clive strolled in, smug grin on his face. Not a special smug, just his Tuesday face. She thanked him for the coffee cup he'd put within her reach as she set her laptop up and began to synch it with the other two computers in the room.

Recht entered, looking around, nodding in acceptance. She hid her smile, pleased he'd approved.

David returned and together with Gemma, set up some display boards they got the maps pinned to.

As a group they all seemed to click well enough. Each had a strength they brought to the table and the rest let him or her get on with it.

Though she had noticed Warren leaving some time before and he hadn't returned. Before she could ask after him, five Nation Vamps strolled in, all wearing some sort of stupid-looking black ops crap that looked like Halloween costumes, with Warren at their back.

"I've brought in some of my people to assist us."

She had to give it to the insufferable prick, he didn't take no for an answer.

Until she taught him to. "No thanks." Rowan turned back to the map and her conversation with Recht. "I want to get a lay of the land. I've been here a few times, but where Nation Vampires hang out and those on the run might be are two different things."

At their backs, Warren interrupted. "If you'll just give the coordinates to my people, they can do your reconnaissance for you and report back. That way we won't need to waste time. It might rain later."

She slowly swiveled her body, trying to keep her temper but there was something stupid and annoyingly Vampire going on and it was totally agitating.

"Back at the Keep we set the team. I've been clear about the makeup of the team from the start. I did not include five Nation Vamps in that team for a reason," Rowan said with what she thought was a lot of restraint.

"Why make more work for yourself?"

And she was out of restraint. "Because this is my fucking job. It's *my* work to do. I want to look at these places with *my own eyes.* I want people whose skills *I* trust to look at these places with their own eyes. I don't know these Vampires, so I don't trust them or their perceptions. You see what I'm saying here?"

"This is stupid. You have a thing about Vampires and I understand it, but—"

"You're riding my *no, thank you* button pretty hard at this moment and I don't know why. Do not ever assume you know my motivations when I have told you exactly what they are already. You do not understand me in some special snowflake way. I don't want these Vamps under my fucking feet. I never agreed to them. They need to not be in my face or my hunt."

"This is impeding the hunt. Your attitude isn't helpful."

Clive moved at her side, letting her fight this one out, but she knew it was only a matter of time before he spoke because he was bossy and this wasn't his territory and he and Warren were already bickering like three-year-olds with one lollipop.

"I'll decide what's helpful. This is a fact and not up for debate."

"Why are you so opposed to the manpower I offer?" Warren tried some sort of charming-rogue thing with his features and she wanted to hit him with a brick.

Rowan curled her lip. "Really? I'm embarrassed on your behalf that you'd come at me like this."

"Like what?" He turned on that extra lilt in his accent, Irishing it up, the shameless whore.

Clive snorted. "Now *I'm* embarrassed on your behalf."

Rowan didn't want this beef with Warren. He was an ally and she liked him most of the time. But he clearly had to have his perception of her shifted away from the Rowan she'd been to who she was now. A power in her own right.

"Yeah, yeah, you're easy on the eyes, and still, fuck off. You think to yourself that I'm the girl you've watched grow up serving The First. And I get it. But I'm in charge and that's that. You coming at me with some dumb line about extra manpower is an insult to my intelligence and your power. I'm not measuring my dick against yours. I don't care about your territory. I don't care about where you sit in relation to me at the table with Theo. This is pointless. Everyone here knows why you brought these guys in. Wrap it up and get them gone because there's work to be done."

"You could show more trust, Rowan."

"Good Lord, man, stop." Clive, more agitated than

she'd seen him in some time, was clearly done being quiet.

Warren glared Clive's way. "You're the reason she's suddenly so distrusting."

"You need to back the fuck off or end up bleeding out." Clive's snarl was laced with violence.

Whoa. Well, that level of vehemence was unexpected. Clive rarely tossed around the F word like that.

The Nation Vamps all milled around the small room, making her more and more agitated. David touched her elbow, drawing her into the hallway.

"Why don't you and I go out? We'll go to the first location. They're going to be at this for a while and you're only going to end up having to file paperwork with Hunter Corp. if you actually kill one of them. You can burn off your annoyance and we can get work done. We can even take Alice with us."

"It's good you bring that up since she's standing around the corner trying to hear what's going on."

Alice poked her head around and then came out with a sheepish smile. "I think that's a marvelous idea."

Rowan knew she'd never be able to shake both of them and it would be good to have a few more sets of eyes so she agreed.

"And I've taken the liberty to arrange for a car as well," David murmured as they left the main house after letting Gemma know they were headed out.

"You know me so well."

"That's what they pay me the big bucks for."

"Oh, you made a joke! I'm having such a good influence on you."

The car was waiting for them just a few blocks away and it was nice to use her Czech since she'd gotten rusty. She'd also be able to park it securely in the same location, which meant freedom from Nation politics at least in that one thing.

"So, do either of you want to hazard a suggestion on which place to head to first?"

"I don't think she's going to be sleeping rough. That's not her style," Alice ventured. "Given the relative importance Vampires as old as she would place on the opulence of her lifestyle, she's not going to opt for anything but the very best."

David nodded. "I'd like to think she's sleeping in a crypt under the Bone Church, but I have to agree with Alice. She's going to be close to the city if she's here. Otherwise why do it?"

The thought of Enyo hiding out in some country house when Prague was so fabulous? Rowan agreed with them both.

"We can walk to one of the addresses so let's do that. If a bunch of pompous Nation Vampires have a fully stocked and staffed villa up here, it's not a stretch to imagine Enyo doing the same."

The streets up near the castle were lush with trees. There were people out and about but it wasn't exceptionally crowded. Enough to provide some cover as they shifted from group to group as she circled the block where the large, gated home was located.

There were plenty of Vampires in the area, Rowan knew that much. Their energy was easy enough to locate. This was a good lead, though she didn't really feel any power as ancient as Enyo's.

But they weren't all baby Vampires either.

Alice separated from them, linking her arm with a

man standing outside a quiet little café. She spoke in an undertone but Rowan felt the wave of her persuasion.

Rowan took note of a few places to get a better view of the other side of the tall stone wall surrounding the house.

Alice leaned in close to the man and then kissed him, walking down the street away from the house. At the end of the block she tipped her head and Rowan headed down the parallel street to meet up with Alice several blocks away.

"He says there was a lot of activity last week at the house. Mainly in the evenings. Pale skin. Expensive cars. He never saw a female though."

"There's an apartment building across the street. I'm going to see what sort of view I can get from the roof. I want to see what's on the other side of the wall." She paused and looked up at Clive as he approached. "Good evening."

"Have a nice stroll?"

Rowan took a quick look, noting the lack of blood. His hair was still perfect and after he fought it was mussed up. "I take it you handled your whatever with Warren. As for our stroll? As a matter of fact we totally did enjoy it."

Clive's smile changed and she could tell he was amused. "There's a lovely little wine bar we're expected in shortly. Why don't you come back to the house and we can all talk about it."

"Because there's a lot of posturing and dick measuring and it's boring and makes me want to punch every one of you people in the nose. Except for Alice because she's a superior specimen. And Recht because he would punch me back and clean my clock."

He put a hand over his heart. "Even me? I'm wounded."

"That was some pretty decent sarcasm. It's the British thing, right?"

He took her hand and tugged, bringing her down the sidewalk along with him as Alice and David followed.

"Don't think we won't discuss the way you snuck out of here earlier," Clive murmured as they got back to the house and David and Alice had gone inside.

"I'm up for that," Rowan said with enthusiasm.

He nearly tripped over his feet as he came to a halt when she'd responded that way. Which made her laugh even harder. She bumped her hip to his.

"Just kidding, sport. I don't negotiate with terrorists."

"What on earth does that mean?"

"It means fuck off. I do what I want."

"Of course it does. How could I not know that?" His tone was dry, but he was amused. Deep down.

"I don't get it either. It's like you're new here." Rowan went inside, smile on her face.

CLIVE WATCHED THE confidence in her stride—along with her arse—as she headed into the operations room.

Warren looked her up and down. "We've got a meeting set up with one of my sources in about forty minutes. It's not far. Where did you go?"

"I went to work. It's why I'm here." She looked around the room but said nothing, accepting the Nation Vampires had been sent away because she'd insisted.

And being exactly correct because that's who she was.

Rowan got to work. "We've done some reconnaissance at this address." She pointed to the map. "Alice spoke with a neighboring business owner who says people who can pretty much be described as Vampires were there last week but it's been quiet for a day or two. There're a few spots I'm going to attempt to get a better look from so I'll head over just before dawn and get into place. Plenty of Vampire energy though. I'm sure you've got plenty around here, Prague being the perfect gothic wallowing spot for all the Vampire emo types. So, it could be that. But I don't think so. Don't know who they are or why they're here, but there are a fuckton of Vamps in that house."

She looked from the map back to the rest of the people in the room. "You said we had a meeting with sources? We'll handle that then I'll head back to that house. After sunrise will do me nicely."

Warren started to argue and Rowan stared at him, daring him to make an issue out of the way she'd taken control again.

They all knew she'd only take so much Vampire politics before she dealt with things on her own. There was no reason to be surprised or even offended by it. She was driven and couldn't possibly care less about hierarchy within the Nation except to protect her father and, Clive had to admit with great internal satisfaction, him as well.

"I assume we'll head to this meet with your sources early? So we can get a look at the layout before we walk into it?" Rowan asked.

"I'm not freshly turned, Rowan." Warren did this thing to his voice that embarrassed Clive on the other male's behalf.

Rowan only snorted at Warren. "I suppose not. What

I'd like to see is a map of the Vamp population within a twenty-five mile radius."

"You're mad to think the Nation would share that with a Hunter!"

"I'm going to get you a string of pearls to clutch every time I say something outrageous. I'm totally mad. Barking. And yet, if that villa I was just at regularly housed older Vampires I'd know more than I do now. It could be a guest house. An estate owned by some old Vampire family and people use it when they come to Prague. Whatever it was, I'd have more information. Which would help me track her down. The entire point of this exercise, remember?"

"Give her the data," Recht said with a scowl.

"This is my ground. I am Scion here. I make the decisions regarding this sort of situation." Warren faced Rowan when he spoke, but it was clear he meant his reply for Recht.

Rowan threw her hands up in the air. "You see, this is why I fought the idea of a team with the Nation to start with. This stupid, pointless display of feathers and power game nonsense. I don't have anything to prove to you, Warren. I'm going to tell you the same thing I told Hunter Corp. I'm going to find her and kill her. I'd like the help but it's going to happen regardless of your feelings on the matter. Killing Vampires, contrary to whatever you have in your head, is a huge pain in my ass. There's paperwork. If I wanted to scamper about the planet gleefully lopping off heads and stabbing Vampires to death, I'd be doing it and I wouldn't need a map from you, or a paid position from Hunter Corp. to make it happen."

Clive pushed away from the wall. "Enough. Rowan,

you'll get the data. There's no reason to hie off on your own."

"There's a reason right here." She flicked a hand at Warren. "We've known from the start that to get hunting we'd be in someone's territory. One of you Scions would be dealing with a hunt on your ground and the others in the group would have to suck it up that they weren't in charge at the same level. You all repeatedly assured me this was not going to be a problem and yet, it totally is."

"Rowan, will you excuse us for a moment?" Clive asked. He thought they'd handled this but apparently not. "Five minutes. Alice, please get her the data she's requested."

Warren didn't argue.

"You have six minutes. If this issue still exists when I walk back in here? I'm done with every fucking one of you. Well, not you." She looked to Clive. "But this hunt."

She left, David at her heels. Alice nodded at him crisply and he was sure she would handle this as well as she did everything else.

Recht held his hand up. "Scion, if I might."

Clive waved a hand.

"She's not yours." Recht tossed this at Warren hard enough to bring both Clive and Warren's attention snapping into place.

"What are you talking about?"

"I understand. She's exceptional. But she's made her choice and her choice is Clive. She's had enough to manage, I won't allow you to make this worse. We need her and she needs her focus. Her focus is this hunt."

Well. That was unexpected.

"I have no idea what you're talking about. This is my land. Of course I take control here. And she's not with Clive. She fucks him."

Before Clive even thought it through, he'd rushed the room, grabbed Warren by the throat, lifted and thrust up into the wall hard enough to knock things down. Cold, detached rage seemed to ice through his veins. That part of him that would never be close to human surged to the fore to protect what was his. "Think upon your next words very carefully. *She is mine* and I will not tolerate your speaking of her in such a way."

"You haven't claimed her."

Clive squeezed tighter. "Stop struggling because you need to hear me and also get as much oxygen as you can to stay alive."

Recht sat, watching but not intervening.

"I don't need to mark Rowan so *you* can see it. It's enough that *she* sees it. Which is why a Vampire like you doesn't have her and I do. You should also understand I would do anything to protect her, because, as I just told you, she's mine. Your feelings are irrelevant but for one point, you need to accept right this moment that you have no chance. None. You're making a fool out of yourself, you're making her job harder—which displeases me—and you're still not going to have her."

Clive let him go, stepping back but not turning around.

"One last thing. I will kill anyone who is a threat to her."

Warren glared as he straightened. "She'd be angry you didn't trust her to take care of her own business."

"You can't bait me, Warren. Get yourself in order

and stop acting like your incisors just descended. I'm going now, I'll meet you all in the foyer in ten minutes so we can get to the meet early and size the area up."

Then Clive turned his back and left the room.

TEN

As they came up the sidewalk heading to the wine bar, Clive slowed as he realized the sounds of evening had stopped. The silence hanging in the air was ominous. Hesitant and afraid. The street was deserted and the hair on the back of his neck pricked up as his incisors elongated, readying.

Something was wrong and in another breath, that was underlined as the sticky-sweet stench of death blood hit Clive's senses.

He glanced toward Rowan, whose expression told him she knew the same. With a few hand signals, they all fanned out.

Clive pushed everything from his mind but the moment. His senses rocketed out, heightened hearing, he could smell the fear, the death, the pain and anger still in the air. There had been other predators in the area and not very long ago.

The wine bar had been shuttered, but it was clear something had happened inside.

Recht held up a hand to stop them as he peered closely at the catch where the shutters had been hastily closed.

He shook his head. Traps were part and parcel of what they did so it wasn't so hard to be wary when it came to opening those doors up.

From the corner of his vision he watched Rowan hop up on a tall stone wall, nimbly walking along the edge. Just as nimbly she leapt from there to the second floor balcony above the wine bar and disappeared inside.

In moments she'd showed up downstairs, pushing the front doors open. "It's bad," she murmured as they passed her and entered the wine bar.

She'd been right.

There was no other way to describe the scene but as a massacre. Blood spatters and bits of gore covered every conceivable surface including the ceiling and the underside of tables and chairs.

Limbs had been strewn around, torn from the human victims heaped here and there.

They hadn't even fed really. This…destruction was wanton in the worst sort of way. It disgusted Clive to be associated with any being who'd do this.

He met Warren's gaze as the other Scion cursed and took in the scene. "Looks like six human victims, given the various parts. Three scorch marks and some dust. Sound right to you?" Warren asked.

"That was my estimate as well." Clive nodded.

Recht came in through the back. "Blood trail leading through the kitchen and out the rear door. There was a fairly crude booby trap but I handled it. I did a cursory sweep but found no more. There's a three car lot back there. The blood leads to one of the spots and disappears."

"So they flew or got in a car," Rowan said.

"That would be my best guess. Once I'm done here, I'll head off to see if I can pick up that blood scent anywhere else."

Warren thanked Recht and pulled his phone from an

inner pocket. "Let me call a team to clean this up." He headed off to a corner while the rest of them checked the remaining bodies in the room for any identification.

The fury rolled from Rowan in waves so hot he sensed them from across the room. She took in the mess with a curled lip.

She put her toe on a scorch mark. "I hope the human who killed this one made it hurt. A lot."

"Some of these might be my sources. They were good Vampires, Rowan. They wouldn't have done this. Not to innocents and surely not in public. Prague is full of Vampires, yes, but older ones. Less emo as you claimed and more Byron and Keats. This is *sloppy.* Not their style at all. This is repugnant." Warren waved a hand, disgusted.

She sighed. "You're right. I apologize."

One warrior to another as was appropriate. Warren nodded, accepting the apology, and they moved on, getting back to work until the cleanup crew arrived.

FROM THERE THEY headed back to the house. After a quick cleanup, they re-convened in the ops room and worked until Recht arrived, wearing a dour expression.

"Why don't we do an update on everyone's status?" Warren asked and when they all agreed, he went first. "One of my people has handled the police. The owner of the bar was one of mine. His brother will take over tomorrow. He's also promised to help in any way he can."

Rowan nodded, pacing as she listened. "Did he have children?"

"Why?" Warren eyed her carefully.

"Because Hunter Corp. has a fund for the children

of parents who've been slain in Vampire-related violence. This most assuredly was, wasn't it? Even Vampire kids have to eat and need new clothes and stuff."

"I'm the one who has to apologize now," Warren said. "I misjudged you and your intentions."

"It's fine." And it was or Rowan wouldn't have said it. Like he'd said her name aloud, her gaze cut his way for a moment. Once they'd connected she put her attention back on the job. "Shitty night all around." Rowan paused. "And I'm about to make it worse when I tell you it looks like your source was exposed so where's the leak?"

Vampires killed one another all the time. They were a contentious group. The young were impetuous but powerful and the old got progressively disconnected with the rules and filters that kept one from pulling someone's spine out over a minor offense.

But for the most part, they killed one another clean. There were rules. That scene was an ultimate violation of everything the Vampire Nation stood for. The risk of exposure from a scene like that? The fact that it had happened in the presence of a Hunter alone brought Clive's hands into fists of rage. Multiple Treaty violations bringing Hunter Corp. squarely into their business. And rightfully so.

"I'm not going to report this to Hunter Corp.," Rowan spoke at last.

All four Vampires looked to her, surprised.

"It serves nothing to report it. First, I'd have to deal with Roth the asshole. And he's an asshole, as I said. Second, it would eat up time. I have little of it. Third, it won't bring any of those humans back. Lastly? You need to understand I will kill each and every Vampire

I find responsible for that unholy mess back there. I need no warrant. If you're clear on that, I'm clear and we're good."

"I find no fault in that. Though if I find them first, I will kill them. This is my ground, this happened to Vampires under my protection," Warren said.

Rowan shrugged at his words. "Dead is dead."

Recht filled them all in on his activities. "I managed to track at least one of the fleeing Vampires to the front of the Four Seasons. He didn't go inside. There's a streetcar that runs out front as well as numerous busses, cabs and two metro stops within easy distance."

"Let me set about getting the information as to what cabs were called from the bell desk at the Four Seasons." David tapped Rowan's arm and she nodded before he left the room.

"He's awesome at getting people to do things he wants them to," Rowan murmured as she looked at the papers on the table before her.

"We could call, but I think it's better if we pay a visit to my source in person." Warren looked down at the phone in his hand. "The one we were meeting at the wine bar was sent on orders of another. He'll be skittish if he's heard about this. You can cover me. We have to go in quiet. He'll run if he sees us coming."

Rowan took a deep breath. "I suppose that's also a good sign she's here. Or she was and they want to keep us here so she can leg it elsewhere. Whatever the case, her stench is all over this city. I can't wait to find her one-eyed ass and kill her dead, dead, dead."

Clive moved past her, breathing her in as he did, sipping her power. She gave him a look under her lashes and he smiled, just a brief one for her eyes only.

Bloodthirsty. Mmm.

A GIANT, BLACK luxury SUV waited for them as they left the house. Rowan eyed it but said nothing, though it was laden with judgment.

Clive disagreed. This vehicle was big enough for all of them and it was clearly armored.

He came to Prague frequently enough that he knew, too, that SUVs like the one they were in dotted the city all the time these days so there was no reason not to be comfortable and safer too.

They headed away from the city center and toward the big blocks of apartments ringing it. Hundreds of thousands lived in these mini cities under communist control and even now nearly forty percent of residents of Prague still called them home. Plenty of lights were on all over the blocks. But after they parked and began to head into the heart of the jungle of buildings, it was fairly quiet.

Once Warren had them all come to a halt at the edge of a building, David handed a pair of binoculars to Rowan, who waved them away. "Don't need them anymore."

Clive sent her a raised brow but didn't comment. He'd save it for when they were alone.

David watched through the scope in the high-powered rifle he carried. Recht had taken position across the courtyard, perched on someone's balcony. Clive passed Rowan to settle in south of her and the apartment Warren was headed to. Alice was back at the house, coordinating all the various arms of that night's operation.

And suddenly Clive knew something was wrong. He sped from his place, keeping low, noting Rowan had left her place and was running across the small concrete courtyard, moonlight glinting off the edge of the sword she'd drawn.

He followed and knew Recht did the same as they burst into an attack in progress inside that flat.

Clive let the animal part of him take over, let the teeth tear from his gums, let his muscles take over to propel him into the room to tear a Vampire off Warren's back.

"Thanks, mate. Don't kill that one if you can help it," Warren called out right before he ripped the throat of one of his attackers.

Rowan pinned their prisoner to the wall with her blade through the Vampire's chest. "Don't move or the blade will slice your heart and you'll die."

"So romantic, darling." Clive drew the curtains back over the broken-out window. No one moved or made noise outside, but they could only hide it for so long, so they needed to get this wrapped up.

"I'd rather he moved and died." Rowan shrugged. "But if I can't kill him, I guess knowing he's freaked is a little bit of a salve to my agitated nerves." She leaned close to the Vampire she'd impaled. "What's your story then? Didn't get enough love as a kid? Mom never tucked you in? I can relate. My dad liked to whip me bloody. And I'm not a Vampire like you so it took me a long time to heal up. It's the root cause of my general crankiness and dislike of Vampires. But I did something positive with all my rage. Look at you and your bad choices."

He dropped to the ground with a pained grunt when she pulled her blade free, bending to wipe it on the Vampire's shirt before returning it to the sheath.

Once that was done, Rowan grabbed the prisoner

by the hair and hauled him behind her like a bag of laundry. Clive made sure the way was clear for her to get their captive back to the car, which she did remarkably fast.

He got in on her other side and she scowled.

"This is some real bullshit, Scion." She pointed to the leather jacket she wore. "I really love this coat and now it's covered in Vampire goo." Her scowl turned into something else. Something dirty and his cock approved mightily.

"I'm sure there are papers you can fill out to get it cleaned at Nation expense. Or I can buy you a new one."

"You sure know how to spoil a girl." Rowan's satisfied tone made him smile.

"I've got centuries of practice."

She laughed and bumped the slow healing Vampire between them as she did. "He's a card, that one, right? What's your story? What's your name? You should tell me or I'll make one up and it won't be nice. I should do that anyway because your friends made a mess with their internal organs all over my clothes."

"Your name," Warren barked. And as that Vampire lived in Warren's territory, the compulsion to obey was too strong for any but the strongest to deny.

"Szabo."

"Really?" Rowan snickered.

"That was my father's name!"

Rowan shook her head. "You don't get to be indignant with me, Szabo. That makes me cranky. *I* didn't name you something weird. Blame the mom who never cut the crusts off your bread."

He started babbling, this time Clive recognized Magyar.

Rowan cut him off. "Don't care about your name really. What we do care about is why you were in that flat attacking Nation Vampires."

Once back at the villa, they loaded the prisoner into the house. Clearly impatient, Rowan gave them all a censuring look. "This is your deal. Crack Szabo here so we can get moving."

"Tell us what you were doing at Gabor's flat." Warren's voice was smooth and calm, but the command in it was unmistakable. As Scion, Clive had the same hold on the Vampires who lived on his grounds in North America. But lone wolf Vampires were harder to crack because they never cleaved to any leadership.

Harder, but not impossible. Clive had his own range of skills and gifts that came from his line. One of them was the ability to go in and take whatever he wanted from a Vampire's head. It was messy usually and quite often fatal so he rarely used it.

Clive gave Szabo a glare, rarely didn't mean never. Fatal or not, they'd have answers.

ROWAN PRETENDED TO be relaxed as Warren began to interrogate the Vampire but really, she was in a killing mood. Not that being in a killing mood was unusual for her, but it meant that she had to accept that this was more than Enyo, damn it.

This had conspiracy all over it. Conspiracies took a lot of time. People who plotted them were usually assholes she needed to kill or maim.

Rowan didn't have the time for this to be a conspiracy.

Recht stood near the doorway, his presence scary and threatening. Even if Warren didn't have the mojo to get Szabo to tell all, Recht could have done it in moments.

Clive as well. She knew he had a gift from Theo's line. One that enabled him to reach into memories and take what he needed.

Szabo at least got the idea he should give the appearance of cooperation. "I got a text. It told me to go there."

Warren slowly raised one brow and Rowan settled in.

"One of the things that irks me most, Szabo, is having to play semantics with my subjects to get them to obey me. I don't like it. Describe exactly your purpose in going to Gabor's flat," Warren ordered.

"I was told to go to that address and kill anyone inside."

"On whose orders do you act? Do not attempt to avoid answering."

Szabo's mouth hardened but he was weak already so he didn't hesitate long. "I don't know who sent the text. But the orders usually come from Lacoste or his people."

Everyone froze at the name of one of the most influential old lines in the Nation. And it was the name they already had from Theo's little jaunt into vengeance-town.

It was Recht who spoke then. "Francois Lacoste?"

Szabo nodded. "Yes."

Recht and Rowan shared a look. Theo was going to lose his shit so they needed to handle Lacoste before Theo got it into his head to do it first.

"How are you involved with Lacoste?" Recht used his super spooky whisper. She'd spent years trying to mimic it but she never came close.

"Blood Front." The words were torn from Szabo's lips and she wanted to beat him bloody with them.

He looked to her, terrified, at the sound she made. Recht smiled and that was a blue ribbon she'd remember forever.

"Who else do you speak to in the Blood Front?"

Szabo gave the names of three other Vampires but didn't have much more. The Blood Front appeared to work in blind cells, which limited their exposure in situations just like this one.

"Who died in that flat tonight?" Recht continued.

"She's going to kill me!" Szabo screamed and Rowan slapped him hard enough to shut him down.

"Who is *she?*" Rowan demanded.

Szabo shook his head, gaze frantic and fearful. Rowan didn't have their nifty power of compulsion so Warren stepped in and repeated the question.

"Gabor died. We killed him when he opened the door to us. There was another in the flat with him. I don't know who. He and Pavel struggled but Pavel killed him. That's when you burst in."

She may not have Vampire compulsion, but she had other tools to get some compliance. Rowan reached down into her boot, slid the stiletto from its sheath and stabbed his hand through the table before he'd even realized she was moving.

Szabo screamed and Rowan leaned in, taking his jaw in her now-bloody hand and squeezing. "Be quiet. I know just how to stab you and not do permanent damage. Which means I *also* know how to stab you and make sure you'll never be able to use this hand again. Shall I tell you which method I prefer?"

Once the violence hit that level the power in the room rose and crackled against her skin. She dug her nails in deep and stared into his eyes. Brigid rode through her then, that magic flowing effortlessly once Rowan called on it.

Szabo went very still, his eyes gone a little dreamy.

Rowan leaned even closer, her hands gripping the arms of the chair. "I'm done fucking around with your bullshit. You think Enyo is scary? She still only have one eye?"

He nodded.

"*I* did that. You get me? You've been commanded to tell your Scion what happened and why. Instead you're dancing around wasting my time. My time is valuable so that offends me. When you offend me and then play shitty little word games to get around the question like you think you're smart? That makes me want to choke you with your intestines. You're a pawn, you stupid fuck. You're a handful of pebbles she tossed my way because she knows I'm coming for her. I don't need to kill you as scarily as Enyo, I just need to do it first. But I *am* scarier." She shrugged and let go, wiping her hand off on his shirt. "Talk or I'll rip your jaw off. Then it'll grow back and I'll ask you again."

And he talked.

ELEVEN

Once they'd cleaned up the mess in the situation room, they'd begun to add all the information Szabo had given them to what they already knew.

Recht came back after he'd made a call back to the Keep. "The Lacostes will be apprehended and questioned."

Which meant the Nation was sending the Five after them. Since Recht was with them and Nadir would need to stay back at the Keep to monitor The First, it wouldn't be all of them, but these were The First's personal guard, one of them could more than handle it. Three? A hearty good luck to anyone who thought they could withstand that.

Rowan sighed long and annoyed. "I *knew* this Enyo crap was going to have politics all over it. Here's my question, boys, how the hell did this Blood Front group get so comfortably funded? And now all these old Vamps are jizzing all over themselves to get a special invite to the party? Maybe I *should* let Theo come out to play more often to keep you dumbasses afraid of him like you should be. This was going on in pretty plain view. Why was no one looking?"

"Are you insinuating I can't hold my ground?" Warren asked.

"Put your dick away, Warren. Do you need a hankie

for your tears? What I'm saying, because I don't need to insinuate, is the Nation has been asleep at the switch and now this is a big ass mess that I'm going to have to clean up and this will most assuredly mean paperwork. And we all know how I feel about paperwork."

"You just make David do it anyway," Recht teased.

She sent a glare to Recht and then snorted. "Yes, but I still have to deal with Hunter Corp. bullshit and politics and I have to be nice and not punch anyone at the office even though we all know Roth Wesslyian needs a punch to the face." Rowan smirked. "Well, another one. Also, this conspiracy stuff means I'm going to have to talk on the phone. A lot."

"Why didn't Hunter Corp. know?" Clive countered.

"That's a good question." And it was. This part of Europe had a Hunter but she was retiring, and Rowan had quite often felt she'd been pretty damned ineffective when she *was* active.

The problem was, if Rowan started poking around and it was obvious, she'd get dragged in to some quicksand Hunter Corp. administrative rules stuff. It would take forever and Enyo would have an even bigger lead and more time to dig in without Roth getting in her way.

She'd find out why, but she'd be sneaky and quiet about it until she had more information and after she'd handled Enyo.

"Sorry you made me send my Vampires away?" Warren said in such a smug voice she had to grip her pen tighter to keep from popping him one.

"Let me give you an essential Rowan Summerwaite truth. I'm never sorry to see less lackeys. I'm never sorry to not have to hack my way through Vampire ridiculousness in the form of entourages. We clear?"

"You're very cranky." Warren lifted a shoulder. "You're far too powerful a being to be so angry all the time."

Rowan paused. "I'm angry all the time because I'm a powerful being. I think about how hot Jared Leto is to keep from going nuts on everyone. We all have our ways of coping."

"Who is this Jared Leto?" Clive demanded and she nearly giggled and swooned because it was so hot and unexpected.

"He's Jordan Catalano, Clive. My heart is yours, but sometimes, a tiny part of my other bits think about him. Not while you're in the room, I promise."

"He's an actor and a musician," David said mildly as he placed a cup of tea in front of Rowan.

"Honestly, you spoil all my fun, David."

Clive didn't look any less unhappy though, so without thinking, Rowan smiled at him. "Even if he gets less than twenty percent of all my pop culture references, he's pretty all right. I prefer him over Jared and those mile-long lashes of his."

Total surprise burst over Clive's features and then there was nothing else to call it but love. This man loved her. And as freaked out as that made her that she'd fuck it up royally, it also pleased her. And maybe she should let herself be something more than angry all the time.

Her phone buzzed in her pocket and she looked at the text on the screen. "*Motherfucker.*" She put her phone down and opened her inbox to find Carey's e-mail and attachments. She downloaded them all and managed to get the document she needed ready. "Here's a thing. Before I left the Keep I had Carey working on figuring out who owned each of those properties on our list of leads. Not surprisingly it was a shell of a shell of a shell with layers of corporations and trusts. Thankfully, Carey is a beast and he managed to finally distill it down." With a few keystrokes the graphic Carey had made showed up on the whiteboard so everyone could see. "That villa we looked at earlier is owned by a front company that's owned by someone else and that's owned by Sangre International. Which is you guys."

Warren looked down at the records he'd given her hours before and then back to her. "We can't. I'd know."

She shoved her laptop his way so he could take a closer look. "Because I'm so compassionate I'm going to say it as nicely as I can." Clive snorted and she gave him a look. "It's impolite to interrupt with your noises of derision, Scion."

"Which is why you do it so often?" he replied.

Someone was feeling sassy. She got the feeling he was all worked up over the way she'd interrogated Szabo. When they finally got naked later it was going to be the kind of session that left her bruised and sore. Which was just dandy with her.

Rowan snickered. "When I do it though, it's necessary. You guys just do it because you're Vampires. Like *oh no!* There's something I don't know? It can't be!" She clutched her chest dramatically as she flailed.

"I thought you said you were going to be nice."

Rowan rolled her eyes at Recht. "This is me being *super nice.* I *want* to punch people. There I was, feeling tender about my Vampire boyfriend. I was attempting to not be perpetually angry, wasn't I? And you guys did it again so my tender feelings are all gone and I'm left with all the grumpy ones."

She took a deep breath. "Look, it's clear there's a whole lot going on that none of us knew about. Hunter Corp. has its own set of complicated issues so I'm not throwing stones like that. But if you have a problem within Sangre, that's Nation business and that means your leak is pretty highly placed."

Clive spoke up. "She's right. We need to get on this and ferret out all our problems before we have too much to slog through and it spins out of control."

Rowan shrugged one shoulder. "I'd planned to get some reconnaissance done from rooftops and stuff, but as you own that villa, I say we just walk in."

"They won't expect it. And if she's in there, we won't be wasting any more time," Clive agreed.

Warren paced. "This is appalling. You know that, yes?"

He was as shocked as everyone else had been. He wasn't faking it. His distress that this occurred and was happening on his ground was real and she took pity on him. "I do. Look, as annoyed as I am, Hunter Corp. didn't know either. So, there's nothing to do but handle it *now.* How you discipline your people isn't my concern as long as they keep their shit together, consensual and in private. That's not happening so I'm assuming you'll deal with them or I will."

"Understood. This will be dealt with on our end. Let's go," Warren said.

Everyone else left the room but she and Clive waited a few moments. He touched her arm and leaned in close. "You and I have some things to address once all this is done."

"That so? Will you lecture me while naked?"

"*You'll* be. But we both know you'd ignore a lecture, even sex based."

Touched by his silliness, she cupped his cheek for the briefest touch and he smiled.

She let herself be happy and accept what they had. "I might pretend. If you make me come hard enough."

The arrogant expression he wore then made her all hot. "I'm insulted you felt the need to say that."

She laughed and he hugged her to him, one armed and then stepped back.

"You do a fine job, Scion. But sometimes you need to be kept on your toes or you might take me for granted."

His teasing look faded into something dead serious. "I know what I have in you. I'd never take that lightly."

He was supposed to always be an arrogant ass so she could manage him and pretend it was just sex. But he of course had to go and be impossible not to love.

"I know. Thank you. Now, I'm uncomfortable being nice so let's move this along because if all goes according to plan I get to work out my pique with my fists so we can get back here and you can address me while naked."

TIME, WHEN DEALING with a Vampire's world, took on a different set of expectations. There were about four hours to sunrise, which would be prime work time when most humans would be sleeping.

It just didn't seem odd to be heading over to that villa at this late hour and once they reached the front gates, though the street was quiet, it was clear the Vampires inside the house were up. Lights shone through the windows and there was some visible activity.

Warren didn't bother with the intercom or a request of any sort to be let in. Instead, he shoved at the gates so hard they groaned and fell away with a puff of dust as they sagged to the sides.

"Nice trick. That was some superhero shit right there." Rowan followed them through the rubble and up the drive, though she and David weren't as graceful as the Vampires, who just sort of hopped over it easily.

Vampires came flooding from the front doors of the massive residence but they sure as hell weren't expecting to see two Scions and a Hunter standing outside and stuttered to a stop.

Rowan smiled at them, showing her teeth.

"What are you doing here?" one of the biggest Vampires demanded.

Rowan didn't even see Warren move, but the other Vampire was on the ground, bleeding, and Warren stood over him, eyes going amber. "You dare question your Scion? On what authority?"

The Vampire on the ground froze against Warren's words and the rising power of those standing in the courtyard just then. His eyes went wide and very round at the realization and then panic chased it away and Rowan knew they'd come to the right place.

"My apologies, Scion. We didn't know to expect you."

"I don't need to RSVP. This property belongs to me. Every Vampire inside it belongs to me too. I don't seek permission for this." Warren grabbed him by the collar and dragged him, up the steps and into the house where other Vampires were busy arming themselves.

"Disarm and stand down immediately." Warren's command froze everyone in place before the weapons they'd been holding fell to the marble floor.

Warren pointed at one of them. "You, bring me whoever is in charge here. Immediately."

Rowan flanked left, Clive went right. Recht stood in the front doorway still, his gaze flicking around the space. No doubt measuring the threat level of everything in sight.

Then he moved, heading past them and into the heart of the villa. Rowan motioned for David to take her place before she followed Recht, getting his back.

"She's not here," Recht said as he paused at the top of the stairs they'd just ascended.

Rowan had been listening for the power signature of every being in that house and she agreed. "You're the oldest Vampire in this house."

He nodded. "But there's older energy here." He opened a set of double doors, revealing a posh, light tight suite beyond.

Rowan found herself in the space before she'd thought about moving. "She was here though." Brigid stirred within Rowan, agitated.

Recht smiled then, sending a burst of fear skittering over her skin for a moment, even though all that violence in his expression had nothing to do with her.

He closed his eyes as he moved slowly through the room. Rowan studied him, as she always had. Learning.

After several minutes he opened his eyes and looked straight to Rowan. "She was here no longer than a day ago, maybe two. And she's weaker."

Rowan harrumphed because the whole topic agitated her.

"You'll get there, little goddess. She's on the run. I bet she knew we were on the way and got out fast. You sent her scampering off. Well done."

"I want to be as scary as you when I grow up," Rowan declared.

He laughed then. "Everyone needs goals. Let's clear the rest of this floor."

They did, finding two Vampires hiding in a closet, a bunch of weapons, some laptops and several cell phones. Which they brought downstairs.

Warren was still pissed, arms crossed over his chest as he glared at some Vampire who'd claimed to be in charge.

Clive leaned against a pillar, his foot on the throat of a Vampire on the ground. She wondered what that story was and was disappointed she'd missed seeing him deliver a smackdown. He was really fucking sexy when he did that.

"This Vampire claims he doesn't know who Enyo is." Warren's tone was amused, but it was only a thin veneer over his anger.

Rowan moved to Warren's side to look the Vampire he'd been questioning over. "That's a disappointing answer, huh? What's your name?"

The Vampire actually sneered at her. "I don't answer to you. My Scion is in charge."

"In charge of killing you because you harbored a criminal the Nation has issued an execution order for? Yeah he is. I'm bummed naturally, because I'd love to kill you myself. But I can live with it as long as the killing you part happens. Your Scion's been at it longer anyway. As far as you needing to answer my questions though?"

She punched him in the face. Twice.

And then wiped his blood on his clothing. She said, *you're so beneath me I won't even let your blood remain on my skin.*

When he got that message he was even angrier that she'd punched him. He started to move to attack, but she pivoted on one foot, delivering a fist to his temple, sending him stumbling back to his ass, more blood on his face.

"Are we done yet? Sun's coming and I would like to relax before bed." Clive's bored delivery made her want to grin at him over her shoulder. But she retained her *I will kill you* face as she glowered at the Vampire who'd tried to attack her.

"Because I'm a lot like Ms. Manners, I'm going to introduce myself first. I'm Rowan Summerwaite. I'm a Hunter. Now you."

He flicked his gaze to Warren and she kicked him in the side hard enough to break some ribs. They'd heal soon enough. But it would hurt.

"You don't need to look anywhere but at me. What. Is. Your. Name?"

"Klaus Krier."

Rowan managed not to send a raised brow to Recht.

So the Lacostes *and* the Kriers. Important old families who apparently hadn't learned much in their time on earth.

"Well, Klaus, you're a liar as well as guilty of treason against your own people. I was just upstairs in the room Enyo used until yesterday. Should we try this again or do I need to hurt you more?" She held up a hand. "I should stop you by saying I'm totally good either way. Hurting you would probably help me sleep better."

"If you don't tell me what the hell has been going on, Klaus, I'm going to kill you so slowly it'll take years." The power and command flowed from Warren like a shove.

"This is about the health of our people. Go on and tell him, Klaus. We should not be ashamed of our goals," one of the Vampires Alice had been holding shouted this out with the fervor of the newly converted.

Beings with as much power as Vampires were dangerous enough. Give them a cause or a belief and it had sent them into fervor more than once over history.

It was how the war originally started between the Vampires and the group that eventually formed Hunter Corp.

"If she wanted them to know she'd tell them."

"May I?" Clive asked Warren, indicating the Klaus with a wave of his hand. He wasn't the Scion here so Rowan noted his manners and was pretty impressed given the level of friction between the two Vampires.

Warren's face took on the same bored mien as Clive wore. "You can if you don't leave him such a mess he won't know I'm torturing him for not cooperating."

"I'll do my level best. But." Clive's shrug was elegant and menacing all at once. He rarely got this way but holy shit it was so hot. She wanted to be back at the villa, behind a locked door naked and being sex lectured, not playing this dumb game.

"Oh for fuck's sake! Klaus, this one over here? He's the Scion of North America. That one?" Rowan pointed to Recht. "He's one of the Five. You can't win. We already know this is Blood Front activity. We already know Enyo was here. We already know you were behind the attacks tonight at the wine bar and a private residence. She left you all exposed but she's gone and we're here. A distant threat as opposed to a blatant promise. Don't be more stupid than you already are. I thought you creatures liked to pontificate about your plans and machinations like you're all Machiavelli? If that's not true and it's only in the company I keep I'm going to be super pissed at how much pontificating I've been listening to over the years."

"I do find it incredible that Clive can get you to shut up long enough to kiss you." Warren rolled his eyes.

"He's magic that way. Anyhow, Klaus, you gonna tell us all the master plan or tell us anyway but have it ripped from you and leave you a lump? You can't brag if it's the latter."

The Vamp on the floor kept swiveling his head to look back and forth between them, confused. He could resist Warren's power to answer a general question by avoiding a subject or trying to change the topic. Which meant Warren would have to ask him very specific questions, which would take longer and she was done waiting for Vampires to make up their minds on stuff.

"Yo, Klaus." She knelt in front of where he'd remained partially on his back. "Tick tock. I have things to do. This is a one-way street. You know it. You knew it when you threw in with the Blood Front. I bet you all made a big deal of it. How brave you are to stick it to the man. So tell me about it. Go on. Impress me with your master plan."

"Make fun all you want, but your day is done, human. The time when Vampires look to Hunter Corp.

or humans to exist is over. We descend from kings! Why should we have to bow to humans?"

Oh goddess, this one. Rowan kept her features impassive. They always said too much when they bragged. "Sure. So how you do plan to make that happen?"

"You started it!" He pointed to Warren and Clive. "You didn't have to agree to let the Hunter Corp. be our masters. You signed us over to them. Again. There are those of us who are tired of waiting. She came to you in good faith and you pursue her. It is you who violates the law!"

Rowan thanked her luck that night when neither Scion argued back with Klaus.

"How long have you been with the Blood Front?"

"Fifteen years."

Fifteen years? *Years?* What the hell? Why had they been so quiet until just recently? Yes, the Joint Tribunal and the addition of an amendment to the Treaty had stirred up people on both sides. But this was more. That sort of agitation could explode into action, but it was also shallow and easily dealt with and extinguished.

Rowan knew right at that moment that while the Vampire Nation hadn't known Enyo was about to crack open a can of governmental overthrow, they had known more about the Blood Front than she'd assumed.

Or been led to assume.

SHE COULDN'T GET a look at Clive because she had to keep herself locked down and she didn't want Klaus to see any weakness in their team. But she'd get her answers all right.

"Why not declare war then? If you're sure your path

is righteous, why do you not take it boldly and openly?" Warren asked.

"Because this would happen. You would stamp us out. Like you're doing now. So we act smart and when the time comes we will reveal ourselves. We've been around a long time. We can be patient."

"How long has the Blood Front existed?" Rowan asked before Warren could speak again. The jagged change in his energy hit her shoulder and arm as she got her own damned answer.

"Centuries. It's an exclusive club you know."

Of course it was. *Every* Vampire organization ever was an exclusive club because they were all assholes that way.

"Have the Kriers been Blood Front all this time?"

"No."

Warren snarled. "Answer the question!"

"My father and I were the first. My grandfather doesn't know but my uncles and brothers do now."

"Where do you think Enyo went?" Warren leaned close, his voice the barest whisper but it cut through her on the way to Klaus.

If he'd asked where Enyo went the Vampire could say, and honestly so, that he didn't know. Enyo wouldn't tell any of these lackeys where she was going and leave herself vulnerable.

But ask what he thought? Rowan was impressed with Warren's skill. Also, he'd shifted the conversation away and if he thought she hadn't noticed she'd take all that impressed stuff back.

Klaus visibly attempted to clamp down on the words. His body tightened as he fought it.

"Enyo loves sorcery. I bet she put a pretty little geas

on everyone here. But it can't defeat what is in his very cells, allegiance to his Scion." Generations of allegiance. Century upon century of obedience and loyalty. Even though he appeared to have shifted his loyalties, he couldn't resist the magic he was born to.

"Italy," burst from Klaus' lips.

"What city in Italy do you think she went to?"

"V-Venice."

"When did she leave Prague?"

"She was gone when I awoke tonight."

"What's the household feeling on when she left?"

The Vampire Clive was stepping on yelled and the sound died on a gurgle as Clive bent to grab him by the throat and gripped tight enough to choke off air.

"No one saw her go to rest at sunrise. It could have been any time after she left the house to feed at nine or so that night."

"Why do they think that?"

"We got news you were coming." Klaus was defeated by that point. He'd expended all his will, which Rowan thought was disgusting. He lay there, staring up at Warren, answering questions without even trying to protect Enyo.

"Keep going. What did you do tonight?"

"We were sent to dispatch the Vampires at the bar who were going to betray her and the Blood Front. And then we heard about the one in the apartment block in Chodov. They haven't returned so we wondered if you had found them. That's how you found us here?"

Warren's features went so hard and sharp Rowan leaned back a little. "We found you here because this house belongs to Sangre International, which apparently no one saw fit to tell me until a *human* had to. For that humiliation alone I would have killed you."

They got some more details from him, but the nature of their organization meant they really didn't know a whole lot about specifics other than what their own cell was up to.

Before they left these Vampires to Recht though, Rowan had to correct some misperceptions.

"Oh and, Klaus? You don't descend from kings." Rowan made air quotes around the last word. "You descend from Theo. The First. Every last one of you descends from him. Your disobedience is to your *king.* The Kriers have taken an esteemed place of trust in the Vampire Nation and broken it. You betray the oath that has kept you safe and prosperous for generations. You have consorted with a being who attempted to shame all Vampires with the laws she's broken. And you didn't even do a good job with that. You will not die well and your family will be hunted down until every last collaborator is no longer. Know this before you take your last breath—that's all your fault."

She stood tall, dusted off her pants, glared at Clive and walked out, David in her wake.

TWELVE

"DO YOU WANT to talk about it?" David asked as they headed down the street, away from the house they were staying in. She wasn't ready to go back just yet.

"We were aware the Vampire Nation had knowledge of the Blood Front when they showed up at the Keep for the Joint Tribunal meeting. They have a hundred dumb, shadowy clubs of eight haughty old Vamps who sit around, drink aged bloodwine and talk about how humans were all cattle who should be bowing down to them. It's their version of bridge club. But I clearly don't know all the details they do."

David sighed, following as they headed down the steps leading to the tiny island nestled between the castle district and the Vltava River. Kampa Island, so pretty and quiet and the perfect place to get some space to think this over before she said or did something bad.

"They don't tell you everything. You don't tell them everything. In and of itself it's not alarming you don't have all the details. Do you feel as if you've not been given something integral to this hunt? Or is this internal Vampire Nation business they'd keep to themselves because that's how they are. And? It's *not* your business unless it does concern the hunt. And if it does, I'll arrange our travel to Venice myself after you tell them all to fuck off and we head off to handle this ourselves."

She threw herself onto a bench with a sigh, looking across the river toward Old Town Square. "It's disturbing and amazing to watch you be so smart and in charge."

"I'm not a child, *Deese.* You don't have to protect me like that."

"David, you don't need to be a child for me to protect you. You're my family. Mine to keep safe and nothing you say will change that. I'm proud of you. I'm always proud of you. I know you're skilled and tough. Letting you come was not about me accepting that because I knew it already. It's more that you're taking on this expanded role with so much aplomb and thoughtfulness that I'm proud in a new way."

She heard his swallow as he processed all she'd said. Hell, she was trying *not* to process it right then because she wasn't prone to this sort of sharing and over the last few weeks the intensity of her relationships with the important people in her world had gotten so much deeper. Killing and punching and being angry was easier ground for her to stand on. She knew that, was comfortable with it. But if that's all she felt, she had no room for all this other stuff like pride in David and love for Clive. And also upset that she felt he'd held back. Which seemed so stupid and simpering, but she felt it nonetheless. Which made her cranky.

"Is it that you love him and feel like he lied to you?"

He'd changed the subject, which meant he accepted what she'd said and they were moving on.

"I do love him. Goddess knows why, but handsome, powerful, intelligent, rich, arrogant asshole seems to be my favorite flavor. And yes, I suppose part of it is that." It stung. Did he think he couldn't trust her? She who'd saved them all from Theo just two days before? She who'd come to do *their* work and dispatch Enyo and deal with their internal shit that could be a threat to their very existence?

"After all Vampires have done to me I still seek to protect them and they hold back. It's fine for me to take out the garbage but not sit at the dining room table?"

David settled back against the bench and they were both silent for a time.

"It's my belief that this increased contact with your father and all this Nation business will raise the threat factor toward you immeasurably. I'm not exceptionally comfortable with that. But to tell you honestly, I also believe you need them."

She'd done this to herself by allowing all this Vampire Nation stuff back into her personal life. "As long as I was killing them everything was fine. Once I started letting one sex me up and doing family dinners with the other one this has all gotten out of control." But she did need them now. She'd opened the door and they'd come in and made themselves at home. Damn it.

"And there's something hinky going on with Hunter Corp."

David sighed. "Yes. Why didn't they know about this? They have to. Which means they didn't tell you. Do they all know or is this a matter of a faction knowing and not telling everyone else?"

"I only know I can trust Susan and Rex. She pulled that weird thing about you petitioning to come with me but it wasn't to harm me. I haven't been able to get her alone and off the Hunter Corp. grid to ask her what's going on. But I need to initiate some contact, so if you can start the process by reaching out to her valet I'd appreciate it."

"I'll do that when we get back to the house. Or do you want me to book our travel to Venice?"

"I think I have to get an answer to my question first. And yours. Does it have anything to do with my hunt and if so, yes, we'll be leaving."

"You'd leave him for that?"

"I don't think I could live with myself if I thought we had this deeper level of trust and we didn't when it really counted. How could I respect myself if I don't walk away from that?"

They stood and he hugged her. A quick thing but she'd needed it more than she'd thought.

"Let's go back so you can get answers. He's going to start looking for you once they get that house cleaned up."

"Oh I have no doubt he knows I'm pissed."

CLIVE KNEW SHE wasn't on the premises when the Vampires got back to their villa. He shot a glance Alice's way and she gave him a replying expression that told him he deserved exactly what he was getting.

"Where the hell is she? Leaves us to do all the work and she's not even here? Check her rooms to be sure she hasn't left," Warren said to Gemma.

Alice spoke up, stepping to Warren. "With all due respect, Scion Farrelly, you can't do that. If you send someone into her rooms she's going to get very angry. You can't check on her that way."

"Why is that?" Warren's surprise was another point in Clive's favor. At least he understood why Rowan would not take her rooms being searched in her absence well.

"Because she's not an animal or one of our servants. You can't invade her private space and not expect there to be repercussions."

Warren's sputter of indignation was priceless. "Repercussions? For what?"

Alice huffed a breath and Clive wanted to demand she admit he was far less annoying then Warren. "You honestly haven't even realized she's angry over not being told everything about the Blood Front?"

"We told her what she needed to know," Clive said. Moreover, he'd been instructed *not* to share anything more than he had to about the history of the Blood Front. The First had insisted she be informed of anything that would be integral to the hunt and her safety, but also that she was not to be given any information otherwise. The Blood Front had been around a long time but most of them hadn't really taken it seriously. It had been an Old Vampires Club as Rowan would say. Elitist, yes. Violent rhetoric, yes, but mainly they'd never done much more than whine so The First had decided they were less of a threat and more of an annoyance and he preferred it that way.

Clive couldn't argue with that reaction because he'd have had the same one. Better to let that sort of thing happen and stay in the nattering, prattling stage instead of give it attention and make them all feel as if they *had* to act.

And the problem with that stance was what they all drowned in just then. They'd been doing far more than talking and the Nation hadn't known it until it had gotten this out of hand and boiled over at the Joint Tribunal.

He had wanted to give her the whole file about the Blood Front but had been overruled not only by three of the four other Scions—Warren had sided with Clive—but The First as well.

There were limits even Clive had to obey.

In the pit of his belly he felt the swell of her power. She was on the way back. *Interesting.* He hadn't felt her like this before she'd given him her blood. Part of his concern eased back a little. Their connection was still strong.

"We told her what we were *allowed* to tell her," Warren corrected. "If she has an issue with that she should take it up with her father because that's where the order came from. In any case, she knows now so we don't have to continue to withhold it."

"And we still don't need to enter her quarters without her presence." Alice kindly referred them back to her point. She was right, of course. Clive never would have allowed such an invasion of her space and more likely than not Warren was just blowing off steam. Not that Clive planned to save him from Rowan, who was inside the house by that time, heading to them.

"She can't just take off without telling us where she's going. What sort of team is this if she doesn't even check in?"

Gemma's eyes widened and she stepped back as Rowan's energy rushed into the room right as she did.

"Yeah, because *knowing* all the background information is necessary. I totally get that. Too bad you fuckers still don't. If you want my help—and let's be totally clear that you *need* it regardless of want—you really should be attempting to be sure *I* have all the information *I* need so *I* don't end up getting hit in the face with it. Or say, have it ambush me in the dark while I'm unarmed. I thought we'd gotten past all this holding information back business after the last time you did this and I nearly ended up dead because of that. How many times is it, do you think, that I'll need to nearly die before Vampires figure out it's totally cool to tell me stuff that could prevent said nearly dying." Her normally cutting tone had gone very flat.

He'd been feeling her energy but she must have locked it down. She gave off nothing, though it was clear she was pissed. No, this sort of blank calm shook *Clive's* calm in a very serious way. Rowan refused to meet his gaze for longer than a few seconds as she looked back and forth between the Vampires in the room.

He'd known she'd be angry, but *this* was different. Closed off was not acceptable. This had to be worked out because he had no plans to let her slide away from him and back into lone Hunter mode.

"We told you what we were allowed to." It was Recht who stepped between both Clive and Warren to take the brunt. "You're no stranger to how Vampires operate. You had to assume you didn't know everything."

"What I assumed was that if you trusted me enough to do your dirty work and to draw fire, you'd have done me the courtesy of simply telling me the Blood Front was more than just some twice-a-year country house party a bunch of Vampires stuck in Victorian England went to and complained about humans at while they ate watercress sandwiches."

"You don't need to know that." Recht shrugged and she sighed.

"You know what? Maybe I didn't. I can't look at it from here and know if it would have made a difference. And neither can any of you."

Warren scrubbed a hand over his face. "We don't have time for a philosophical discussion right now. We can never know what we can't know. Et cetera. The First was very clear about what we could share. When something comes up we think you need to hear, we seek the permission to share it. That's how this works, which is no surprise to you."

David stood at her side and Clive flicked his glance to the other man who looked less angry at Clive than concerned for Rowan.

Clive leaned close to her. "Rowan, may I speak with you privately?"

She cut her gaze his way. "No. We *spoke* privately earlier. I think that's enough."

That was *more* than enough, just not in the way she meant.

He looked to David. "I do hope you'll pardon me for this." And then grabbed Rowan around the waist and tugged her toward his room.

"I said I'm not interested in private anything with you, Scion," she growled through her clenched teeth as she dug her heels in. Still, she hadn't gone for her sword. Yet.

"Yes you are and unless you want everyone in this house to hear how much, you'll accompany me to my rooms where we can speak privately," he said quietly.

"Go ahead and get close enough. I'm going to punch you in the dick. I'm happy for everyone to hear that."

Relieved that her anger had filled in the blank canvas she'd given him before, he grinned and kissed her temple as they finally reached the doors to his room. "There's my Rowan."

"I'm not *your* anything."

He opened the doors and pushed her though, closing and locking them at his back. He engaged the daylight locks as well as he kept an eye on her, making sure she wasn't really going to punch him in the penis.

"You're far too good at understanding Vampires not to have known this was coming." He stalked her way and for the first time she appeared to realize she'd pushed a master Vampire too far and that he was coming for her.

She kept him from flanking her so he just took her down, his front to her front, landing on the bed, his body pinning hers.

"I imagine that blade and the sheath are uncomfortable underneath you. Obviously I value my life so I didn't attempt to remove it before you landed. I could be convinced to let you remove it yourself if you promise you'll listen to all I have to say."

"I'm not interested in *anything* you have to say. It's over, Clive. Thanks for the sex."

"I think not. Hush or you're going to make me cranky. Why do you have to be so difficult even when you finally admit you love me? You know I told you all I could. You know I told you more than I was supposed to. I would never put you in danger if I had something that could help you. At the same time, outside that very narrow exception, it's not up to me to choose how much to tell you. What I *am* sorry for is upsetting you and having you find out the way you did."

She tried to give her Hunter face. A detached mask. She'd used this face on him before and he hated it. But her emotions crashed over him, wave after wave of sadness, of anger and a little fear. The Rowan beneath him was vulnerable and hurting and she couldn't hide it.

"I don't care anymore. It's fine. Whatever." Her bottom lip actually quivered just the tiniest bit.

Or, maybe she could hide it. Most likely she could, actually. But she wasn't trying that hard. And that meant she wanted to get back on track with him. At least enough to not stab him.

Now that he'd cleaved himself to her the way he'd finally stopped fighting, the need to fix it, to make her happy—scratch that, she was, after all, still Rowan—keep her satisfied and not in pain, beat at him.

"Yes you do care. And I want you to." He risked a quick kiss but the violence in the way she responded, the edge of her teeth, a growl of sound, was going to lead to her undoing. He let her see it in his eyes, the way he meant to claim her until she was a trembling mess of muscles and skin once they had worked this out.

"Foreplay already, darling?"

She snarled and he continued speaking, amused but not letting her see it. "But you have to remember who I am. *Who we all are.* Including you. Vampires have built an empire around secrecy. It's kept us alive. It's a revered duty to us. As you know. Also, I hasten to point out that I am certain you don't tell *me* everything about Hunter Corp." Her frown only underlined what he already knew. "I know you're puzzling over something with them right now but you haven't said much about it. I don't push. I assume you'll tell me what you can."

"I don't tell you everything, but I'd never hold back something important. I trust you. I thought you trusted me too."

He sighed and rolled to his side, his hand on her waist to keep her from running off. "I'm here with you in the place I am most vulnerable. How many times have I trusted you with my very life? I love you, Rowan. Those aren't just words for me. There's no one I'd rather have at my side in my life and at my back in a fight. But I'm a Scion. I have many responsibilities and I'm in charge of upholding the laws of my people. I was told what I could and *couldn't* tell you, by my leader and your father. You have my heart and my trust. He's got my allegiance and my Vampires have my diligence and protection. We both have myriad responsibilities and commitments and this will take work on our part, but there's no reason we can't continue to be together and face these things head-on."

"This is a lot of work."

"Rowan."

"What?" Her surly tone returned and made him feel a great deal better.

"You can only push me so far."

She went to her elbows. "Is that so?"

"There's still quite a lot I can get to before the sun comes up, you know." He eased closer, pulling the sheath she wore to keep her blade hand free.

"You must be feeling quite lucky to be getting this close." She bared her teeth. "I'm still angry, Clive."

He cupped her cheek. "You're good at anger, darling. I'm good at making you come when you're angry. It's obvious how perfect I am for you."

She blinked slowly, one of her brows sliding up.

"Earlier tonight you were quite the one to watch."

She tried not to smile for a brief moment and then gave in. "I knew that got you hard. You like it when I'm rough."

"Watching you interrogate a prisoner is one of life's finest pleasures."

"Some men want threesomes. You get off on me beating people bloody. We're a pair."

"I never said I'd turn down an offer of a threesome. Should you ever be driven by the desire to have one, of course. It's all about your pleasure."

She rolled on top of him. Her sword still on her back because she might still want to use it. "Yeah? So I could invite Warren in here and you'd be down with that?"

His eyes flashing was the only real warning she got before she was on her back, the sheath and her shirt gone as he kissed her senseless.

She wrapped her legs around him, holding him close. "My goodness, that got a reaction. Is that because you like three ways with dudes? I could probably work with that. Just for future reference."

"Don't joke about that." His voice had gone snarly and growly, the cultured silk of his accent a memory. "Your ex can proposition you for a three way with me and then also try to kill me and I can't respond to a three-way joke *you* made?"

"Life isn't fair. You told me that more than once. I'll happily admit I know exactly what you mean now. You're mine, Rowan. I share you with your Goddess and your job, but I don't share with anyone else."

Some part of her knew she should be offended and horrified. But that part was drowned out by all the hormones a declaration like that seemed to elicit from her in response.

All her life she'd been treated like a thing. A weapon to the Hunters, a weapon to the Vampires. The monster in the closet Vampire parents used to keep their young ones in line. A Vessel for Brigid. People saw Rowan and thought of her in terms of what she could do for them.

But Clive—though of course he knew what she was and how much power that came along with—saw her in a way she was pretty sure no one else ever had. It wasn't just that he accepted her bad manners or looked the other way. He got off on her rough edges. Respected her talent and strength. Loved her mind. But he wanted Rowan the woman just as much, if not more, as he enjoyed and appreciated Rowan the weapon.

Thinking on what he made her feel dissolved a little more of her anger at him. He was right, she had known there were things the Nation hadn't disclosed about the Blood Front. Information was power and Theo wasn't going to idly give that away, even when Rowan was helping.

Still. Part of her was a little petulant, she admitted it. Knowing Theo had ordered Clive not to tell her things hurt her feelings. She wasn't surprised. She understood how they all were.

She hadn't lied when she'd said the entire situation was complicated. "This should be easy."

"What should be? You? I think you are. When you want to be." He kissed across her collarbone and against the sensitive skin at the hollow of her throat.

"This relationship stuff. Love."

He grumbled and lifted his mouth from her skin

so he could meet her gaze. "Love is the most complicated thing in the universe. And you're an exceptionally complicated person. We won't be easy. Nothing worth having truly is. But you know that."

He brushed his lips against hers, coaxing her open so he could slow dance right in and rev her up so she kept forgetting to be mad at him.

"You wouldn't be happy if it was easy anyway. You like being annoyed. It gives you an excuse to step in and fix things for people."

"I kill people. Don't romanticize what I am."

He had the audacity to roll his eyes at that.

Roll.

His.

Eyes.

"Another plus to being on top is that your ability to whip your head around when you get angry at my audacity is hindered," he said.

"I said it was an accident!" That time anyway. Make a guy's nose bleed *once* and he cries about it like a baby for months. "Is this ever going to be all right for you? Do you need to go journal about it?"

"I find that even when I have no idea what the references you're making are, I can still understand your tone. You're mocking me, which means you're not in a twisting-Clive's-head-off-like-an-apple-off-the-tree mood anymore."

"That's a commendable way to throw shade. That means clever insult, by the way. And as you have painted such an evocative picture in my imagination of exactly how I plan to rip your head off when you're being insufferable, I'll let you slide. This once. But you've ripped my shirt and we have to go back out there."

He frowned and one wayward lock of his hair dared to fall over his eyes. "We don't have to do any such thing."

"We have to plan our transit to Venice. I haven't been updated on whatever else you may have found after I left. Or is that a Vampire Nation secret too? It's not a recipe for fucking fudge or a secret sauce, you know. Holding back is petty and dumb and it wastes my time. I hate having my time wasted."

"Warren's cleanup people came over once they'd finished up at the flat. Alice has the electronic devices you found and is having them all looked over. She said the data cards were still intact."

She sat up and he frowned. Good.

"I should connect her with Carey. He's a whiz with all this. And at least you guys and your perpetual distrust of technology is in my favor. Those data cards should give us some good intelligence."

He banded her waist with his arm and she let him. She'd go whenever she pleased, so it wasn't as if this little game was really keeping her there.

"She's already acquainted with Carey so I'm sure she'll loop him in. Warren will handle the travel arrangements."

"Maybe for you, but I want to handle my own travel."

He gave her a look. "And why is that? Talk about a waste of time. He's got the pull to do it faster than you and to keep it light tight and safe for us."

"I don't need any of that. David and I can go right now and get working while you all catch up."

"Rowan. This is a team. You're angry right now because we didn't inform you of something you felt the team should have."

"I'm not hiding the fact that I'm leaving though."

"I used to think it might be nice to see you agitated over something silly for once. Now I realize the error of my ways. Not that feeling like we hid things from you is silly, so let's not argue that part again."

"Isn't this the place you'd throw something shiny at one of the chicks you banged before me? Shuffle her out with a new bracelet. Thanks for the pussy, now get the fuck out."

"Darling, you're so much more than a *chick* I bang. Such a delicate flower. I do adore your pussy. Far too much to send you, and it, packing. In any case, I don't waste my time on jewels for you unless they also come with a weapon. When we get back to Las Vegas I'll make it up to you with something that carries bullets. Or perhaps I'll mix it up with something other than a handgun. Maybe a crossbow."

She shivered and he chuckled.

"So easy when it comes to things that maim." He kissed her ribs and let go. "Would you like me to send Alice to your rooms to get a replacement shirt?"

"No." Rowan rolled from the bed and rifled through the shirts hanging in his closet until she found one she liked best. It'd be a little big on her and everyone would know it was a different shirt than the one she'd worn earlier. But there was no helping that part.

He put a hand at the small of her back as they headed

out to reconnect with everyone else. "I like seeing my shirt on you."

It smelled of him, which made her smile. Inside. Outside, she was still miffed.

THIRTEEN

"Any luck?" Warren asked as Rowan and David boarded the private plane they'd be taking to Venice.

Rowan had managed to chat with a few sources in Italy, as well as send some pictures from her phone to Susan and Rex with an encoded WTF message asking them to contact her by private channels.

Carey had sent a file with hard copies of all the data they'd put together, as well as a flash drive to London in the luggage of a family member. Rowan wanted to be sure Susan and Rex saw it all without any interference from Roth or his ilk.

"Just shook some trees. No sightings of her in Rome, as we figured."

Clive and Warren continued to bicker over every little thing as they made it through takeoff and got under way. Rowan sighed, as she took them in. This was partly her fault. The presence of another power on the team, one that had a foot in both worlds and didn't have to answer to anyone, was bound to get them all worked up.

Warren made a cutting remark straight out of the Rowan playbook, but before she could call him on it, Alice sat on a nearby chair and leaned toward Warren. "Are you channeling Rowan now?"

"Are you all out of your minds?" She looked to

Clive. "We need to talk." Then to Warren. "I'm sick of listening to you bicker. I have work to do and since we have to take the same plane instead of David and I traveling ahead on our own and getting started, I have a few hours to do it but you two just won't stop."

"We were waiting for you so we could depart."

Warren's delivery was so bland and yet baiting at the same time she started forward, but Clive caught her around the waist. "You said you wanted to talk to me? Come, there's a stateroom back here."

He pushed her, although gently, down the hallway and into a small room with a banquette that could be made into a bed. He shut the door and gave her a measuring glance.

Rowan held a hand out. "You, stay back. You got me all addled last night and then I forgot to be annoyed with you. There's something more than the usual Vampire power games going on. Spill about this situation between you and Warren."

His expression, which had been arrogant and totally assured he was getting some, hardened.

"Don't even think about avoiding the topic."

He sighed. "I'm not. I'm just trying to figure out how to tell you."

"This isn't giving me any sort of closure. I think your reaction is making me nervous. Yeah, that's it. Just say it, my goddess."

"It's you. Warren and I…this unpleasantness is because you're bright and powerful and compelling."

Then she got it. "Oh! You and Warren are swinging hammers over me?" She laughed at the horrified look on his face. "Is your look I said hammers and you think I mean penises? Or because you're embarrassed to be fighting with Warren over me like we're in grade school? Also, ew. He's like my uncle."

"I go out of my way to respect your world, Rowan. Do you think this is funny?"

Rowan paused, surprised by his vehemence. Did she hurt his feelings? Was it the penis thing? Gah! She was totally right about how complicated love was. She had no idea what the hell she was supposed to do.

He groaned. "Your face right now, as you argue with yourself about whether or not you want to feel bad for my anger. You make it impossible."

She deserved that. "Listen, I make lots of things impossible." How could he not understand the level of her commitment to him? "I'm with you. I shared my blood with you. Do you..." As she spoke, the emotion of it hit her unexpectedly deeply. Mortification as tears threatened. The question, the answer, what if she asked and he said the wrong thing? Why did it matter so much? Rowan opted to clamp her lips closed before she started oversharing or crying or whatever.

"Do I what?" Clive asked.

Rowan shook her head. "Never mind."

He stood and was on her so fast she found herself nearly gasping. Clive breathed deep, taking her in, and then he spoke and she fell so hard and fast her stomach lurched with it.

"I'm here, cut open. For you. Because of you. Tell me. You're the bravest living creature I've ever met. Take a risk. Be real with me now. Honest. Let me be worthy of your trust. Do I what?" he repeated.

Rowan remained frozen for what felt like forever. Her pulse raced though she knew she could have hidden it from him. But it would have felt duplicitous.

There was so much right then. So much emotion. Pain. Anger. Fear. Love. Damn it. *Love.*

"Do you realize what it meant when I gave you my blood? I haven't willingly shared my blood since I left the Keep."

He cupped her cheek. "Rowan." Just the word. Her name spoken like it meant something. Clive cocked his head, smiling. "Oh yes, I do know. I was honored then, as I am now. I'm continually felled by the way you love me. I adore you."

Confused, she asked, "So why are you so shirty right now? You said I was impossible."

"There are times," Clive began, carefully, "when the nature of your childhood and the distrust you have because of it really gets in your way and it makes me so angry. It makes me want to confront your father and make him see what he's done." He stopped himself, took a deep breath and continued. "When I said you *make* it impossible, I meant *to stay annoyed with you.* As in the tenderness you evoke in me makes me want to fix you. And I know you don't need fixing so we don't need to have the feminism discussion again."

She snorted a laugh. "Don't do that. The confronting part. You'd die and then I'd have to get a new boyfriend. Took me this long to find you. I can't imagine there's anyone else out there I'd want to be with more than I want to set on fire."

He shook his head. It was a compliment. A beautiful one and one only she could have delivered.

Rowan sobered. "So explain this to me. Obviously this isn't just a run-of-the-mill problem or I'd have known about it. What's going on?"

"You grew up with Vampires, how could this be a

surprise to you? Two Scions with an equally powerful female? Of course he's pushing."

"I'm *with* you. I mean, it's all you whiny ass Vampires talk about! You're the biggest gossips around. You and your information hoarding." Her gaze narrowed and he knew she was remembering the night before. *Danger.*

With one last glare, she appeared to let it go and kept talking. "Anyway, it's not like they gave me a manual on Vampire mating habits in my biology class. I left at sixteen. I knew pretty much nothing about sex, much less how Vampires did it with one another and why. Apart from the obvious I mean like boobs and hair."

She was so adorably befuddled by this. Out of her element. And she was doing it for him. When he'd told her he was laid open before her, he hadn't been dramatic. She amazed him multiple times every night since he'd known her.

"And it's not like anyone ever, you know, fought over me before." She paused and locked her gaze on his. "So tell me the rest."

"What do you mean?"

She licked her lips, as nervous as he was.

"I told you I'm bad at this. It wasn't like Theo had lovers, or whatever, not in my presence. Apparently Enyo and her magic screwed him so hard he wasn't looking for it again. Or he took it elsewhere. Who knows? I just…I know how to kill you and prod you into a rage—Vampires I mean. I don't want to kill you personally. Not usually," she amended. "I thought we *were* together. We're open in front of your people. All the Scions know because they saw us at the Joint Tribunal, including Warren. So I'm not doing something

I'm supposed to. Or you aren't. Vampires are endlessly on about your fucking steps and rituals and hierarchies. If Warren is flirting or showing his tailfeathers or whatever it is, it means he doesn't recognize what we have as official. Still grossed out by the way. Tell me what needs to happen to satisfy even the most finicky of Vampires that you and I are in a relationship."

Her brilliance was so sexy. But she hadn't heard what he was going to propose to her yet. As scared as he was, he realized she had to own what they were openly or they'd never make it. And he wanted her to be totally sure she knew that. "Are you sure you really want that?"

She frowned. "When you say it like that I'm less sure than I was before. Stop it. I know Vampires are exhibitionists. Goes with the vanity. But I'm not fucking you in front of a bunch of people like we're extras in *Eyes Wide Shut.* Which is a freaky sex movie, only it's not sexy in any way."

He wrestled a smile back. "All right, we'll scratch that off the list."

"Oh *you're* mocking me?"

Clive thanked his centuries of training as he kept a smile from his face. Instead, he took her hands and unballed her fists, bending to kiss each palm. "I'd never dream of such a thing. I don't need to have sex with you in front of an audience. Wherever do you get these things? Usually you're the most Vampire of all Vampires I know."

"Hey, fuck you sideways. I'm trying here and look what I get for it."

He risked getting close enough to taste her lips. "I

apologize. I'm teasing, not mocking, and I'm still sorry I upset you."

She sighed. "This was easier when we just banged and pretended to hate each other."

"Not for me." He shrugged. "You don't need to do anything. You've given yourself to me and that's enough."

Her smile was wry. "Sure. Because Vampires never care what their friends think about the people they've collected."

There it was. The warmth she brought to his belly. She *understood* him. Understood what he was and she didn't run from it. Even better, seemed to find it attractive. No one knew him like she did. It meant a lot in no small part due to the way they'd stumbled on one another.

"Do you know how hard it makes me when you accept and understand me this way? Who else but another Vampire could? And yet after centuries with Vampires it was *you* who understood me best. You know the beast inside me and you're not afraid."

The light in her eyes was all his. Her Goddess had retreated and it was truly just Clive and Rowan.

"I'm a monster. You know that, right?" Her voice was so soft. Soft enough the hum of the engines as they made their way through the sky nearly swallowed it up. "I'm stumbling and I don't like stumbling. I do this all wrong. I don't have the right words like you do. I'm also not a nice person. I kill things at an alarming rate. I really hate Vampires sometimes. Most Vampires all the time. I say bad words like it's my job. I'm The First's daughter though. Is that good enough for them?"

He cupped the back of her head as he spun her and walked her over to the plush couch near the windows.

"Darling. I'm a monster too. Remember? That's why you're perfect for me. I love you not because you're the daughter of The First. I love you because you survived. You rose above it. My phoenix."

"Love is fucked up."

Clive had ceased to take her seriously when she said things like that. She might mean them at that moment, but Rowan, while she guarded against vulnerability with all her might, loved him with the same intensity she did everything else. And with her own unique take.

He sat and she joined him with a wary look.

"There's a great deal of room right here in my lap."

"Should I tell you what I want for Christmas?"

He patted his thigh. "Come over here and let me show you."

Chuckling, she sat astride his body, knees tucked against his thighs. The weight of her was just right. Her scent—he moved closer to breathe her in—spicy. Oranges and cloves.

Like home.

He'd thought long and hard about what sort of gesture would satisfy any lingering questions regarding his relationship status. About protecting her as much as he could while he did it.

"During the Joint Tribunal meeting I publicly claimed you to the other Scions. In front of Enyo and Victoriana. I said I'd draw blood to protect you because you were mine. That should be enough. It *is* enough, actually. The problem is more of whether or not another Vampire at my level believes you're also as committed to me as I to you."

She kissed him quickly. "So Warren's calling me a liar or he's saying you're too weak to keep me?"

Already breaking the problem down so she could solve it.

"You do know how much I adore your mind. So clever. You're an independent woman. You make your own rules and there's an element of you openly acknowledging you're mine."

She growled. "*I* want to openly acknowledge your being *mine.* How come we're not talking about that? Also, Warren is a tool."

Clive agreed. But if he couldn't have Rowan he'd be sad and petty too, he supposed.

"It's clear I'm yours." Scions didn't go declaring their affections for someone the way he had so openly unless it was genuine and permanent. And he quite enjoyed how worked up she got at the idea of people not knowing he was claimed.

"How come *you're* clear and I'm not?"

"I'm a Vampire and our rules are pretty defined on such things. You should know this. Since the last instance of Warren crossing the line—after I'd spoken to him about it—I've been thinking about what it would take. About what to do that would be effective and still protect your privacy as much as I can." No need to share with her that they'd had a physical altercation over it more than once.

"One thing I'd been planning for a while but it dovetails with the next part so be patient. Would you consider wearing a piece of jewelry bearing my crest? Some Vampires have marks, like your mark of service, but I understand why that's not possible." He would never ask that of her. The mark she bore on her wrist identified her as a protected member of a Vampire household. It said she owed fealty and it was also a warning to anyone not to harm or otherwise interfere with that human.

He knew she saw it as being owned. And it was true. The mark was a mark of ownership.

The Hunter's mark was also a stamp of fealty in a sense. He didn't want her to feel shackled by their relationship in any way.

"Like a fox or bagpipes or whatever it is you guys put on your crest with diamonds around it?"

He sniffed, affronted. "I have taste, Rowan." He hesitated and then pulled a ring from his pocket. "Don't panic." He held it up. "A necklace might get caught when you were fighting and choke you. A bracelet might impede your movement when you use your blade. You don't wear earrings very often. I want you to wear it, not for Warren, but because it means something to me that you would."

She nodded her head slowly. "Okay. Okay." She blew out a breath and he slid it on her finger. "I like it. I'm glad it doesn't have a gigantic diamond in it, or a fox or bagpipes."

Clive was about to finally lose his patience and explain bagpipes were Scottish and he wasn't, when she just stared at her hand and the ring, awe in her eyes.

"I'd only break it or lose the stone." She traced over the lines in the platinum band shot with threads of amber. "Like fire."

"Yes. The full crest has a dragon breathing flames." Not a fox to be found.

Her eyes widened. "Really? How did I not know that?" She grinned. "That's amazing. And the way you brought the elements of that into this design and still made it something I'd love? Thank you, Clive. Yes, I'll wear the ring."

He kissed her. "I'm glad you like it." And he was. Giddily so. Hopefully this trend could continue as he told her the rest.

"Well."

She started to laugh. "You're blushing. As hot as that makes me, I'm not jerking you off in public either."

A horrified guffaw came from deep in his belly and he was helpless to keep it from escaping. "See what you do to me? The deterioration of my manners is marked."

She shrugged. "It's on my warning label I'm sure. But I do take some solace in your reaction to that. So you don't need me to sex you up in front of an audience. Why are you hesitating?"

"If I take you right now. Here in this room, and we go back out to the salon where they're all waiting and you're wearing that ring and…"

"If I smell like a lady who was just rogered by a Scion we're good?"

He sighed.

She put a hand on her hip, brows raised. "Oh I'm supposed to say the scent of your lovemaking or something like that? You're with the wrong female if so."

To shut her up—and because he loved her taste—he stretched up to take her mouth in a kiss.

She arched as she ground herself against his cock. His need for her—always there just waiting for the opportunity to touch—swelled as he loosed it, let it free.

A rush of magic and power filled the space, enough that Clive knew everyone on that plane would have felt it.

He smiled against her lips.

"You're cocky," she murmured as she got her pants unbuttoned and unzipped.

"I'm about to be inside you. If a man wasn't cocky over that achievement, he's not much of a man."

"You're especially gifted with saying things that expedite that."

"I haven't lived centuries without learning a few things." He yanked at her pants and they overbalanced, ending up on the floor, the hum of the engines vibrating through them both.

She snarled, but not in anger. He managed to get his trousers open but the damnable woman didn't want to wait for foreplay, she grabbed his cock and squeezed just right.

He groaned.

"Give it to me," Rowan urged.

"You're so bossy."

"You know it. Demanding too. So get to it."

"I'm a gentleman. I'm not just going to—" He lost his words as she rolled them so he was on his back and in one more movement, sank down on him. The heat of her body arced up his spine as his back bowed.

He sputtered a curse and she laughed. "Fuck being a gentleman. You're not when your cock is out so let's stop pretending."

Clive bucked enough to stand, spinning to back her against the windows. "A gentleman always makes sure his partner is ready before he fucks him or her."

She grinned. "Okay, I'll give you that. But in case it escaped your notice, I'm ready."

He thrust deep over and over for some time before he replied. "Yes, yes you are."

Her nails dug in at his shoulders as he kept her pinned. The icy cool of the windows and wall at her back only seemed to make her hyperaware.

Rowan didn't care if she was supposed to be embarrassed or worried about getting caught. She wanted Clive pretty much all the time, and this? This Clive—hot, ready and driven—melted her butter. That he wanted her so much he lost all that smooth veneer and got down, teeth bared, the muscles in his neck and forearms strained as he sought his release? Damn.

The amber threads in her ring caught the light and she looked for panic and found none. The ring didn't make her any more in love with Clive, though it was a beautiful gift. It didn't make their relationship any more real.

No, that ring was a symbol. It was roots. She didn't have a lot of roots, which made it easy to move around when and wherever she wanted. But at the same time, without roots you floated around.

It was...nice.

For all their bickering, he was her safe place. And that meant more to her than she wanted to contemplate right then.

One-handed—the showoff—he held her up while the other hand found its way between them so he could get to her clit. He bit her too, hard enough that she'd feel it for hours, not so hard he drew blood.

He did it over and over. Nips, some so hard it brought tears to her eyes, but the pain warmed into something else. When she came so hard she cracked her head against the window behind her, the pain seemed to amplify the pleasure until she yelled out so loud she was sure everyone heard it. And she didn't care.

Clive spoke in her ear. Dirty stuff that only sounded even sexier because it was in French. He needed her more than his breath. That wasn't dirty, just sweet and tender. All the good stuff about how hot and tight she was nearly burned her skin.

One, two more thrusts and he stayed deep, hips jutted forward as he came, his focus on her so intense his emotions filtered through to her. She smiled because what else could a woman do when someone like Clive felt that way after being with her? He left her helpless against the way he saw her.

He helped her stand, bending to grab her clothes.

"I may have given you a love bite." He looked at her neck and colored slightly. "Or three."

She decided to find it funny. Why not? The entire situation was so ridiculous all she could do was laugh. "I'll heal by the time we get to Venice."

The look he gave her made her think about grabbing him and tossing him to the couchette so she could go at him again.

Then he smiled. That smug Scion face she used to get so mad at. Maybe because she found it hot even when she hated him.

"Careful now, Hunter. You go looking at me that way and we'll never leave this room."

Though she'd just been thinking the same thing, she didn't say it. "Wouldn't want to miss out on letting Warren sniff your jizz on me."

His lip curled at the word jizz and it made her snicker and resolve to use it again.

He pulled himself together as she re-braided her hair and they headed back out to the salon where she could hear the tap of a laptop's keyboard and the steady murmur of a phone call.

David's eyebrows rose for a brief moment but he quickly recovered and went back to his screen.

Rowan's phone buzzed and she looked at the screen. It was Susan. "I need to take this." She walked past Warren, letting him get a sniff and tried not to roll her eyes at how stupid the whole thing was.

"Susan, it's good to hear from you." Rowan paused a ways down the hall, pausing outside the room she'd been in with Clive so she could hear what was going on in both places.

"Hello, sweetheart. I'm sorry it's taken me so long to get back to you. I've had a bit of a time trying to get off the grid so to speak." The sound of Susan's voice made Rowan feel better even if she wasn't pleased with what she was hearing.

"You're being watched?"

"Before I get to that, let me apologize for the way I brought up David going with you on this hunt. It's our belief—mine and Rex's—that David was to be a target while you were away. I had only learned of it right before our call started so I couldn't warn you. I didn't know if he was with you or not and I felt if he wasn't I didn't want to call attention to his being unprotected."

She'd gone cold. Very. Cold. "My David a target? Who would dare?" Even as she asked, she knew it was Roth and his little wing of Hunter Corp.

"Who do you think?"

Well, Enyo wasn't the only being she had to kill then. *No one* attacked David. Not who'd be living to tell about it. He was hers to protect and she took that oath very seriously. Also, she didn't like Roth Wesslyian so it wasn't a chore to be angry at him.

Though he was protected back in Las Vegas. No one else had to know about it, but she and Brigid had made a deal with the Dust Devils. Carey and David were under their protection when Rowan was away.

"Okay then. I'll put that on my to-do list." Maybe she'd swing by London on her way back home. Clive had been at her to meet his parents, which meant she'd have to do that too, so she could do it at the same time and tick off some more boxes on that list.

As long as she didn't have to do this weird sex smell thing with them. Rowan had her limits.

"I need to courier you and Rex something, Susan. There are things you both need to know. Things I believe Roth *did* know and has not shared. I don't want to send them to the office or your townhouse." Rowan explained about the Blood Front's activity level and what they'd found out after interrogation.

"How soon can you get the file to me?"

"It's in London now with one of my contacts. A relative of my tech guy brought it over. Just tell me when and where and I'll get him there within an hour."

"There's a bookshop down the road. On New Cavendish Street. Give me three hours."

"What are you going to do?" Susan had been at Hunter Corp. since the age of nineteen. She'd met Rex the next year when he joined at twenty-three. They'd been a very important part of Hunter Corp. governance and direction. This sort of thing had to be upsetting for them for all sorts of reasons.

"We need to see how deep this rot goes. If he's playing at politics, or if he's laying the groundwork for a coup and a declaration of war. Either way, it needs to be called out and ended. How are you through all this?"

"I warned you all Roth was up to something. He tried to blame all his behavior on the spell used against him, but this information just proves he's been actively undermining the Treaty and Hunter Corp.'s stated goals. Long before he showed up at the Keep and certainly since he returned. I don't like that I can't count on Hunter Corp. in the field because I can't trust everyone."

Deep inside something began to fray.

"Sweetheart, I'm sorry. I do know how you feel. Rex and I are worried for you, of course. But we also have every confidence you'll find this creature and cut her down. If you need backup, call my office. I can't promise Roth or his people aren't listening, but I can promise everyone in my direct employ is trustworthy."

Rowan sighed. "All right. We're on the way to Venice now." She nearly shared her fear that Theo was losing his shit. Before she and Theo had reconciled, it would have been natural for her to talk to Susan. Bounce ideas off her. But now it felt like she was betraying a confidence and putting Theo at risk.

"The palazzo has been prepared and staffed for your visit but if I were you I would find myself alternate accommodations. Let this leak of ours waste some time looking for you."

Rowan had already come to that conclusion but hearing it from Susan just underlined that it was the right choice. There was no way she'd risk Clive and the other Vampires when they were most vulnerable.

Susan continued, not bothering to wait for Rowan's answer. She knew Rowan would do the smart thing and that confidence buoyed Rowan's resolve. "Keep me apprised, both officially and privately. And do be careful. The number of times you've been nearly killed in the last year is far too high already."

"*Everyone* who isn't following in line with Roth and his ilk are exposed and at risk. You be careful too."

"Rex and I have already altered our schedules and tightened our security at home and at the office. I know some of the others are as well. Factions are settling together so we're keeping an eye on where everyone is lining up."

Roth's little anti-treaty group didn't care that the people they were selling out were the very people who laid their lives on the line to not only enforce the Treaty, but to keep the fragile peace. It didn't bother them that open war would be disastrous with huge casualties on both sides and worse, spilling into the general human population.

And for what? They were power drunk and willing to burn everything down rather than face the truth.

Shit was complicated.

As much as people continually tried to make every religious, political, geographic, whatever issue an us versus them thing, usually it wasn't that simple.

The truth of the planet was that there has always been a spectrum of things people did, believed, worshipped, not worshipped, found beautiful, ugly, worth celebrating, worth respecting and worth fighting and dying over.

It was larger and a million times more complex than right or wrong. It was a balance so delicate it kept all the beings co-existing on the planet from doing something so disastrous it destroyed *everything.*

Rowan realized Susan had been talking to her and she sharpened her attention. "I apologize, I was just caught up in something I'm trying to work through."

"Just more nagging at you to be careful."

"All right. Heads up that I'm going to have someone looking into Roth and this threat to David."

Susan hummed in agreement. "Would you like me to recommend someone to you?"

"Much appreciated, but someone very bad, but very connected, owes me a favor."

"All right then. I do love you, sweetheart. Stay in teams. Don't let them get you alone."

Rowan didn't bother arguing. Sometimes she hunted alone. If she felt the need to do it, Rowan would. Susan was just being motherly or whatever.

They hung up, and she made a few more calls before she sauntered back into the salon where Warren had settled himself. She narrowed her gaze his way but he smiled and raised his glass her way. "Congratulations."

"Thanks. Now. Ew." Rowan shuddered. "Ew. Ew. Ew. You're like my *uncle*. I'm scarred forever."

Warren waved a hand her way. "You're a grown woman. A power in your own right with connections to the very highest level in my government. Of course I was interested. But you've made your choice and I honor that."

"I made my choice a while ago." She held up a hand realizing she actually had no interest in talking about this anymore. "Changing the subject now." She turned to Recht and filled everyone in on the conversation she'd just had with Susan and her subsequent call to the investigator she set on Roth's tail.

David's eyes got wide and then very narrow and

Rowan approved mightily. He *should* be pissed off that someone he worked with was trying to have him killed. It would keep him sharp and focused.

She'd take anger over fear any day.

They planned their next steps as they began their descent toward Venice.

FOURTEEN

CLIVE KNEW HE wore a smug expression but he didn't care. She was his and she'd declared it in her own way, loud and clear. And she seemed content to let him be smug though he was sure her patience would fray soon enough.

Still, he loved it when she indulged him.

The boat that had met them at the airport took them up the Grand Canal a short bit until heading up several smaller and increasingly quieter back canals.

Rowan had kept her eyes closed the entire way, her nose up to the wind. Hunting. But when they got close, she opened them and took in every detail, gaze flicking from spot to spot.

Their driver expertly deposited them and their bags on a dock just outside an impressive palazzo. A tall man came out and bowed.

Rowan's expression changed once she recognized him. A smile replaced the intensity. "Ciao, Marcelo!"

Marcelo took her hands and squeezed, speaking rapid-fire Italian. But not. Venetians spoke their own dialect and clearly this Marcelo had grown up or spent a great deal of his life there.

Rowan followed him inside, listening to him, nodding. The rest of them followed into what was an unexpectedly lovely space with high, exposed-beam ceilings. Clearly the original structure. The house felt older than Clive was. It held a great deal of energy in the walls and floors.

One of his favorite things about Venice was that he could stay in a place like this, rich with the lives of generations. It seemed to feed him the way extreme emotions fed him. Not as complete as blood, but it was the sort of energy that seemed to settle in his bones.

Candles lit the space, casting a pretty glow over the furniture, an eclectic mix of restored antiques and newer pieces.

At the entrance to the kitchen, Rowan hung her coat up. "Welcome to my home. This is Marcelo, my house manager."

Clive blinked.

"Surprise. I only made the decision as we were flying here. I thought about a hotel, but this is safer. I can't trust Hunter Corp. Not while you're sleeping and we're all working. It's too big a risk. So I told Hunter Corp. we were headed to a smaller town away from Venice and that we'd handle our own accommodations."

Clive wasn't angry or even hurt. He knew how she worked and that she'd made choices to keep him and the others safe satisfied him deeply.

"Marcelo and his brother use the front of the house as their workshop. He keeps the house running while I'm gone."

"We have donors for the Vampires and a meal for David and Rowan," Marcelo said in English, indicating a set of double doors. "The stairs are just through there. Head around them to the workshop. That's where the donors are. Your things will be taken to your rooms."

He turned to Rowan, switching to Italian. "You said he was your man so I put him in your room."

She nodded and looked to Clive, knowing he understood every word. Which had to be on purpose because Marcelo said it slower and more clearly than his rapid-fire delivery when they'd first arrived.

Clive liked that. But he liked it even more that she'd told her house manager about their relationship. Let them into her home and was feeding them.

He kissed her cheek. "I'll be back shortly." A small dip of his head to Marcelo. "Thank you for accommodating us so well."

The workshop, as it happened, turned out to be a place the brothers created clothing of some sort. Bolts of fabric were stored in racks, clothing hung, half finished on dressmaking forms. Most likely costumes for Carnival.

Each new thing he learned about Rowan only made him hungrier to know her better. And the people she came across in her life before Clive had known her. The fabric of her life fascinated him, including the people who'd formed her—good and bad—into the person she was today

"This is a lovely home," Alice murmured as they headed back into the kitchen area after feeding.

It had good energy. Rowan was happy in this place.

David was at the counter when they entered the kitchen. "Your things have been put in your rooms. There's wine and food in the salon too."

Clive grabbed the basket with the bread and David shrugged, opting for a carafe of limoncello. "Marcelo's wife makes this. It's very…potent. Just thought you should know in case you sipped it in front of him."

Alice laughed, delighted, as they followed David up a gleaming staircase. At the top they spilled into a far more intimate space than below. Here the wooden floors had beautiful rugs and the couches were sumptuous and inviting. Framed art hung on the walls, like the furniture downstairs it ran the gamut in style, and like the downstairs, it worked.

There was a table at the end of the open space where food had been laid out.

"Let me show you where you're sleeping." Rowan had changed into a T-shirt and soft pants she often wore to work out. He approved of those pants a great deal.

"Alice, you're here." Rowan pushed open a door to reveal a room that faced the canal. "The windows all have light tight shutters that lock down totally. No one can enter unless they have the code." She handed a sticky note to Alice. "I have an override. I won't use it unless there's an emergency."

"This is a remarkable view." Alice went to the windows facing the canal.

"There's a bakery just around the corner. They'll start at about three so you'll all get hungry as you go to sleep." Rowan's voice held a tone Clive rarely heard. Content.

"Come out to the living room and have some food after you freshen up. Marcelo's wife isn't here tonight, but she sent over a feast. Plus, she's magic." Rowan paused. "Like really magic, actually. She's a conjurer. Anyway, good food. People you should know. Come out if you like."

David stayed behind to show Alice how to use the shutters as Rowan led Warren and then Recht to their rooms and finally turned to him.

"You. Come along." She took Clive's hand and he followed her up another set of stairs.

Her bedroom was nothing like her place in Las Vegas. This space was one created for relaxing. An oasis for Rowan the woman more than Rowan the Hunter or Vessel.

Her movements were suddenly a little shy as she motioned to the bureau. "I tried to tell them not to unpack your stuff, but Marcelo ignored me and did it anyway. He liked your ironed underwear. I'm not joking. He said it was a good indicator of your character. I tried to tell him you were a bossy prick but he said that was all right as long as you knew how to fold fitted sheets. Then I stopped taking anything else he said seriously. Because hello."

"Your mind is a twisty, nonsensical place, Rowan."

"Says you."

"Indeed."

"All right, professor. But right now your things are in there and in my closet. It's a big bed and I've got an office set up through there, which also connects to the main hallway so I can come and go in the daylight because the room next door is a safe way to do it."

"What I find so interesting," he stepped closer, pulling her in with hands at her hips, "is that you have security shutters. Did you have special Vampire visitors before me?" He realized after he spoke that he didn't really want to know if the answer was yes.

It couldn't be.

He was sure. Mostly.

"I did it to keep you all out so I could sleep at night. I usually can only get here once a year, though I spent a lot of time here for the freaking year the Nation poked at me after I staked the shithead Scion before you. But I like to sleep easy and make it impossible to break into my house while I'm sleeping and unarmed."

He blinked, realizing he'd totally forgotten that she must have been a target for younger Vampires looking to make a reputation for themselves. Or maybe older Vampires who'd lost someone they'd loved or made, or had a difference of opinion with her. Which were all easy to believe.

"I wasn't hiding it from you," she replied like he'd said it aloud instead of the petulant thoughts rattling around in his head. "I hadn't really wanted to stay here originally. It's one thing for you to know about this place, but now so do Recht and Warren. Recht would tell Theo the location if asked. It's his job. So I figured the Hunter Corp. palazzo would be opulent, like you Vampires prefer, with fourteen staff people to each guest. But I wasn't comfortable with my location being known by Roth. And I especially don't want *David's* location known now that I've learned Roth wants to kill him. Oh, I'm going to enjoy crossing that fucker's life off my to-do list."

"If you feel that way about Hunter Corp. why do you still work for them? They don't treat you right, Rowan, and it makes me angry."

"I don't know why it would. It's not happening to you." She turned away but he knew her game.

"Don't lie. Of course you know why I'd be angry."

"I work for them because they were a way to make the difference I want to." *Maybe they weren't anymore.* He heard the unspoken words and the churn of her emotions brushed against his heart.

She slashed a hand through the air to cease the discussion, trying to run again. "I'm going back down to eat. There's scampi and scallops and oxtail soup. And fresh bread. I plan to get my carb on with bread every few minutes while I'm here."

He stood, watching her, gauging how far he could push before she punched him in the temple or stomped off.

"Stop." The word was quiet, but there was emotional force behind it and he licked his lips but didn't break his attention on her. "Why? Why do you let them treat you like this?"

"Why do *you* let my father tell you not to share information with me when you knew I'd be mad?" Rowan asked.

"You're stronger than I am." That was nothing more than the truth as he saw it.

But she paused, cocking her head. He'd expected a quick, bitchy retort, but she was thinking, which was far more dangerous.

"You think so?"

"Even growing up as you have, you think for yourself."

"And you think you don't? Or that being a centuries-old Vampire who now holds a significant part of the planet means you're too obedient?"

"It means I'm powerful enough to hold that land, but if I hadn't been obedient I wouldn't be Scion."

"If you hadn't been obedient you'd be dead. There's that." She shook her head. "The reality of a Vampire's life is obedience to his or her master. Theo isn't going to fuck around with disobedience. He saw in you the power and cunning to hold North America. That takes plenty of thinking for yourself. You make decisions on the ground every day. It's not the same."

It wasn't, no. But he wanted her to see that too. No one was harder on Rowan than Rowan.

"I'd tell you, you understand? If there was something I felt would have endangered you."

She cupped his cheek. Just a brief touch. "I decided earlier that yes, I do know that. But that doesn't mean I'm not going to give Theo a hard time about it. Once he's...better."

"I'm sure you will and I'm also sure you'll be very careful when you do."

"There's no other way to be with him." She stepped back and pulled herself back together. "I'll deal with Hunter Corp. in my own way. In my own time. Everyone needs to understand that."

"I'm not the only one who has brought concerns to you." His words weren't a question.

She shook her head. "No, you're not. But you all need to back up and trust me to manage my own shit."

"Darling Hunter, this is not about us not trusting you to manage yourself. This is about the people in your life wanting you to be treated with the respect you deserve."

She frowned, so delightfully confused it was nearly sweet and also a little sad.

"Come on down or they'll think I'm nailing you again."

He caught her, his hands at her hips. "We could make that reality."

She laughed. "You just did!"

"*Hours* ago."

"Cool your jets. I have to go meet a source at sunrise and I haven't eaten yet."

He kissed her, deliberately taking his time until she relaxed into him, her arms encircling his neck until they broke away long moments later.

"Why not before sunrise so I can go with you?"

"My source doesn't know you. Plus she's human so she sleeps at night like normal people."

"Don't pretend this isn't me asking you to be safe."

They started back down. "It'll be daylight in Venice so you really haven't seen it. But trust me, the garbage collection will be running full swing. Lots of people out and about. Barges, boats, shops opening up. Also, I'm sort of a badass. Or so I hear."

He hid his eye roll as they came out into the main salon area where people were drinking wine and eating. She broke away, heading back to the chair she'd left when she'd gotten up to show the Vampires to their rooms. She was greeted by smiles. Clive sat back, drinking wine and watching her interact with the others. After this mess was finished, he wanted to be here, just the two of them, to get to know Venice as Rowan and Clive.

It only meant he needed to redouble his efforts to locate Enyo so they could take her out.

FIFTEEN

FROM HER PLACE next to Rowan at the sidewalk café, her source, Donna Goldoni, Marcelo's wife, murmured quietly, "Across the bridge, three down. That palazzo with the closed shutters."

Rowan sipped her espresso as she looked the place over from behind her sunglasses.

She took note of the outside alarms as well as the cameras and every few minutes a human guard would patrol along a roof level walk. A lot of security for a random rich person. "Who owns it?"

"Here's something you'll find interesting. I started searching for the owners of each place I'd identified. That one over there took longer because it was a tangle. More than normal. Companies owned by trusts, owned by corporations, owned by, you get the idea. That palazzo? At the very end of that very long list of several other corporations remained Sangre International."

Motherfucker.

"That's some silence. It's true then. Marcelo told me but I have to say I was skeptical."

"What's true?"

"You're mated."

Rowan allowed herself the small joy of showing the ring off. But just a moment before it got sappy.

"While you're planning how to get in that palazzo, tell me about the Vampire."

"I figured Marcelo would have given you a briefing."

"He's a man. He doesn't listen seventy percent of the time, and even then only if it's about food or fucking. I know there's someone and that this Vampire of yours irons his boxers and had tailored shirts. It's love." Donna rolled her eyes.

Rowan laughed. "He's the Scion of North America."

Donna's delighted exclamation loosened Rowan's spine. "He's the British one, right? I've seen some pictures of him. He looks quite nice in a suit. He should try Italian next time."

"I'm sure he'd need medication and therapy to change tailors. He's very...precise."

"*Precise.*" Donna thought that was quite funny. "You must make him insane. This is good. Men love women who drive them crazy. You must make it into an art form."

Rowan hid her smile as she thought about how she'd spent the first eighteen months she'd known Clive trying to provoke him into developing a neck tic. She hadn't abandoned the plan entirely, but he was pretty nice to her most of the time so she kept that in reserve for when he really got on her nerves.

"When I'm doing my job right, yes. And you know how much I like a job well done," Rowan said.

"Is it the sex? I hear things." Donna waggled her eyebrows.

"The sex is quite fantastic. But..." Rowan paused as a platter of meat, cheese and eggs was brought out to them along with still-warm bread.

"But?"

"It's more than the sex. I like him. Most of the time anyway. And he knows my family and is still around."

"Of course he is! Your father is their First." Always blunt, was Donna.

Considering how borderline violent and crazy Theo could get, it was a double-edged sword to be in a relationship with the one person he considered his child. There were times she felt like it was her who held him, kept him from setting everything aflame.

"He's influential and powerful without me." Rowan drew up one shoulder briefly. "And," she blew out a quick breath, "we're together. Like *together-together.*" She held up her right hand. "It goes on my right hand because that's where I hold my blade."

Donna's eyebrows raised. "He said that?"

"He didn't make it up. I mean, it's customary in their world if one of the spouses is a warrior of some type." It was that he'd put it there without hesitation. She wondered if he'd even noticed it when he'd given her the ring. *She* hadn't really thought about it until several hours later.

"He accepts who and what you are. That's a good sign."

Which was exactly why it meant so much.

"Yes. Despite the whole Vampire thing, he's…he's nice. I mean, he's still one of them so he's arrogant and bossy and thinks he's the only person capable of doing anything right. But I like him more than I want to kill him. Most days."

"Considering what a wretched bitch you are, that's not a bad thing."

A laugh bubbled up from Rowan's belly as a rush

of gratitude hit her. She only saw Donna once a year, maybe two, and yet, she was someone Rowan trusted. Trusted enough to give her admission to Rowan's home, and to her life. It was good to be teased by a friend like her.

"I'll probably tell him this story. If I'm feeling nice," Rowan said.

"So maybe never?"

"You're so mean," Rowan said around a snicker.

"My ex said the same thing when I spelled him so that his butthole itched every three hours for six days. My mom taught me that spell." Donna's smile was proud.

"What?" Rowan had to put her espresso down because she shook so hard with laughter. "Man, I wish I knew that spell."

They finished their breakfast as the city came alive all around them and then moved to stroll along the canal, over the footbridge and around the palazzo.

They headed away from the area, back over Rialto and into Costello, where the Goldonis lived.

"Here's what I know." Donna spoke quickly as they weaved through the already growing crowds fresh off the cruise ships that docked nearby. "I started asking around about new long-term tenants who may not have been human."

"As you do."

"What?"

"Sorry. Americanism. It was a way to comment on the absurdity of putting the word out for non-humans being totally normal for us. He—Clive—only gets about half the references."

"Naturally you do it even more often."

Rowan nodded, mock serious. "It's like we're sisters."

Donna's smile brightened. "I understand that one."

"You're quick that way."

"I am. Which is why I had two suspects within three hours of finding out she was possibly coming here."

"Also one of your finest qualities."

Donna unlocked the main door to the building she and Marcelo lived in. Her parents lived down the hall and Marcelo's brother lived a floor up. It was like a magical fortress in there. Whatever she had to say to Rowan, Donna wanted to be sure they weren't overheard.

The entry to their flat welcomed Rowan with the scent of yeast and something fresh and green.

Window boxes lining the entire living room burst with all manner of living things. Herbs, flowers and vegetables filled the space with so much vitality Brigid approved as mightily as Rowan did.

They got morning sun but at the end of the day, when it was hottest, they got shade. It made their apartment even more soothing to be in. Rowan had spent hours in the kitchen with Donna and her mother the last time she'd been in Venice. Cooking. Drinking wine or tea. Rowan liked to watch Donna create the complicated potions she used for her magic. The energy of the flat embraced her, made her feel safe.

A conjuror worked magic through spellcraft. As they learned and their control grew, their ability to work more and more complicated and powerful spells also grew. Most never got past dabbler levels, but Donna and her mother were both fairly strong.

In fact, Donna led the gathering there in Venice.

A gathering was a group of conjurors who worked together. She was sort of an ambassador, president, judge and teacher all at once.

"Sit. I think tea is in order for the rest of the telling." Donna indicated the scarred kitchen table. Rowan did and after she set the water to boil, Donna joined her.

"I wanted to come here so that we could speak privately. There's quite a bit of Vampire and magical power in my city that's recently arrived from the outside. It makes everyone else nervous. The practitioners have been asking around but no one seems to know the source. Not for sure. But whatever is in that palazzo we were looking at is my guess."

Rowan would have to take Donna's word for it. She had her own sort of magic, but no talent for that sort of working.

"Shortly after learning Sangre International owned the property, my cousin had finally gotten back to me. He works for a security company. They got a service call for the system in that palazzo. One of the panels had water in it so he had to tear it out and put another in so he was there for several hours. He said there were three Vampires, one female. He told me she smelled like almonds."

Rowan blew out a breath. The very oldest Vampires smelled like almonds. Enyo definitely fit that bill.

"Two human security. From dawn to twilight they patrol the exterior every hour at the quarter after. They're not using any specialized equipment. No body armor though they're carrying sidearms. They also have food delivered to the outer gate. Idiots." Donna got up to pour the hot water into teacups and bring them back to the table.

"It's got to be her. We won't know for sure until dark though. She's bound to have a fortified resting chamber, so I can't just go in and stake her while she's at rest or even count on her dying if I burned the place to the ground. It's such a beautiful building I'd hate to destroy it. And it belongs to the Vampire Nation so if I do destroy it they'd demand to be compensated for it. Even though it's their property this woman is in to start with. This is the level of ridiculous my life has gone to."

"Fire jumps from building to building too easily anyway." Donna patted her hand with a smirk. "So when are you going in? I have some rudimentary plans for the building that should help us."

Rowan shook her head. "I appreciate your help. I've already transferred your fee plus an additional fifty percent for the speed and thoroughness of your work. I'll take over from here."

Her friend's amusement slid into hard lines. "My mistake. I shouldn't have made that sound like a request. You're family. There's to be no argument."

"It's one thing to sneak around and gather intel for me. This is something else." Enyo was the scariest thing she'd ever come up against other than Theo. Rowan was sure she'd kill Enyo or die trying. But the humans she cared for were fragile. So, so vulnerable.

"I'm not saying anything negative about your ability and power. You're a badass. But she's like nothing you've dealt with before. I can't risk you."

"Those of us in Venice who are practitioners have a loose organization. As I said, we've noted the rise of some new magical power. Poison on the breeze sometimes. We believe this is connected to your Vampire and as such, it concerns us. Today, while it's daytime and safe," she added before Rowan could argue, "at least let me walk with you back to your villa. We'll take a small detour past that palazzo. Just so I can get a little closer. You'll be with me. It's daylight. I might be able to tell if it's a Vampire working magics or if she's got them with her as part of her retinue."

Rowan groaned. "We can go now if you have the time. I appreciate your assistance." Help freely offered was something sacred. While she wanted to keep them safe, she didn't intend on insulting these women and the truth was, the expertise they had to offer would be valuable.

After tidying up the kitchen, they headed back out. The warmth of the earlier morning had gotten heavier as rain waited somewhere nearby. The scent of it, in Venice like nowhere else, already hung in the air.

Before they'd even crossed the footbridge to the other side of the canal, a faint hint of dark, sticky magic laid itself against the breeze for a brief moment. Donna's muscles tightened up. Brigid, too, rose and her power unfurled slowly, filling the space in a warm wave.

Donna paused, turning to Rowan, looking her over carefully. "Well."

"The last year has been intense." Rowan turned her back, looking carefully at the rear corner of the building. It also helped not to look at Donna.

Each threat she'd faced had made her stronger. The distressing thing was that she kept having to tangle with super-old Vampires who kicked her ass sideways, nearly killing her, before she'd been able to vanquish them.

It *hurt* to nearly die. But worse than embarrassment and all the pain, it filled her with outrage that she hadn't vanquished Enyo.

Things wouldn't be balanced until Rowan had erased the ancient Vamp from the earth. And it wasn't only Rowan who burned with the need to end the Vampire. Enyo had killed the last Vessel who carried Brigid, which meant She hated Enyo as much as Rowan did.

The score to settle was one of those big, giant holy mission type things and Rowan was totally okay with that.

"Sometimes the path to greater power is a painful one," Donna said, understanding in her tone.

There was always a balance to keep. It would never *not* be a part of her life. It hadn't been a happy, bouncy road to get to that point where she'd not only accepted what it meant to be a Vessel, but she embraced it.

It was then, that moment where she accepted her path and took it up like a mantle, that she and Brigid had kicked open the last doors between their power and became something else. Something stronger and faster and ultimately more powerful and deadly.

But the path had been lit with a whole lot of pain and anguish. Donna was right about that.

As they circled around to stroll along the narrow walk at the front of the palazzo, that sticky energy nearly touched Rowan.

Donna spoke under her breath as she hustled Rowan along about three times as fast as they'd been moving before.

Down narrow alleys and through the tiniest of courtyards and Rowan realized they'd ended up at the canal her house looked on.

"I've never come home this way."

"I know a thing or two."

Rowan smirked at Donna. "I bet you do."

Once they'd gotten inside her villa and the doors were locked behind them with the wards in place, Rowan finally asked, "Okay, mind telling me what just happened?"

Donna brought a bottle of red wine left over from the dinner the night before and poured them each a sizeable glass and nearly drained hers in a few swallows.

Well, that was alarming.

"I haven't been that close to it before. I suppose I thought it was superstition but really it was most likely self-preservation to keep my distance. There is something *profane* in that palazzo. Wrong. Yes, there are Vampires there. But I can't say if it's yours or another," Donna said. "Whatever the case, it needs to be routed and driven from here. Even those who practice dark energy have lines they won't cross. There are rules you don't break without risking a great deal." She made the evil eye with a nimble flick of her wrist.

"Let's hope it's her and not an entirely new and separate threat. I sort of have a lot to do right now." Rowan finished her wine.

"Trouble likes company."

"I'm trouble's best friend."

"How long has it been since you've slept?" Donna asked.

Over a full day by that point. "That's on my list. But I have other things to do first." Like call Hunter Corp. and report in because even if Roth was being a treasonous asshole, not everyone there was. This clusterfuck was Hunter Corp.'s job and she had no plans to let them sidle away from their responsibility.

After that rousing call, she'd check in with her investigator to see if he'd heard anything of use to her about Roth and this business with David. Then she might just be able manage to grab a few hours' sleep before the Vampires woke up.

Right then, Rowan pushed away her exhaustion and began to put together an angle of attack. "You said you had the plans for the palazzo?"

"We aren't done negotiating yet."

Rowan shook her head. "Nope. I'd appreciate the plans, but I'm sure Carey could get them too. I'm not going to let you put yourselves in the line of fire."

"I can help you, Rowan. Me and the other practitioners in Venice. We can put our magic to good use."

Rowan's power seemed to fill the room in one hard burst. "It's *my job* to protect humans from creatures like whoever is in that palazzo. It's *my job* to kill it and end any threat. This is what I'm going to do."

Donna blew out a breath. "I understand you want to protect us."

Affection was one thing; she cared for the Goldonis. She'd protect them, even if they were unhappy about it. "The sentence needs to end right there."

David came into the room but instead of leaving, he came to stand with them, a brow rising as he caught sight of the wine.

"You've been busy today."

They filled him in on what they'd learned. David made notes and sent several texts to Carey, who coordinated with his counterpart at Hunter Corp.

"Donna is right, *Deese*." David said this respectfully, but he was firm.

"I liked it better when you were perfectly obedient." Rowan frowned his way.

He bowed slightly, hiding a smile still showing in his eyes. "I am yours to command. As ever."

"Look at you! Was that sarcasm? I wrote that book, mister. Don't try it. You're not even afraid of me anymore. I'm slipping. I used to make people weep with a look and now you're giving me puppy dog eyes. It's like I'm in hell."

David ignored Rowan. "How close do you have to be for your magic to be effective?" he asked Donna.

"We can all stay at least several houses away. My mother and I can access the third floor of the café where Rowan and I sat earlier today. Across the canal from the palazzo. The others can position themselves similarly." Donna turned her attention to Rowan. "All of us, across traditions and practices, are standing against this abomination and rooting it out. Let us be your shield. You'll be gone in a few days. Venice will still be here. We'll still be here. And it'll remain *our* job to keep it safe. We've already been working—all of us with the gift—together to find it. We're no small power and we're at your disposal."

They were right. But damn it, the more things she had to keep track of, the slower her response would be.

Rowan had allowed herself to be soothed by this sense of camaraderie, and of course she was appreciative of Donna's expertise. But Rowan was responsible for her and all these other practitioners. Didn't they get it?

Rowan blew out a frustrated breath. Trying to manage people was a pain in her ass. "I need to take a walk to think about it."

"You shouldn't go out alone," David admonished.

Rowan's eyebrow slid up very slowly. Sarcasm was one thing—and she was proud he was so good at it—but he needed to remember what she was. "I'm a big girl."

Chastened, he nodded. "Of course. I'm not questioning that. Merely requesting that you be safe. Which of course you will be because that's your job."

"Nice recovery. Get back with Carey and then have Susan's valet set up that call with Hunter Corp. I don't want you dealing with Roth, or anyone else but Celesse or Susan. Oh and for that conference call, make sure Carey's included." He'd know bullshit in ways Rowan wouldn't even think to be suspicious of. He was crafty in ways she wasn't. "Anyone starts trouble while I'm gone, shoot them in the face. And then text me."

She headed back out, needing to be alone to parse over all the stuff in her head.

The desire to simply go over to that palazzo, kick the doors open and hunt until she sliced Enyo's head off rode her nerves, made her jittery. Like a bead of water skittering across the surface of a hot pan.

The Rowan she'd *been* would have done it a year ago.

Now she had all these people to juggle. Some to protect, others to mollify, fear or deceive. And some of those people were all those at once.

Her life before Clive came into it had been free of having to ask people for permission to do things. Or to seek their input.

Clive had changed things.

That was pretty mushy, she realized, cringing. But there was no denying it. He'd come along at a time when everything in her life had been in flux. Any other man and she'd never have considered him.

But he'd gotten all up in her head and her life and her heart and there wasn't much else to do.

He'd changed *her* and then the intervening year a hundred other things had altered her life.

And six months ago her loyalty to Hunter Corp. had been unquestioned. Sure she had annoyances, but most things annoyed her and people being in charge of her had always chafed.

The Joint Tribunal had changed things. Roth trying to harm David had changed things. Hunter Corp's foot dragging when it came to investigating the role of one of their own in this leak they so clearly have within their organization had changed things.

She didn't trust them anymore.

She headed down to the Grand Canal so she could grab a water taxi. Rowan had already walked up and down the bridges and back alleyways so at least she could cruise through by water while she was doing her thinking.

Rain was coming but that hadn't stopped the crowds. Rowan waited her turn in the lineup for the water taxis, neatly defending her turf when a young couple tried to cut in line.

"I think you'll find it easier to locate the end of the line back there." Rowan jerked a thumb.

Inordinately pleased with the opportunity to deliver a dressing-down, she turned, grasping the hand of the guy on the dock and stepping down into the boat.

"Off we go, Sally!"

SIXTEEN

ROWAN RUBBED THE bump on her head. He'd gunned the boat and she'd knocked the back of her skull against the gleaming hardwood at the back of her seat. Like a fucking rookie. She was so agitated it took a moment to find her manners.

"Carl." Otherwise known as Crazy Carl, a sage who turned up in her life from time to time to deliver some mystic advice. In his own, taxidermy obsessed, totally mad-as-a-coot manner.

On his own timetable. And not if she got shirty. He had something to say and she had to be patient until he said it.

"Lottie, you look a little ragged."

He also never got her name right. It was on purpose. She thought.

"Yeah, I've been getting that one today." She took a look around the taxi, noting the swank details. "Did you do something naughty, Carl, and take this pretty boat from someone who owned it?"

"It's mine now. That's all that matters."

Okay then.

"What brings you to Venice?"

He zipped around a corner so fast Rowan was pretty sure they'd have hit the wall if he hadn't had some sort of magical mojo to keep from doing it.

"I'm a world traveler. We already covered this back in London. Did you bump your head harder than I thought?"

He grinned back at her over his shoulder, his usual orange camo cowboy hat had been replaced with a jaunty short billed ball cap.

She raised a brow at him but he didn't give one tiny fuck. Which was why she loved him so much, even when he was a giant pain. He was like a kitten. Even she couldn't stay annoyed with a kitten.

Cosmic protection most likely kept him alive, just like kittens and babies. If they were cute enough you couldn't be annoyed and they'd make it through to adulthood.

"If it would fit into your plans, I need to look around." She was just going to assume he had some sort of internal GPS and wouldn't get lost. Or maybe he would. She just wanted him to cruise around the back canals where Venice was quieter and she could get a better feel of who and what was a threat. Or not. Though the latter was clearly wishful thinking.

"I've created a trip itinerary, Maisy. Just you be patient."

Maisy was a new one. "Isn't Maisy a cow's name?"

"My mother's name was Maisy."

Rowan cringed. "Oh. I'm sorry."

He cackled and she realized he'd totally lied to poke at her. She shook her head, scanning the buildings as they floated past. The further they got from the Grand Canal, the less frequent the calls from one gondolier to another as they came around a blind corner became.

"You're a sneaky old bastard," she muttered and he laughed more.

"I got into town last night. Isn't as clean as it was the last time I was here."

He didn't mean litter. He meant power.

"I'm here to sweep it clean."

"Like in that movie with the cab driver with the hair?"

She paused before she realized he meant *Taxi Driver.* "Sort of. Only without the penis. I don't have one."

He nodded, very seriously. "Well, that's a question I don't have to ask in the future."

"Can we?" Rowan pointed for them to turn but he waved her away.

"I have an itinerary, Lola. What you need isn't down there."

She sat back, willing patience. She had so much to do. Daylight was wasting.

"Patience isn't your strong suit. You have a lot of years in you. More now after your tussle with that rabid beast. Rabies is a death sentence you know. Can't rehabilitate rabies away. Brain gets damaged."

He slowed down, letting the force carry the boat through the canal.

"Anyway, as I was saying. Lots of years in you. Patience means you pay better attention. There's always something to be done. I understand that. It's busy time down at the library."

He wouldn't actually come out and say anything plain. He had this sideways, meandering delivery that at first listen didn't mean anything specific. But after many years of Carl taxi rides here and there, she'd gotten the hang of it. Mostly. He was a sage after all so it came with being mysterious.

"Heard your little friend lost an eye."

Rowan snorted. She didn't bother to ask him where he'd heard it. He would have told her if he'd wanted her to know. They probably had a gossip website.

"That's what she gets for invading my space bubble."

"Glad you still got your sense of humor. You'll need it before this is over."

She moved forward to hear him better.

"I never figured her for Italy. I had Greece in the pool."

"You guys have a pool?"

"Like fantasy football, not one to swim in. We got the ocean for that. They like to talk big while we play a round of golf."

"So, a golf club for ancient wise ones? That's pretty cool."

He growled. "They're weird. Some of 'em are flat-out nuts."

Rowan gave him a look, which he ignored. "Yeah, I'm sure *some* of you are."

"So I lost three hundred dollars because I figured your one-eyed friend would run to familiar ground. Don't know who chose Italy. Probably Monty, that stupendous oaf. As I was saying, the last time I was here in Venice it was a lot cleaner. They got themselves an infestation. I expect you know how to exterminate some pretty nasty creatures. But this time."

He trailed off.

"See that wall over there? At the corner?"

Rowan nodded. Generations of gondoliers and other boaters would have bumped into it over and over. The layers of plaster and paint and whatever else had worn away to the brick beneath.

"There's a great bakery near my hotel."

Rowan struggled through, knowing he was giving her some sort of clue or clues, but not having any idea what it was, she gave it up for a while. If she let it stew a little it might make sense later.

"Where are you staying?"

"I just told you. A hotel near a bakery. Aren't you listening?"

"Yes. Of course."

"Cakes."

"At the bakery?" Cake for breakfast would be really good. She needed to stop by the bakery near her place and bring back cake. Maybe she'd share with everyone else. If they deserved it.

"Layers. All the elements line up, make it better."

She mulled that over a minute or two before she got an idea what he might mean.

"Like say, if you combined magic with Vampires?"

"Recipes are just chemistry. Magic is just chemistry."

"Are you ever allowed to just say what the heck is going on?"

"Where would the fun be in that?" He pulled up at the dock in front of her house.

"How do you do that?"

"Magic." He grinned for a moment and then darkened. "Do not speak her name until you are face to face."

"She's here in that palazzo, isn't she?"

"Why ask me when you know the answer already?"

"Because everyone gets mad when I kill the wrong

Vampire. If I make extra sure, the less likely the chances of me having to spend hours upon hours in a meeting, going to meetings, coming home from meetings or waiting for one to end or begin."

"You're never going to be as powerful as you can be if you don't stop questioning what you know here..." he tapped her temple, "...and here." He tapped her chest over her heart. "You were made to do your job. Nature made you perfect from birth. All you need to do is own it and be it."

Wow. He'd actually been less mysterious this visit than he ever had been before.

"Are you here to fight against her?"

"Sometimes I like it when a fox is posed, teeth bared and ready to rumble. Other times maybe he's sleeping or laying on a log. You see what I mean?"

"Um. Give me a second." She cast a quick look for one of the dead, stuffed things he seemed to carry with him and spied a lizard of some sort on a shelf to his left.

"My son is an engineer."

She stepped away, repressing a shudder. "The one who isn't talking to you anymore because you keep trying to get him to go snake hunting with you?"

Carl, in addition to whatever he did at this mysterious clubhouse with other sages, had several ex-wives and three adult children. He seemed to forever be agitating one or all of them at the same time.

He chuckled. "That's my younger son. Just like his mother. She doesn't like me either. Though she liked me well enough for a bit of time." His laugh went a little bawdy for a breath or two.

And just like that, she got what he had meant. "Everyone has a different role to play." Even his creepy taxidermy projects apparently.

"Now you're talking, Sally."

Since he was being pretty coherent in some of his answers, she decided to press a little more. "There are people, friends, who want to help me. They could be of use, but they're human. Fragile."

Carl pushed his super shiny wrap around sunglasses up his nose a little. "*Cake*," he reiterated. "Remember? Now go on. Daylight's wasting and you have things to do."

She had no idea how long they'd been gone. He had a way of altering her perception that way so she could have spent ten hours or fifteen minutes with him.

He helped her to the dock. "Keep wary. We talked in London about deep, cold water." He referred to her stop, on the way to the Keep, nearly three months before. He'd warned her about Enyo. Well, via a slightly meandering story, which was pretty much his standard operating procedure. "Trouble can be like an iceberg. What you can see isn't the most dangerous part."

He stood across from her, also on the dock. Brigid rose like a cobra flaring its hood.

"Speak plainly, *Sophos,*" Brigid warned.

Carl's grin went from slightly goofy to a little dark, and maybe a little reverent too.

He lifted a hand in surrender but it was soothing as well. "Whoa there, Bride. I mean no harm. You know that or I'd have seen this before now. I'm allowed to urge her to remember that revenge breeds haste. Haste breeds mistakes. The real enemy is not a one, but a many."

Brigid had more than one name, had been revered

by more than one culture, more than one religion, more than one time period. Bride was one of Her incarnations and it pleased Her to hear the sage use it.

And it pleased them both to realize he'd answered the question. Brigid stepped back enough for Rowan to continue. Rowan didn't reference that whole thing with Her, getting right to the point.

"I knew this was more than about that one-eyed skank. The Blood Front business is a problem."

He tipped his hat her way. "You're a bright one. Engineering is like magic. It's like lots of things. A recipe for how to get something to work in any case." He looked into her eyes, seeing Her there. "Nice to see you again, Bride." And his jolly was back when he turned to Rowan once he'd gotten back into the boat. "Be seeing you around, Lolly!"

Before she knew it, he'd swept her into a hug, kissed her smack on the lips and had jumped back in his boat before speeding off, leaving her to stare at him as he left her sight.

"What a weird fucking day," she mumbled, moving inside.

SEVENTEEN

AFTER ANOTHER RIDICULOUS teleconference with Hunter Corp., she wanted to call the investigator, but she didn't have to because as she pulled the phone out, he called her.

"I don't have everything just yet, but I wanted to relay what I did have. This Wesslyian cat, he's had feelers out in the magical black market, looking for some people to perform off the books jobs. I don't have the link yet. I'm still looking."

"Any idea what types of off the books jobs?"

"I've heard hired muscle, but I don't know if it was magical, physical or what. And some custom spells. No one much wants to talk about that which says to me it was harmful in nature. But that's just guesswork on my part."

She thanked him and headed back out to the office downstairs where David was. Happily he was not only where she hoped he'd be, but had brought her a sandwich and some lemonade. "I can't believe they wanted you to hold off on the raid of that palazzo," David said.

"I can't believe he thought I was seeking permission in the first place."

Roth had brought several of his key supporters to the teleconference, including Hilary Sams, who'd tried one of those *aw shucks, I'm just joshing* things a few times when she'd been ripping Rowan down and Rowan wasn't having it.

He'd known she wasn't at the Hunter Corp. arranged villa, which she'd found very strange indeed. It was quite rare for any of the partners to check up like that. Especially if they weren't an active part of the investigation.

David gave her a wry look. "They continue to miscalculate and underestimate you."

"It used to piss me off. It still does, actually. But they all have to learn the hard way. I don't know how many others besides Hilary and Roth are involved, but I'll find out." She told him what the investigator had reported in their earlier phone call.

David paled, but kept himself together.

"I know he's behind this attempt to harm you. When I get enough evidence, the same as I'd use to back up any other execution, that will be handled."

"You could just work with them to have him jailed or whatever."

Rowan shook her head. "He's playing big-league games now. He's got to face the consequences. He's trying to start a war, trying to engage people to hurt a Hunter Corp. employee. More than one. But you're what I care about. I gave him chances. He's ignoring those chances."

David kept looking at her.

"I get that you think I'm being harsh."

He shook his head. "No, *Deese*, I don't. I'm just honored by the way you treat me. And protect me. I worry for you, how they'll react. But then I realize you don't care. You don't do you?"

"I'm beginning to understand I can continue to do

what I believe in without working for Hunter Corp. if they can't make better choices."

She changed the subject because she didn't want to get into it any further just then. "I cruised by the Hunter Corp. villa earlier. It's being watched. Luckily there are so many magic bearing creatures here in Venice it's not that easy to locate me. But I'm going to head back over there and take them out later on. I want to question them to see what they know. But first, it's Pirate Polly the Vampire Queen we need to handle."

Rowan really did love the fact that she'd poked out Enyo's eye. She couldn't wait to taunt her over it. Right before she used her blade to kill the ancient Vampire.

"Call Donna and ask if she's still willing to help."

He grinned. "I'm glad."

"I don't want to do this. They have no real idea of what they're getting into. But I need them and they're the type to try to do it on their own if I said no and that would be worse. Don't use her name. Pirate Polly I mean."

"Of course. I'll pass that on when I speak to Donna, but I'm going to assume they already know."

"It does come under the magic stuff umbrella. They have this thing about the name of a thing having power. Which is actually true and not just hokum. I love the word hokum."

"You have about two hours before the Vampires rise. May I suggest this is a good time for some rest?"

She'd taken what Carl had said to heart. No matter how badly she wanted to storm in and kill everyone inside that palazzo, it all needed to be planned carefully. Enyo wasn't an ordinary Vampire and there was sorcery involved in some way that was so bad it made the other badass witches she knew pretty much run the other way. To rush because Rowan was impatient would end in disaster. She had humans to protect and Enyo was the most formidable enemy she'd ever faced.

She wouldn't be raiding that palazzo that night. But she would need to be sharp when she was creating the plan.

"You're right. I'm going to sleep. I need to talk to Recht. If he comes down before I do, can you let him know?"

David nodded and she headed up to the room she belatedly remembered Clive was in. She briefly considered the couch in the sitting room but he'd be upset and as much as he'd understand she needed to be alone, part of him would feel rejected and she'd stopped trying to pretend it didn't matter.

She stripped to her panties and a T-shirt before she headed in. All was quiet of course. Clive would still be in the same position he went to sleep in. Nearly totally still. His skin would be cool.

Sliding in bed on her side, she managed to snuggle into the duvet and close her eyes. The house was safe. She was safe. Everyone under that roof was safe and she could finally sleep.

CLIVE AWOKE AND smiled as he realized she was in bed with him. Rolled up in the duvet like a crepe, her hair sticking out the top.

That she was still asleep told Clive she only got to bed a few hours before. He wanted her to sleep more than he wanted to show her just how much he missed her while he was resting.

He eased out quietly. He showered, dressed and

headed downstairs. He wanted to check in with Recht and Warren regarding The First's mental health. Rowan would also most likely be checking, but this was Nation business. They needed to be rooting out the leak within their ranks as well. He had his own people on it, as did Warren. But the Five were far better at this sort of thing. Vampires were terrified of a visit from The First's lieutenants and usually confessed quickly rather than endure whatever plans they had to get a confession from an uncooperative Vampire.

There was a note that donors had been arranged and would be arriving shortly. Clive went in search of Recht and found him speaking rapid-fire German over his phone. Orders to handle something from what Clive put together.

He hung up and nodded to Clive. "Where is Rowan? I was told she wanted to speak with me."

"Resting. I didn't want to wake her just yet. Have you spoken with anyone at the Keep?"

"He's taken to sleeping most of the time. The few hours he's awake he's cranky and needs diversion, but he hasn't left the grounds since the last time." The relief in Recht's tone was clear and that allowed Clive to relax a little.

Clive was at a disadvantage because he hadn't been around during any previous bad spots. He could have asked Rowan. She'd have given him the information, knowing why he'd need the details. But he didn't like to make her relive those dark times in her childhood if he could avoid it.

"The last time this happened, did all the Scions know?" Clive had taken up his predecessor's tenure as Scion of North America just eighteen months prior.

"Things were different then. We relied on her to keep him calm." Recht's gaze had been far away but his focus sharpened on Clive. "We should never have done that to a child. A human. The times before she was born we hid it when we could. The Scions can be volatile. She changed everything. She still does."

Clive realized what a gift Recht had just given him. Not just information, but an entirely new part of her that clicked into place. What would it have been like to have all that on your shoulders? Yes, he held the lives of the Vampires—and to a certain extent the humans—who lived in his territory. But she'd never experienced a time when she didn't have the weight of her father's devotion, sanity and direction to bear.

"Even when she was gone, his behavior was generally controlled. He does not want to disappoint her. He will recover if for no other reason."

Clive dipped his head below Recht's in thanks. He'd been trusted with information few others knew. That showed a great deal of assurance that Clive would not only continue to be loyal to The First, but to Rowan.

Like he was Rowan's husband, Clive realized.

"I did not speak to you before I asked her to wear the ring. I should have. You are her family, after all."

Recht smiled briefly. "She made her choice before you gave her that ring. I suggest you go to her father and tell him you love his daughter and wish to bond with her."

The moment was over as Recht slid his impassive mask back on and was once more one of the Five.

Clive shifted the discussion back to The First.

"The sleeping is good. It means on some level he

knows whatever this is he's going through is dangerous so he's trying to wait it out," Recht said.

"And the leak? There's a great deal of high-level information being obtained by our enemies. All while they're using the Nation's resources."

"We're working on it. We have a great deal of data to go through. But thanks to the North American Vampires, we have some sort of program to comb it for clues."

"Glad to put them to work."

Being the youngest Scion had its merits. He understood the importance of modern skills in his arsenal. Technology was his weapon to make up the imbalance of his lack of years presented.

He knew how to be savage. Knew how to hunt and kill. Knew how a little violence was necessary with Vampires so they understood his rules were not to be violated. He was quite good at it.

He'd forgotten the joy of a different kind of violence until Rowan had come along and he'd been pulled into a world where he rolled up his shirtsleeves and beat the hell out of someone on a regular basis.

Being a Scion was also a political position. A part in a larger, more complex network of power held across the entire Vampire Nation. As a potential Scion, he'd been trained by the Vampire Nation for three hundred years before he'd been appointed. Had learned strategy from the brightest minds. He'd lived and worked in London for several centuries, knowing the key to his success was understanding humans set the direction of the society they were inevitably part of.

That was how he'd continue to build the strength of his land. His inner circle was already more dynamic than the other Scions. He would continue to reign in North America and as each term ended and he moved to a new capital location, he would gather the best of the best.

The others would ignore him for another fifty years or so—it used to be that they'd have ignored him for a hundred and change. But his connection to Rowan had raised their attention.

He'd keep to his plan and get as much in place as he could before they started to consider him a real threat. And by then, he'd have all he needed to hold it against all comers.

Warren came in with Alice. Recht quickly brought Warren up to speed and when they came back to the kitchen, David was there directing Marcelo, who carried what appeared to be a great deal of food.

"Rowan is awake. She just got out of the shower," David said quietly to Clive.

"Did she speak to Hunter Corp. yet?"

"I'll let her bring you up to speed on that."

With an internal sigh, Clive headed up the stairs in her direction.

She entered the main salon as he reached the other door. A quick look around said they were alone so she let him hug her, kissing her slow.

Her eyes had gone dreamy for long moments and it was a gift. He kissed her quickly one last time. "Good evening. People will be coming up shortly. There's a lot of food. David is setting up some sort of staging area. You need to eat. You're pale."

She sniffed, annoyed. And yet she leaned into him for several long moments more. He kissed the top of her head, breathing her in. So vital.

She moved away, putting that part of herself aside until they were alone once more.

"I had an interesting day. I will absolutely eat. You'll get to meet Donna, that's Marcelo's wife."

Before she could say anything else, people came up the stairs and Clive caught her in a totally unguarded moment as she caught sight of David and smiled briefly before she scowled once more.

But David had noticed. One of the things Clive liked about their relationship was the vulnerability she showed around her valet. It was important that she have these relationships in her life. That she be surrounded by people and beings of power who cared about her and were invested in keeping her safe.

Rowan, more than any woman he'd ever known, needed a space to be soft. To be around people who didn't want something from her. Who didn't hate her or judge her or try to kill her. He wanted that for her very much. A safe, inner life where she could be unguarded.

She moved to take a few bowls and carted them over to the large table.

"Marcelo, thank you for moving this larger table in here. I appreciate that," Rowan said as her friend came in.

"We have big dinners every night. You're here so we'll be here." He shrugged. "Donna wouldn't have it any other way."

Another woman came up. "It's your table anyway. It was just down in the shop."

Rowan held up a hand to pause the conversation until she finished eating the bread she'd dipped in olive oil.

After a few more moments, she sighed happily. "Oh

my goddess, that is so good. Sorry. Clive Stewart, this is Donna Goldoni."

"Don't apologize for how good my bread is."

Clive bent over Donna's hand briefly. "It's a pleasure to meet you, Ms. Goldoni."

Warren and Recht came up with wine and water and they all settled at the large table.

"Everyone, fill plates and start eating, I need to speak to Recht for just a moment and then we'll start talking about what I learned today," Rowan called out.

Recht nodded and the two of them headed downstairs.

Once there, she spoke. "I won't keep you long. I just wanted to check in with you about Theo."

He outlined the situation at the Keep, first updating her about Theo and then the leak.

"I think it's an old family. I think it's a trusted family. I also think you know both those things. I can't say more at this time. I will share what I can when I am able." Recht's expression said he wished things were otherwise.

Which meant he was constrained by some Vampire bullshit on what he could tell her. And since he was ranked even higher than Warren and Clive on this hunt, there was only one other being who had the power to deny her information.

"Gah. That manipulative asshole." Theo was still pulling the fucking strings. On the verge of madness and he was keeping her where he wanted. "He's conscious what? Three hours a day? And yet he's got time to tell you not to share things with me. This is dumb. I know you won't violate his edict and I understand.

But I'm caught. I can't call him out. He's not well. It could make things worse. And he knows it."

"On the bright side it means he's getting better. He couldn't plan at this level otherwise."

"Are you kidding me with that? Why does he fuck with my head this way? It's totally unnecessary."

Recht smiled. "Little goddess, he wants you to need him. He's your father. This is what fathers do. Granted, yours can take things to levels far above and beyond what most fathers do. But he's exceptional in every other way as well."

Was that it? He *was* like an alien sometimes—okay all the time. And he was shady as fuck in many, many ways. But then she'd see his madness through someone else's eyes and realize she might sometimes miss nuances about Theo and his relationship with her.

He did love her. In his way, in whatever sense he connected her to his deep affection compared to everyone and everything else. It was terrifying and yet, she'd missed that while they'd been estranged.

It would likely always be complicated between them. Fraught. They would bicker. But she no longer liked the idea of not having him in her life. In some way. She was quite glad he lived on an entirely different continent so he couldn't just drop by.

She sighed. "He's crafty. One of these days I'm going to outmaneuver him."

Recht found that hilarious. "Not a chance." He headed back upstairs and she followed after making sure the security system was armed and all was locked down.

She filled a plate and settled at the table next to

Clive. He handed her a glass of wine and then clinked his to it. "Eat and then talk."

He'd gotten even bossier with her since she put his ring on. It was annoying when he poked at her to sleep and eat and that sort of thing.

But she might have also liked it. Maybe it was nice to be cared about by a man like Clive. A super uptight control freak millionaire Vampire who gave her weapons more often than pretty panties. That wasn't such a bad bargain really.

"Fine," she snarled as she put some more shrimp on her plate. He made that cute stuffy British sound but he had a smile at the corner of his mouth.

They were so dumb.

She'd been stupid back when she was sixteen and lost her cherry to one of Theo's guard. Who then told her the sordid truth of who'd killed her birth parents. Spoiler alert: it was Theo.

But lots of sixteen-year-olds did stupid things. Aside from the bomb he'd dropped into her life, she'd headed off on a path that had been necessary to who she was right at that moment. Who she had to be.

But she was dumb with Clive. Dumb with love. He made her think about maybe one day considering making those noises people used around kittens and babies.

She should be horrified and ashamed of this entire mental dialog but the problem with love was that you found stuff like getting a handgun tucked in a high-end handbag really nice. Maybe even romantic because it was thoughtful.

She'd probably been colonized by an alien pod or something.

"I have no idea what you're thinking about, but you're going to have to tell me later," Clive murmured.

Ignoring him—okay not really, she found him sort of adorable—she tried some of the greens with red peppers and moaned. "So good."

Donna beamed, happy with the praise for her cooking. "You should live here full-time. You can eat at my table every night if you want."

Rowan warmed. Yes, she would be welcome at their house any time. That was nice. Like family, only appropriately weird.

Ack. She was getting so goopy.

"I could. Stay out late, get up late. Eat. Nap. Eat. Go out. Sleep. Yes, that's a nice life." She finished her wine as no one in the room bothered to believe that she'd actually retire and relax.

"All right. Let me tell you how today went."

EIGHTEEN

RIGHT AS SHE slid her blade into the sheath at her back, her phone rang. A look told her it was Susan.

"I need to take this." Rowan excused herself, going up the stairs and into her room.

"That was quite the meeting," Susan said by way of greeting.

"Right? I'm never attending a meeting with Roth again." Being dead meant you couldn't go to meetings, though Rowan bet if he could, Roth would. Suck-ups like him loved tedium.

"I'm not sure that's a promise you can keep. He's trying to stir even more trouble right now."

"I warned him not to come for me. I hope he's got his affairs in order." Rowan told Susan about the information her investigator dug up. "This time I'm handling this like Rowan, not a hunter he works with. He and Hilary are up to something. One or both of them either are the leak or they know who it is. They need to be investigated."

"This all takes time. Celesse and I are working on it at this end. When you're done, come to London and we can deal with every last bit of nonsense once and for all."

Being told to be patient rankled. It was normal Hunter Corp. politics sure, but this was far more serious than the usual petty bullshit she regularly ignored so she could tolerate it and not stab anyone.

"I dropped by the HC villa and it's being watched. This needs to be addressed right now. It can't wait until this is over."

"Rex brought it up, opening an investigation. Celesse seconded. Roth volunteered to head it. I said no. There was more fighting." She paused and Rowan sighed.

"Say it."

"They've tabled it until you come to London to present evidence. He managed to sway enough people. Said he'd only checked in before the meeting to brief himself on what you were up to. They don't know about the threat to David, remember?"

"Are you kidding me? They know plenty about everything else. I'm here now, in danger *because* of this leak. The person who has already interfered and endangered me on multiple occasions is far more knowledgeable about my location than any of you have ever been. I normally handle my own travel arrangements. And when I don't that's the time he's suddenly so fascinated with my itinerary? It's just a coincidence? This is the loyalty I'm going to be shown? I'm here for Hunter Corp. taking out the garbage yet again and the safety of me and the other hunters in the field is not important enough?"

"I don't like the tone in your voice, Rowan. Don't be rash. There is absolutely no reason to believe we won't win on this. You'll come and we'll put down this ridiculous uprising."

"I'm not being rash. I'm finally just facing the truth.

I have some killing to do. And then I'm coming to London. And I won't be sparing anyone's feelings."

"I wish things were different. I wish we had more ability to sway them. The information you gave me is quite powerful. I'm sorry."

"Scrub it for anything that might identify a source's identity. If you can do that and protect my people, you have my permission to share it with them. The relevant bits anyway."

"All right. Hilary seems to have gotten a few more partners behind her. This Vampire you're hunting has made your job more complicated."

"Sure, but that's her job. It's not the job of the other full partners to do it too. I have to go."

"You know Rex and I support you totally, don't you?"

Rowan's anger softened at the alarm in Susan's tone. She and Rex were Rowan's family. She trusted them both with her life. She understood what internal Hunter Corp. politics were like.

"I've never doubted it."

"Excellent answer. All right, sweetheart. Go kill that nasty creature. When you get here we'll have dinner and you can bring Clive as well."

"Yeah, about that. I have a lot to share but I can't get into it now." Rowan looked at her hand, the amber threads in the ring catching the light.

"Did he hurt you?"

Despite all her worried, that made her smile. "He didn't. It's good news, not bad."

"All right. Do be careful. We love you."

"I love you too," Rowan said and then disconnected the call.

She turned around, knowing Clive had come in. "I take it you heard all that."

He nodded. "I've already said how displeased I am with the way they treat you so I won't repeat that."

"You totally just did."

He fought a smile and she rolled her eyes.

"You're powerless when faced with an I told you so, Clive. It's part of your makeup. You're driven to say it."

He stalked over and hauled her close with a snarl, kissing her senseless.

He finally broke away, setting her back from him. "I don't like you put into jeopardy again and again because the very organization you're serving is actively trying to derail you. And it doesn't help that those doing it seem to want to wipe my kind from the planet."

"As if. See, the problem is, they're dangerous because they lack any real intelligence when it comes to how to deal with the results of their little revolution. I'm sure as hell not letting any cabal, not of Vampires, sorcerers or hunters, go genociding around. But I can't do this right now. I need my head on the plan. Let's go. One major threat at a time."

HE TOOK HER upper arms, pulling her close again, locking his gaze with hers. "I will not allow anyone to harm you."

Six months ago she'd have bloodied his nose for this sort of touch. Maybe. They also could have ended up fucking against a piece of furniture. She really was perfect for him.

She had already been protecting *him* for months. Spent her entire life protecting other people, but it was more because it was Rowan caring for Clive. And that she was being attacked by those within Hunter Corp. made his blood boil. She was his to keep safe in ways they couldn't possibly have understood.

But they would. They underestimated Rowan but they had no context to what he was going to do with those threatening his woman.

"I can protect myself." Her voice was a whisper. He saw the fear in her gaze. The worry that this would turn emotional.

"You can. And you do." He pressed a kiss to her forehead. "And the fact remains. I won't allow this to go unanswered."

"This is what happens when you have a Vampire boyfriend," she muttered.

"I'm not your boyfriend. I'm your mate. Your husband. Now that you're delightfully cranky again, let's go."

"Husband?" Her sigh was theatrical and it made him laugh as he followed her out. She called back over her shoulder as she headed down the stairs. "The only thing good about this whole trip is that I get to do crime. That's it."

He waited until they'd reached the bottom before taking her hand. And in full view of everyone gathered there, he kissed her knuckles. "After you get your fill of stabbing and killing I'll take you for gelato."

But she didn't get mad. Surprised delight scattered across her features for a brief moment and he resolved to bring that expression to her face as many times as he could. She needed more of that in her life.

"I know a place. Open all night. You're paying." Rowan pulled her hand back pretending to glower.

"I'm at your service." He bowed deeply and she

flipped him off. He pretended to be offended at her vulgarity and the spring was back in her step by the time they headed out into the night to do some crime.

NINETEEN

CLIVE KNEW THE Villa was one a powerful Vampire had been in recently. Had rested at least once or twice. During the daytime when they were asleep, they tended to leach magic into their surroundings. Over time it created a protective spell in that place.

It was a beautiful sort of synergy and one that convinced Clive that Vampires were as meant to be on this planet as humans. Vampires had carved out their place in the ecosystem.

He made the hand sign for empty and pointed at the villa. Rowan's brow knitted as her anger boiled over through the alley they stood in.

"Darling, you know that that does to me," he murmured as he moved closer.

"This is bullshit. How does she keep one step ahead all the time?"

Clive shook his head. "This is just another delay. But it won't be a long one. Or one we won't overcome. This is winding down to its ultimate conclusion."

He simply knew it to his bones. Anticipation hung heavy in the air. Humid, tense, that inevitable march toward whatever was supposed to happen.

"That sounded remarkably new age."

Said the woman sharing her existence with a millennia old deity.

"Since I'm not prone to such flights of fancy, you should take my words seriously. Let's get closer. If it's empty we should get in there to see if we can find anything to locate and end her once and for all."

"Yeah. We may as well speak with the others first."

They pulled back several canals over and met up with everyone at a tiny church courtyard. Donna unlocked the gate in the little stone fence and they went inside.

Once they did, Rowan nearly gasped at the way the spell simply tightened around them as the gate closed once more. Wards were usually sort of like a gate, this felt like being squeezed into a coat. For a moment it was a little uncomfortable, but then it wore off.

Donna said, "Let's go inside. We can speak freely."

It was indeed a church. The hardwood floors gleamed, smooth from generations of feet shuffling over it. They headed to the front where the altar was to gather in the pews.

"The villa is deserted." Clive didn't waste any time getting to the point.

"I've spoken with the other practitioners who came out tonight. We all agree on this point. There is a great power in that villa," Donna said.

"That I agree with you on. But the wielders of whatever power are not there. If she were there, or whoever that old Vampire was who has been lodging there, all the Vampires here would have known it," Clive explained.

"What you're feeling is the residual magic Vampires leave when they rest in a place for a while," Warren added.

Donna sighed and thought about that for a while.

"You may be right. But if you're wrong, we'd like to be on hand to help. The energy there is so strong I really don't think they've been gone very long."

Rowan agreed. "I'm convinced someone powerful was there this morning when we walked by."

Warren cleared his throat. "All right then, Donna. How about you tell us what's going on because this obviously has a magical component you're not entirely forthcoming about."

"It's not that I'm lying." Donna's tone was sharp. "We're all responsible for protecting something, eh? I've said all along that whatever magic is being practiced in that villa is wielded by someone who doesn't care about the cost. Which is steep."

Practitioners—what they called all brands of witches, sorcerers and the like—had pretty live-and-let-live attitude with one another. Even the ones who worked with blood and other darker elements Rowan tried not to think about. But all the practitioners here in Venice were universally repulsed but whatever was going on. Which made Rowan simultaneously curious and resolved to never know.

"Can we ask about it or is this a secret?" Rowan asked. She was surrounded by people keeping secrets and it annoyed her, even as she had her own.

"It's something none of us, even those who practice the darkest of arts, utilizes."

Great.

Rowan knew that was all she'd get for the moment. Eventually she'd force the issue, but they had bigger issues to deal with just then. "All right. I tend to agree with Clive and the Vampires on this. They're good at knowing if places are empty or not because they have that built-in predator instinct and great hearing."

"You'll make me blush with all your flattery," Warren said.

"I'm sure you're just misunderstood. Anyway, Donna, get your people in place." They'd established that none of them but Rowan's team would enter that villa or even get within a block without her permission. "David, you'll be with me and Recht. Clive, Alice and Warren, you three head—"

"Perhaps David should be with me and Alice can be with you." Clive tried very hard to say it, make it sound like an imperious order but also make it sound like he was asking nicely. Only a Scion level Vamp could do it as well as Clive had.

Not that it worked. But she admired the effort. "David is with me." She could keep an eye on him better that way.

"We know the entry points," Clive said, without referring to the subject again, "so we'll take the north and you the south."

Within minutes they'd headed back out.

TWENTY

It was late, but it was also Venice, so despite the rain—maybe to spite it—windows were opened up and the sound of conversations, of clinking glasses, televisions and music drifted down to the street they walked along.

The villa loomed ahead and each of the three approached it from a different angle. Rowan had let go of David. He'd been trained. He was smart. She could ask for a lot worse than his first fieldwork to be in the company of so many who'd step in if he needed help.

Brigid pushed to the surface as Rowan reached for their connection, wanting to view this from Her perspective. This close, and all the windows remained dark. Some on the third floor appeared to be uncovered, but the first two floors had dark drapes and shutters. Someone could be inside, behind those covered windows.

There was a lip on the edge of the canal leading to a small dock, mostly rotted. The villa's back wall faced it there. It would give Rowan a measure of cover while she got a closer look.

She motioned to Recht that she was headed that way. He paused, looked at her path and then nodded. Did the same.

Now as she walked the tiny ledge over to the dock,

the ooze of broken, misused magic began to stick to her skin.

Brigid didn't much like it. The surface of Rowan's skin burned white hot. So hot she nearly fell into the water when she jerked at the pain. And then it was duller and finally normal again. Except the magic wasn't clinging to her anymore.

Okay, so a little pain was worth that.

The wrought iron gate appeared to be stuck closed with disuse. But it allowed her to get close enough to see the house. She took in the scene. Second-floor shutters all closed but the ones here at the back of the house on the first floor were bare but for drawn curtains.

She didn't need to see in the house to smell it though. Not just death, but very bad death. Pain. Fear.

Inside Rowan knew Brigid had seen this before. Maybe back when Enyo killed the last Vessel.

Once she'd had that thought she was sure that was it. Enyo was there. Oh, not at that moment. Clive had been right. There was no one in the house. But in the city. Rowan scaled the stone wall quickly and walked along the edge until she got past the trip wire that had been left armed.

The shuttered windows were light tight and would be locked most likely, but the third floor had a balcony that looked like it led up to a rooftop deck.

So many people, even people who should know better, forgot how easy it was to hop from a fence or wall to an upper floor window or deck. The sheer number of times she'd entered a place that way because it wasn't locked never ceased to amaze her.

Rowan jumped, grabbing the edge of the casement around one of the shuttered windows. There was no way she could have gotten in there, but that perch allowed her to get a handhold and pull up to the deck and up to the roof. Where, as she suspected, several large skylights had been installed.

After making sure the room below was empty, Rowan got the French doors to the deck open and went inside.

Before they'd left the church's courtyard earlier, Donna had given Rowan a talisman. A coin that made her feel better the moment her friend had placed it in Rowan's palm.

It heated through the material of her pants, burning against her thigh. Rowan didn't have to be told to know it was warding off some bad shit in that house. The stain of what had been done there would not be easily removed. If it ever could.

Moments later, Clive strolled in, Alice in his wake.

They did a sweep of the third floor and then she and Recht met each other as she came down to the second floor and he was coming up. David popped up a second later.

Warren came down the other end of the hall. He hit a code and the doors all clicked unlocked.

While Rowan and the others made sure the villa was truly empty, Warren and Recht headed off to be sure there weren't any alarms or listening devices they hadn't seen and dealt with.

Burnished hardwood and wrought iron curved up a grand staircase. The furnishings were antique and absolutely stunning. Art hung on the walls that the Vampires probably stole centuries before. It was, quite honestly, one of the loveliest homes she'd ever been to in Venice. In fact, there weren't many places in Venice left with this kind of majesty.

Which made what had been done within the walls even more repugnant and offensive. Everything awful in the world seemed to seep from the walls. From the beautiful rugs at their feet. Hopelessness cloyed against her skin as they searched the place. They kept going outside to get fresh air so the nausea could subside.

Rowan wasn't sure that gorgeous art and the antiques could be saved. Or the home itself. There was no telling how that magic was going to affect the people living and working in the vicinity. Would it leak? Should it be neutralized? She was out of her league when it came to this kind of magic. That's when she made the call to allow Donna into the villa to see what her take was.

IT WASN'T QUITE an hour and a half later when everyone came back together to discuss the situation.

"They sure up and got out of here fast. Like they were ready to go at a moment's notice," Donna said.

"That's a basic precaution all Vampires are advised to take. Most of us have multiple bolt holes, caches of money and the like. It's a skill we don't like to let get rusty. If they had anything to hide, they took it with them." Warren paced.

Rowan looked to Donna. "What did this magic? They left that behind. A signature."

Donna wrung her hands a few moments. "You don't understand. If anyone knew what some of us were capable of, all would bear the punishment. We'd be in danger by those who'd seek to engage our services, voluntary or not. We've been drowned and stoned and burned since the first of us. We have laws I won't break."

Like Rowan could argue with that? It was nothing but the truth.

"I did get a call. The other practitioners have all consulted with one another and we don't think any being of a power who could do this," Donna waved a hand, "has left Venice."

"Why is she still here then?" Rowan asked. A boat and they could have been gone from town and on a plane before Rowan had even left her own house earlier that night. "Is there something she needs from here that she can't get anywhere else? As a Vampire or magically?"

"We're looking into that now. There aren't any holy days for at least a month for those of us in the known arts. There are certainly places here that are conducive to personal power and working spells. This is an old place. That's the beauty of old places."

Clive spoke. "I don't know of anything she'd need here that would aid her. Not based on any history or lore that I've been taught."

Recht shook his head.

"Maybe it's not a place she came for but an item or some sort of ceremony. Maybe this is her new thing. Like she declared her candidacy for Empress of Monstertonia and now her gig is traveling around and causing trouble."

"And we caught her in mid trouble and she had to scramble to get out of the way. She didn't expect us to find her here." Clive squeezed the bridge of his nose at the thought.

"At least not yet. We came to Venice early, remember? We were supposed to stop in Rome but changed our mind at the last minute." Rowan tucked that away to stew on it in the background. But she had things to do. "Do we need to stay here or can we get moving? We still have some darkness left so I'd like to get back to it."

"Once you leave, I'll let some of my compatriots in. The more traditions the better. One of us will hopefully see something that can help. In the meantime, we'll be keeping watch for you to see who is coming and going. So we'll be safer," Donna assured her.

"I don't want to leave you without more protection."

Clive nodded. "If she came back..."

"We're no small power." Donna stood taller.

Warren bowed deeply. "Madam, you are of course, very powerful. You have my admiration as a petty dabbler in spellwork myself." His attention shifted to Rowan, asking if it was cool for him to stay there.

It was his territory this was all happening in. He'd want to run Enyo to ground nearly as much as Rowan did. But this was also part of his job. A Vampire in his land, one who owed him fealty, had done this. Left whatever stain this gross magic had by doing whatever secret stuff so awful Rowan couldn't even imagine what it could be.

He was stepping back, giving the hunt over to her for real, and in doing so, he was being a better Scion. Rowan nodded slightly and he turned to Donna again.

"Would you consider letting me stay here with you while you and your friends go through this place? As I said, I'm a petty dabbler so I'm sure you could all teach me a few things."

Donna sniffed and then smiled, flattered. "If it's all right with everyone else, we'd love to have you."

Rowan nodded her thanks and they quickly took off after promising to keep Warren updated.

TWENTY-ONE

RECHT HEADED OFF in one direction, with Alice. He had access to a nice little boat—access meaning he stole it—and they planned to search via water.

"David, I need you to go back and deal with Carey. He needs to know what's going on so he looks where he should. I'm heading to the HC villa. I want to case it a bit. Text me when you connect with him."

David paused a moment. Rowan knew he was most likely trying to figure out if he'd been exiled. He nodded. "I will. And then I'll join you once you let me know where you are." He darted off without giving her a chance to argue.

She pretended to wipe away a tear, sniffing. "They grow up so fast."

"You think this situation with Hunter Corp. and the business with your one-eyed friend are connected."

Rowan sighed before turning to face Clive. "There's a connection, but I don't think I'm seeing all of it just yet."

"I'm afraid you're correct. I'm going to sweep along this way. I will reconnect with you over there in an hour. Don't ignore my texts."

"I don't ignore them. Sometimes I don't see them because I'm busy." Or when she didn't want to deal with him. Which was technically ignoring but not really. Probably. Anyway, she'd go where she wanted, when she wanted. So there.

His expression told her he knew what she'd been thinking. "Whatever you say. So, I'll be texting you to get your whereabouts."

"I'm going inside if it looks safe. This is the job. You knew it before you put a ring on it so suck it up. Go on. I'll see you later." She kissed him quickly before jogging the other direction.

The night was heavy. It had rained on and off over the ten minutes it took Rowan to make her way over to the side of Venice facing Giudecca. The Hunter Corp. residence was on a side canal not too far away from the last gondola yard remaining in Venice. And the roof gave her a place to settle in to watch the comings and goings without being visible herself.

It didn't take much time for Rowan to locate the people watching the villa, waiting. Within ten minutes she'd already started to think of them as the stupids.

There were three of them. They smoked and spoke loudly to one another and on their phones. She knew exactly where they were the whole time and not a single time did even one of them look up higher than street level.

She took pictures with a nifty pocket-sized camera with fantastic zoom. Carey had given it to her before she'd come back to Germany.

Technology being what it was, she was able to then send the pictures directly from her camera to her phone and then off to Carey to see if he could get a bead on who these watchers were.

They smelled human. Moved like it too. But until she'd gathered some more information, she'd hold off on saying it was certain. Which meant she needed to get a lot closer. After she got into that villa.

No one seemed to be inside. And when the stupids on surveillance wandered off after talk of some wine and a snack, she sent a quick text to Clive that she was headed in to an empty house and would let him know what she found.

He called her immediately and she answered after considering not doing so for a ring or two. "I'm on my way. I just spoke with David. He's working with Donna's people and Carey and will stay where he is to coordinate. Wait for me before you go in."

"The stupids sent to watch the place have wandered off to get drunk and eat too much. I should be doing that right now. And yet, here I am. *There's no one inside.* If you're on your way, I'll see you in a bit. Don't worry about me. Also, I've been doing this for a little bit of time. I'm cool."

She disconnected but heard him grumbling about how much he did worry just before the call dropped and she slipped her phone back into her pocket and buttoned it closed.

A quick scramble and she was down off the roof and on the little lane, the villa sat.

She crept across the nearly deserted street, across a small courtyard and circled the entire villa, seeing nothing.

There was something here. Not here as in where she stood. But in the air. In the city. Something wanted to do harm. To her. To everyone.

She eased through the slightly open double doors leading to the house's small front garden. It was kept up well, as Rowan assumed it would be. This property had to be worth quite a bit and whatever their sins, Hunter Corp. took care of things of value. Most of them away.

It wasn't like Rowan shouldn't have been there. It was prepared for her arrival, or supposed to have been. No staff she could see. Maybe they'd been told to go home.

She peeked through a window and seeing nothing, skipped using the pass code they provided for the front door keypad and picked a lock to a side door.

She knew all the Hunter security protocols and after a quick few minutes she'd managed to get it on a loop so that it didn't show any doors or windows being opened.

Nothing of note on the main floor, which was pretty much just organized storage. The second floor was the heart of the house, clearly, just like hers. There were flowers in vases. Which she usually hated. These were roses—she preferred peonies—and they were still relatively fresh as they overflowed from vases all over the place.

She checked each of the six bedrooms on the second and third floor. They'd been readied with fresh linens and more fucking flowers. If she hadn't fixed the security system, every sound in the house would have been recorded she bet. Jerks.

Whatever the case, nothing looked overly suspicious and she wanted to get out so she could position herself closer to where the stupids would be when they came back.

She wanted to know who—and what—they were.

It was as she was rounding the stairs coming back to the first floor that she heard the security system beep off and the front doors opened up.

She edged back up and around the corner, listening to what was happening.

It was the stupids. The average criminal couldn't have managed to get in and these jokers weren't even good enough to be average. They'd been given that code, which meant someone at Hunter Corp. had given it to them.

Someone she worked with, knowing she was coming here, had given people the tools to hurt her. She narrowed her eyes as she added them to her to-do list.

Downstairs they made a call, saying she wasn't coming. Rowan nearly went down there to say hello before she knocked them both out. They moved around and made a lot of noise but made no move to come up the stairs.

Rolling her eyes, she figured she'd just go around, hop out through a window and meet up with Clive as he made his way to her. Amateurs.

Down the hall and out a window onto a decent-sized ledge. There should be plants out there, she thought. It would look better. The neighbors would be happier too.

It was just a matter of a careful climb down but once her feet touched the ground the gravity of her choice hit her, along with a nasty spell that knocked her on her ass.

Luckily, once she'd touched the ground, Brigid had taken over and the magic, though disgusting, seemed to slide off her skin after some more super-hot skin action.

Hurt like hell, but at least she wasn't suffering whatever that spell intended her to.

"You motherfucker." Rowan was back as she rolled out of the way, avoiding another strike of whatever the fuck it was coming from a sorcerer she was going to stomp the hell out of shortly.

All her supercharged blood helped her to open herself up to Brigid so they could work as a unit. It was as if she needed that extra boost to truly create that sort of magical link.

Whatever the case, even at first there was a slight disorientation as Rowan had to fit Her very precisely in her head.

That momentary bit of dizziness had been the break the Vampire who'd been lurking just at the corner of the house needed. He hit her hard, slamming her against the wall.

The air left her with a painful whoosh and he followed up with a punch to the kidneys.

The Goddess fully linked, Rowan gathered her strength and pushed back, kneeing him in the balls as she did.

He flew backward, arms windmilling, and hit the low stone wall at his back, tumbling into the street.

"Piece of shit." She turned her attention back to the sorcerer who'd been tossing magic her way. "Now. We were having a discussion about who you are and why you're attacking me."

He didn't respond, just kept his chanting. Rowan had to be smart and attack at a time when his attention was fully diverted, but not be close when he managed to complete whatever spell he was building.

The Vampire she'd knocked out came back and a few beats later the stupids came around the corner. They all started threatening and making violent gestures at the top of their lungs.

"Dear Goddess, stop yelling. You guys make so

much noise it's a wonder you didn't get caught before now. Well." Rowan jerked her chin at the two humans who'd been casing the house. "They couldn't. But you."

The Vampire charged and she ducked to the side, just missing when she aimed a hard kick at the side of his knee. It landed and knocked him back, but it just slowed him.

The humans came at her from the other side, babbling in Italian that sounded very much like they were from Rome.

She drew her sword and the sound made her laugh with delight. Power surged through her as she connected with the blessed blade forged just for her.

This too had gotten stronger after her attack and recovery.

"I don't like to kill humans, even stupid ones. But I will." Brigid seemed to purr the words but it was Rowan who smiled when they were done.

They cursed at her and she shrugged. One movement. She kissed the hilt and breathed in and out deeply, centering herself.

A flick of her wrist as she stepped to one side, one last movement of her arm and stupid one was dead.

The other human came at her from one side while the Vampire did from the other. Then the sorcerer broke his chant and Rowan had to choose which of those to ignore while she dealt with the biggest threat.

She took the hit from the Vampire as she dropped to her knees and rolled out of the way just as the spell formed and came at her.

Only momentarily deterred, the Vampire picked her up by the back of her shirt and punched her with the other fist and then brought her down hard as he brought his knee up and racked her like he was a professional wrestler.

Sweet mercy, that fucking hurt.

Rowan struggled to breathe through bright bursts of jagged pain as one of her ribs broke. But she didn't drop her blade. Instead she punched stupid two in the temple with her fist wrapped around the hilt. He dropped like a stone and she stumbled from the way as the Vampire came at her again.

Clive rocketed into the yard with a snarl she'd never heard him use. It was a sound of rage, pitched low. Too low for most humans to hear, which made it even scarier.

His eyes had gone amber, burning with violence as he hit the sorcerer from behind, knocking him into the ground so hard he lost consciousness.

Her breath was coming easier as her body was already beginning to knit her rib back together. That hurt, but in a different way. "Don't kill him or the Vampire. I need to know stuff."

CLIVE LOOKED HER over quickly, but carefully, as the other Vampire tried to flank them. Rowan knew Clive was just waiting to strike and it was gloriously ferocious when he did.

His gaze, as it was on her, had been concerned and possessive. Hot. But when the other Vamp got close enough, Clive's energy changed. His features went hard.

Rowan actually didn't see him move, that's how fast he went from facing her to holding the other Vampire by the throat, pressing him against the wall of the house.

"I'll get what we need." Clive's voice had changed as his teeth had elongated.

Rowan knew what he planned and if he was fine with it, she was too. The other Vampire though, he hadn't gotten it yet. He didn't know who Clive was, only that Clive was powerful.

"I'm not going to tell you or this whore anything." He spit blood, but Clive had reached up and slapped the Vamp's face to the side. Again so fast she didn't see the movement, only the result.

"I don't need you to. You put your hands on my wife. You hurt her. I won't tolerate that." Clive's voice had lost its cultured cream and carried razors and briars.

Right as Clive plunged into his brain, the other Vampire finally figured it out. It was too late for more than a brief expression of surprise before he went blank and limp.

"I have what we need," Clive said to Rowan, the tension humming from his muscles. He shifted all that scary attention back on the other Vamp. "I'm looking you in the face so I can watch you as I separate you from your life. Traitor."

The Vampire landed on the ground, a gaping hole in his chest where Clive had punched through his rib cage and taken his heart.

Okay then.

He turned to her as the body began to break down. "We should deal with this human and go. What do you want to do with the body of the other one and the… *bloody fucking hell.*"

Rowan turned to him and realized the spot the sorcerer had been in was empty.

"Deal with the human. Get what he knows. Leave the bodies here. I'm going after the sorcerer."

Clive's jaw may have actually clicked from clenching it so hard. "Let me handle this. It will take moments then *we* will go hunt the sorcerer. Or whoever else we're actually looking for."

Oh yeah, Enyo.

"They were sent by Pirate Polly?"

He sighed and didn't even bring the human back to consciousness before taking a little of his blood to create a link and then got what the guy knew all in about two minutes.

"We're leaving the bodies here? We can clean this."

Rowan looked at him. "Who ordered this attack on the house?"

"Let's get out of here. I don't want to talk outside."

"Do I need to send a message to those assholes in HC? Tell me that."

"Yes."

Rowan nodded. "All right. Leave them and let's go."

TWENTY-TWO

As they approached the church they'd been in earlier that night, Clive put an arm around her shoulders. "I told you not to go in there until I'd arrived."

She snorted, but didn't try to duck away. "It would have been fine eventually. I mean, I was taking them out one by one."

He growled and she laughed for a moment before stopping him, a hand on his chest as she came to face him. "Thank you for coming. I knew you were on the way. It helped."

He couldn't be angry with her. It was her job, after all. She had to work alone all the time, which he knew suited her. But he'd not been pleased to find her fending off three attackers at once.

"I will always come for you."

Her features went tender and he breathed in deep, taking in night, Venice, magic and death. And her. This woman who had changed everything. Who had allowed herself to belong to him as he most assuredly belonged to her.

People came up the other end of the street and they turned to let Recht and Alice catch up to them before going inside where the practitioners were already waiting.

"Here's what we know," Clive addressed everyone

who'd gathered in the church. "She's on Giudecca. She's in a private estate that can only be accessed by water. There's a sorcerer on the loose who knows we took a human and another Vampire who had information on where our target is resting."

Rowan cleaned her sword of blood and dirt and slid it back into the sheath and then spoke. "It's two hours until sunup. She'll either have left by now or she'll wait until sundown tomorrow and get out first thing, before we can get to her. I bet she's going to stay, thinking this is so close to sunrise we won't come for her. But she's wrong.

"I don't think the sorcerer who came at me is the only one around. There's every reason to think we'll have a magical assault as well as a physical one." Rowan thought about Carl's layer-cake talk. Donna and her fellow practitioners were part of the recipe and she'd need them to be successful.

Two other practitioners had joined the group and spoke quietly with Donna first and then to the group. "We want to be included in this plan."

"Before you say no, we can help, Rowan," Donna said. "We know it's dangerous. We know there are risks. We want to help and this is our city."

She was right. Rowan nodded. "Okay. But I'm in charge and if I tell you to do something you need to do it. Even if you don't agree with me."

But Rowan needn't have worried. They all nodded. She guessed having witnessed some of this shit already from the scene at the place Enyo had been staying first had been enough to impress on them the gravity and danger of this enemy.

David stood. "I've arranged several boats to take us."

"We won't need a boat," Warren said.

They could fly, but she hadn't planned to mention that in front of the practitioners she didn't know that well. Too late now.

Rowan gave Clive a look. "Don't move on that estate until we arrive."

Clive nodded before the Vampires took off. She and David headed after them in a sleek, modern boat that delivered them the short trip across the Giudecca Canal to the island of Giudecca. The practitioners had split between three boats and would station themselves around the estate as best they could. Out of reach, hopefully, but still effective.

"You didn't say anything about whether or not Hunter Corporation was behind any of these attacks," David said as they headed across.

"According to the investigator and what we found out from those we dealt with earlier today, Roth hired the sorcerers to watch me. We aren't sure if Hunter Corp. is behind trying to kill me or not. None of them seemed to have orders concerning you." Which meant it was very possible there were more out there meant to harm David and she didn't know where. *Yet.* They couldn't hide forever.

"What we do know is that the humans and the Vampire were together. One Eye sent them. So there's a leak, all right, and we know Roth has tried to harm me in the past so I can't see why it wouldn't be him. But the presence of the Vampire and the humans also casing the place complicates matters. Is Roth working with One Eye? Doubtful."

"The sorcerers are working for both and giving the Vampires information."

Nicely deduced. "I'm thinking that's a contender for what is actually going on. But there's more to find out first." After she killed Enyo of course. And then she'd also figure out who was the threat to David and handle that too. It was a giant game of Whac-A-Mole. It seemed like she had to bop some stupid mole over the head to keep it from trying to kill her or her protected all the fucking time these days.

Ah well, too late to decide to be a hairdresser or a gardener.

She cut the motor as they got close. Rowan wasn't sure of the exact place, but it was impossible to ignore the power, like a beacon, coming from up ahead.

The Vampires waited for them.

Rowan conferred with Donna and the practitioners once they'd dropped anchor and were out of sight. Clive explained that from what they could tell with their Vampire spidey sense an ancient was in the main building. There were four other Vampires of some power. How many others they couldn't tell but after a little surveillance they caught sight of three humans.

"They're with your target."

A simple, short sentence and it was all she needed. "We're going ahead as planned."

"*We'll be more effective if we're close. You have other problems to take care of. Let us do this,*" Donna had urged back on the dock before they'd headed to Giudecca.

No matter how much Rowan didn't want to say they could come along, she knew there was no other choice.

She nodded and made them promise to obey her and stay out of the fray with Vampires.

"We'll be all right. You go handle your business," Donna assured Rowan as they parted.

SHE AND CLIVE headed through a pretty back garden, unusual in these parts that it was so big.

A flare of heat on her skin again and Rowan shoved Clive down as the spell landed with a splat of disgusting stink where he'd been standing.

David headed the other way, landing with a thump, but was otherwise safe a few feet across the paved walk.

"Fucking sorcerers. I'm going to kill Roth twice for this," Rowan snarled.

Clive pulled them both over, out of sight and behind a substantial enough set of terra cotta pots that they'd have some protection from attack.

Rowan craned her neck to see David, who was eyeing another path to get up to the house. She shook her head at him, but he waved her off.

She started to head in his direction but Clive took her shoulder, leaning close. "You have to let David go whatever way he can make it into the house. Trust that you've trained him well."

A series of crashes and shouts indicated the practitioners had engaged the sorcerers.

Clive indicated that they move to the west, to avoid the back of the house where a magical skirmish took place. The other Vampires were approaching from different floors so they could attack from as many directions as possible.

Inside, shouts of warning were raised and the doors

to the main house facing Venice flew open as Vampires ran out and any time she'd had to haul David's ass back to them passed.

The battle had begun in earnest.

Rowan took one out, Clive the other and they made it inside. Enyo had to be there somewhere and she was going to find that bitch and kill her true dead.

"She'll be hiding somewhere, too cowardly to protect her people. And still they do her bidding like weaklings," Clive said loud enough Rowan was sure he was driving her out, or at the very least, underlining that lack of loyalty to anyone who might be in the vicinity.

CLIVE SUSPECTED ENYO would be up on the second floor. This wasn't a space made solely for Vampires. The curtains and window covers did not lock down. They were storm shutters, which would keep it dark enough, but not secure from breach.

He pointed up and Rowan nodded. She'd stopped favoring her non-injured side so he guessed she'd healed up enough that she wasn't in too much pain. He hoped.

Rowan would fight to the death and he wanted her as strong as possible.

She grabbed him before they got to the stairs. "You get the fuck out of here and into a safe place before daylight. Do you hear me?"

"I've got a few bolt holes in mind. Lots of abandoned places in these islands scattered all over the area if I can't make it back to the villa. Go. Don't get killed or I'll make you a Vampire."

"Fuck off. Neither of us is dying because you owe me dinner and gelato."

"What? Did you levy a tax on me? It was just gelato a few hours ago."

"The price you pay for keeping company with a mercurial woman."

"I love you, Rowan." He kissed her and she nipped his bottom lip as he broke away.

"I love you too. Now come on. If she gets away I'm going to kick you in the balls."

"So, back to normal then," he muttered as they crept up the servant's stairs accessible through the kitchen.

At the top the narrow stairwell led to a wide hallway with rooms on both sides. And at the very end they caught sight of Enyo heading around a corner. They followed, keeping some distance just in case there was a trap they couldn't see.

"She's mine," Rowan said as she cleared the corner and caught Enyo trying to get out through a window.

She turned and Rowan noted the eye patch and began to laugh. "Oh wow. This is even better than I'd imagined. Hey, what's shaking, Pirate Polly?"

"You dare?"

"Bitch, I dare you to infinity and back. And I will laugh and laugh that your pretty face is so disfigured now. I'd add 'for eternity' and make it sound all spooky but you don't have eternity. I'm going to go ahead and kill you right now. Never fear though, I'm going to do it extra hard. I wouldn't want to shortchange you the full painful, horrifying revenge-filled death you so richly deserve."

Enyo looked to the window again and Rowan reached back, wrapping her palm around her blade's hilt, and that's when She took over.

Brigid looked at the Vampire, at the blood-sucking

bitch who had killed Brigid's previous Vessel. A young woman who was far softer than the one who held Her essence now.

"So this is what a tick looks like on two legs." She put herself between the Vampire and her method of escape. The blade She held was balanced perfectly, its magic singing through Rowan and Brigid both.

Her Vessel's mate stood ready to jump in should she ask for help. The warrior in Her recognized the strength and loyalty it took to stand back and let the Vessel put herself in harm's way. But he did it because it was necessary.

He was more than adequate as a husband. Even if he was a Vampire.

Inside, Her Vessel let go of her control totally, giving over to Brigid. Either of them could kill her and avenge what needed avenging. But Rowan let Her do it to lay that ghost to rest.

"You can kill me but you won't stop what's already in motion."

Brigid stood very still, focusing, her concentration on the tiniest detail. There were four others in the house. The sorcerers were still outside, battling the others who accompanied Her Vessel.

A quick movement and the blade sliced through the air audibly. "I love that sound. Don't you? This Vessel's heart always beats faster when she hears it." She circled as Her prey did the same. "You made a grave error, pushing this one."

Brigid stepped close, cut three times and danced away as the scent of blood hit the air. She smiled at the thin bloody lines on Enyo's chest.

"Enyo. Oh, I've longed to form that sound but we

kept it in because we needed to get close enough to strike. You ran. But you can't run forever. I can because I'm a goddess. You? You're about to be dead."

The Vampire rushed her and Brigid laughed again at the moment she realized how much stronger and faster this Vessel was than the last time.

"You ambushed her in the dark when she had no weapon. You like to feel as if you are a superior being when you are a bag of meat and skin who has tainted her soul with the magics she's worked."

In the corner of her vision, Clive stood up straighter.

Enyo's smile turned into a sneer of disgust. "You're an old goddess no one cares about, Brigid. All those centuries ago, *that* one had far more power than this. More people believed in you. Now you're nothing more than an automaton who uses her body when she allows it."

Enyo feinted and managed to get two solid hits in. This body would be sore, but it was not crucial that Brigid stop at this point.

She cocked Her head, blinking without speaking until the Vampire began to squirm under the scrutiny. "Usually creatures who bear as much power as you have some sense of honor. You have none."

As She'd suspected, that prodded the Vampire into action. Brigid sliced her several more times, this time deeper. Arterial blood began to seep into the material of the frock Enyo wore. Dark, sticky, all of it running from her body just like her life would be.

"Blood from a killing wound always smells so much better I think."

Clive barked a laugh and Brigid appreciated that he'd found Her humorous. A warmth inside said Her

Vessel approved as well. This one had connected to Brigid in a way no others had for a very long time. Brigid would not let Her Vessel down. *This time* She would protect her.

"My Vessel would say something like, you're not so tough now, are you, bitch?" She got the words right, but Rowan had better delivery.

The stench of tainted blood began to fill the space. "I think perhaps you're realizing how slow those wounds this blade made are to heal. Distressing, is it not? To feel your life running from your veins? After so long being the one to bring this to others at your hands, aren't you fortunate to understand it from this perspective? My Vessel says it's a teaching moment."

"Your time has passed!" Enyo screamed, putting power behind her words, pelting Brigid with it as she followed with a series of swipes with her nails, her jaws snapping as she tried to bite.

"*My* time has not passed. Your time, however." Brigid made a face and then let Rowan take over the swordwork. She and the blade were bound, much like Brigid and Rowan were bound. They all worked together at that moment in a perfect rhythm.

Once that had happened, Brigid slipped back fully, grateful that Rowan had been willing to let her take this kill to honor the Vessel she'd lost. But in the end She hadn't needed it the way She felt She had for so long.

It was obvious to Her then that Rowan needed to do this. Needed to fully open herself up to her power and truly stretch the limits of her skill and succeed. She was capable of so much more than what she'd been doing and it was integral that she understand it.

Rowan felt the tide of Her power recede enough that

Rowan was fully in charge again. "It's nifty when She does that," Rowan said as she flowed into the movements, blocking Enyo's attacks.

"Hunter, welcome back," Clive called from her left.

"Scion."

"You must know this is bigger than me and you, you silly girl," Enyo taunted.

Rowan took that anger and channeled it and she moved just a little bit faster, nearly avoiding the attack entirely. Rather than tumbling to the ground with an ancient Vampire on her chest, she just got tossed to the side. Unfortunately it was in the path of the footboard of the bed. Which she hit at a high rate of speed with a great deal of force. Against the rib that had only healed from being broken a few hours ago and nearly broke again.

It hurt so bad a wave of nausea flooded her and then receded soon after as she righted herself, grinning at Enyo.

"Either I'm faster, or you're slower because of your unfortunate work-related accident." Rowan motioned at Enyo's ruined eye. "I really outdid myself with that. Do you know how much easier it is when I can say, *hey have you seen a really old Vampire with bad taste and one eye?* They know who you are right away. I need to start doing that with all of you. Just mark you so I can locate you when you act up."

Rowan sliced deeper and the blade sizzled as it cut through Enyo. "Bag of meat indeed." Then she laughed. "Isn't that what you've been wetting your pants over? That the big bad Hunter Corp. was going to put cameras in every nest and document your every move?"

"Your precious Hunter Corporation who hired sorcerers to *watch* you. Don't mistake your obedience to them as anything of value to you."

Some of the other wounds were healing up so Rowan opened new ones. The more Enyo bled, the worse she stank.

"Your blood smells like rotting garbage." Rowan wrinkled her nose.

"It's rot. The first cuts were shallow. Now that you're deeper and she's healing and having to generate that power, the depth of infection from the magics she's been using is irreversible." Warren spoke from the doorway at her back.

When the heck had he arrived? She didn't have the time to think about that. The moment was right to push Enyo and see what they could find out before Rowan executed her.

"I know Roth was having me watched. And I know those sorcerers were giving you the information they gave him. But I wonder if they gave you everything or if they're playing you the way they're playing Roth?" This was what her biggest question was now. Were the sorcerers in league with one of the sides or only with themselves?

"It doesn't matter." Enyo was going to die and she'd accepted it but the hate still shone from her eyes. She wasn't going to tell them anything willingly, the petty, stingy bitch.

Enyo's smile was edged with malice as she continued. "You'll be flooded with problems. The chaos of it will be beautiful. Humans, Vampires, magic wielders of all types, at one anothers' throats, bickering, confused. Humans do get so violent and irrational when they're confused and afraid. It will weight you, Rowan Summerwaite. Like an anchor around your neck and you will drown in it. You'll be nothing but bones. In the end, that's all we are."

"You won't even be that."

Clive spoke up, "Wait. Let me see what I can get from her."

It had been her impulse to ask him to delve into her head and take her memories, but the way Enyo's blood smelled was freaking Rowan out. It was an infection of sorts and the last thing she was going to allow was Clive taking that sort of risk of exposure.

"Warren, will whatever she's become after all that magic infect Clive or otherwise endanger him?" Rowan called out as she kept her eyes on Enyo.

From the doorway at her back Warren answered, "I don't know. She's very old. She's been practicing the darkest of magics for most of that time."

That's what she thought. Anger, vengeance, seemed to boil over and pity tempered things once again. Not that she wasn't going to kill that one-eyed twat, but deep inside the Vampire had such a gaping hole of need to feel special and important. That drove her and that was just sad. Regardless of who it was.

Rowan brought the hilt of the blade to her lips as she murmured a blessing and then as Enyo opened her mouth to argue, she spun, striking out with her blade, through Enyo's chest and then up.

The stench of putrid blood and terrifying nightmares oozed from Enyo, bubbling over the blade and onto the beautiful rug at their feet. She slowly turned to dust around the sword and Rowan leaned in close and whispered, "Die well, Vampire. I hope death brings the peace you could not find in life."

TWENTY-THREE

WHEN VAMPIRE WARRIORS dueled and one was killed in battle, the other said those words as the dying warrior turned to dust. It was a time-honored way to wish your adversary the ease of death.

Clive had seen Rowan give that blessing before, even when she hadn't liked the Vampire she'd had to execute. He wondered if it wasn't her way of letting go of the guilt and accepting it was necessary. Though he also believed she bore the weight of those deaths anyway.

It was a mercy to have done it. Even for just the last moments of Enyo's life it would have been. And his esteem for Rowan only rose.

Clive pushed away from the wall and moved closer. Strolling so it looked casual to those gathered in the doorway behind them.

She allowed her gaze to lock with this for a few moments before she hardened up, her body language broadcasting loud and clear that she needed her space.

This ending had been coming a long while but it took its toll on her. Clive wanted so badly to sweep her away. Once he had her alone, he could take care of her.

But she had to soldier on and he knew she wouldn't give in to any of her deeper feelings about the fight and the entire hunt until she was finished with all her investigatory work.

He'd let her keep her armor on until he had given her a safe place to let go. And then he'd let her pick a fight and then fuck her. After that he'd bathe her and feed her before tucking her into bed and making her rest.

They hadn't been able to talk in detail about her situation with Hunter Corp. But he knew her. And he knew she was hurt. Worse, she felt she'd been betrayed and he wasn't so sure how she would deal with that. He'd support whatever she wanted to do, but if one of the options was separating herself from Hunter Corp. he'd love to throw his lot in with that option.

"Boom. Next item on my to-do list is that you and the others need to go. You have the time to get back and into bed before the sun rises but it needs to be now."

"I—"

She shook her head. "Don't waste time. Just do it. I'll see you when you wake up. We need to be here, need to talk to witnesses."

"I can be far more effective with witnesses than you can."

"You can't steal a sorcerer's memories. Not without exposing yourself to their rot. That's what Warren thinks. Go back to the villa. I'll come to you when I can." She pushed him toward the door. "Thank you."

Before he could say anything back and make her appear—as she liked to call it—dumb, she squeezed his hand one last time and turned to face the group now gathered in the hall.

"Where are the sorcerers? I trust we left some of them alive?" Her voice was sharp, taut, and people began to snap to attention.

Clive didn't want to go, but the sun hinted at the farthest edge of the sky. With one last look, he and the others left to rush back to safety.

After his quick shower he just fell onto the mattress, pulled her side of the duvet back so it would be ready for her and let himself sleep.

"WE HAVE ONE sorcerer alive. He's in a sort of magical stasis. It won't last forever so you need to speak to him," Donna said.

"And then what?" This was her witness; she wanted to know what the hell they thought was going to happen.

"And then we will handle our problem here in Venice," Donna replied. "We have a Vampire too but we're going to have to work fast or wait until sundown."

Rowan wiped her hands the best she could on a wet cloth David handed her. "Let's go see this Vampire and I'll make my decision after that."

"He's in the light tight room down the hall," Donna said.

Rowan hadn't argued with her about the sorcerer. She wasn't so sure she would. First though, she had to see the Vampire.

When she walked into the room a few doors down from where she'd just finally separated that cow from her life, she made a nearly comical halt when she saw who was inside.

With a muttered curse, Rowan rushed back out and dialed Nadir. The Five wouldn't go down to rest until the sun was up completely. They'd be sure Theo was going to stay in place first. But she was cutting it really close.

While she waited, Rowan asked Donna, "Who took this one prisoner? Did another Vampire see him?"

Donna pointed at the other guy she'd met earlier.

He came forward and spoke, "I knocked the Vampire out. First I dropped a rock on his head from a balcony and then I hit him with a spell. We brought him inside a few minutes ago. I don't know if any of the Vampires you were with saw him. I don't think so. We were in separate places. This Vamp was with the sorcerers. Protection while they were working."

"Are you going to tell us who this is?" Donna asked.

Rowan shrugged. "I will if you tell me what the hell kind of magic they were doing."

Donna nodded after thinking it over a bit.

"All right. This is one of the guards from the Keep. He serves The First. As had his family for generations. I need to—"

Nadir answered and Rowan turned her attention there. "You have a problem. Giancarlo is working with the Blood Front." She gave a quick rundown. "I have about five minutes before he loses consciousness so I need to go."

"I will deal with that immediately. Keep me updated." Nadir disconnected.

Rowan went back into the room where the Vampire was being held. She shook her head as she took in a face quite familiar to her. "By now you've probably guessed I'm not going to kill you. Yet anyway. You're going to be unconscious shortly and you'll be my prisoner. Before that I'd like you to know I am really beyond sick of this whole situation with you and this dime store knockoff of an idea J.K. Rowling did like a billion times better. So, you better wake up eager to enlighten me. You'll tell me either way. It's really up to you how the script goes. I'm quite vexed that someone who has held such a position of trust and honor would choose to use it in this way."

She stood, moving to David. "Make sure this room is light tight and then strap him to the bed with that rope in your pack. It's got silver just under a fine surface dusting that protects unless the Vampire struggles and wears it away." This she made sure to say loud enough for Giancarlo to hear. She wanted him alive and he seemed willing to stay that way.

What happened after she found what she needed to know was another story.

Donna then took Rowan to the main salon where they'd been keeping the sorcerer in magical stasis. Whatever that meant.

Before they went inside though, Rowan halted the practitioners she was with.

"You said you were going to tell me about what kind of magic fuckery Enyo and her little gang of castaways were up to?"

Donna came over. "There are, as you know, many ways to access magical power. There are methods I find ridiculous, some I find disgusting, even reprehensible. But we have a few things we simply don't do. Not any of us."

"And so one of those things is what Enyo did, which is why you all got together and kicked these sorcerers' asses."

Donna nodded. "I ask that you keep what I'm going to tell you from as many people as possible. We know you might have to share this information, but please be careful with it."

Rowan nodded, indicating she agreed.

"Do you know what a shade is?"

A chill worked over the surface of her skin. Brigid stirred in the pit of her belly. "Basically. It's sort of like a ghost."

"It's what happens when a soul is torn away from a living being. The body will die a short while later, but there's no *transition* for that being. A shade is a restless, voracious ghost, empty, searching, in pain and misery. It is the worst sort of dishonor to create such creatures."

Rowan blew out a long breath. "So, she's making them to get power? Or to use in her bidding? What?"

"The kind of power a practitioner would gain from such an act would be tremendous. All that life force would have made Enyo and her group strong. Or the sorcerers strong. She can't command a shade. No one can. They're not sentient that way. Just suffering."

"Is this an Enyo deal, or a sorcerer deal? Can you tell? It's a problem either way, but the source affects how I'll go about correcting it." Though she hoped it was the former, Rowan had been around the block enough times to know it rarely worked out that way.

"That I don't know. It's not like this type of magic is performed even rarely. It's not done! The knowledge of how to do these workings isn't readily available. When we combed through the other villa we came across things I'd never even seen before. We had to consult with some elders to get more information."

"I imagine if you were a super-old Vampire you probably had the connections. All sorts of weird stuff happened every day when Enyo was young so perhaps it was easier back in her day to get in on the ground floor and she's been doing it over the centuries maybe?"

"Given the state of her when you killed her she'd been working with and around that magic for a very long time so that's likely."

Rowan stretched a bit, popping her shoulder and cracking her neck, feeling better immediately. "Well, seems like the only way we can know is to talk to this joker and see what he's going to share. So what's the protocol? How does this work?"

TURNS OUT MAGICAL stasis was pretty much like a medically induced coma. When they went into the room, the sorcerer was lying on a table, strapped down. Several very large men watched on warily.

One of the practitioners slowly brought the prisoner to consciousness and Rowan sat across from where he'd been restrained.

"I'm not going to waste time pretending to be your friend." Rowan shrugged. "I'm not. You know it. So, you can talk to me, or not. But I'm going to recommend the telling me option. The other one is a lot more painful and I'll still get the information I need."

His features remained impassive.

"It's cool, you'd be surprised at how many people manage to continue to be brave at this point in the discussion. Bear with me. I'm going to start with what I know. Share information, so to speak. I know someone at Hunter Corp. engaged your services to watch me. But you little fuckers have been doing a lot more than watching. I don't know about you, but repeatedly being attacked and nearly killed makes me cranky." Rowan growled his way and he flinched, which cheered her.

She sat back a little, taking his measure. "Sorry, got sidetracked. Like I said, I know about the connection to Hunter Corp. But I also know you're working both sides of the fence."

He might have had some admirable physical control at keeping his facial features pretty blank, but his eyes told Rowan more than his face would have anyway. He was a liar-liar-pants-on-fire.

"Now, what I'm wondering is what shape your problem is." She cocked her head.

He didn't know where she was going but there was the dawn of some genuine fear in his gaze.

At least he was smart on some level.

"I'm now going to ask you questions. You're then going to answer them. I have all day before the Vampires will awaken. No one is coming for you for fifteen hours or so. At the earliest. Lest you think your compatriots will make some heroic attempt to free you, they won't. You're the only one left alive."

Rowan stood, looking to the practitioners in the room. "If you're squeamish I suggest you get out now because he's going to make me prove just how serious I am before he starts talking."

A few left, taking up positions in the hall, at the ready if she called, but out of sight.

The dude stayed, as did the two who'd already been in the room. Donna shifted to see better, but kept her distance.

Rowan shut the door and removed the jacket she'd been wearing, draping it over the back of a nearby chair. She left her blade at her back as she circled the table and came to a halt at his feet. She wanted him to have to strain to see her. Wanted him to know how helpless he was. And she wanted him to believe she would hurt him for hours and hours and hours if she had to.

Mostly the ones like this sorcerer made her give them an example.

She let her hair down and then rebraided it, keeping it tight against her head and neck, tucking the end into her shirt.

"That's better. Have you seen *Pulp Fiction?* What's your name, by the way?"

He remained silent so she shrugged. "Okay, I'm going to call you Ernesto. You look like you could be an Ernesto. Have you seen the movie?" When he didn't respond she continued. "You really should. Anyway, there's this part where Samuel L. Jackson is getting ready to kill someone and he's got this great bible verse he says to be spooky. While I've done that a few times to see how it fit, I ended up with a basic script. A disclaimer, if you will.

"I know you're thinking that you can take whatever I'm going to do to you. And you think that because you have no idea what I'm going to do to you. None of you ever do. I warn you every time and most of you make the wrong choice. But I'm giving it to you anyway, because that's how I roll. This is fate and choice and chance and all that big cosmic stuff. Make your choice knowingly."

Just as she thought, he said nothing.

She didn't bother with something in the low end of the pain spectrum. The lesson had to be swift, furious and resolute. Most of them learned after that.

She buried the small knife she kept in her boot in his side, narrowly missing anything vital. Close enough to be very painful. She pulled it out as she chopped him in the throat with the edge of her hand.

He cried out and then choked, shuddering from the impact. Rowan got close enough to nearly touch his nose and dug the knife back into the wound. "Do we understand one another now?"

He screamed and then started nodding furiously as tears streamed from his eyes.

David handed her a warm, wet hand towel and took the knife, cleaning it as she got rid of the worst of the blood off her hands and wrists.

"If you can behave yourself and not try any magical bullshit, I'll let someone staunch that wound. Otherwise you'll probably stop bleeding soon. Probably. Or you'll bleed out and die. Either way you're going to be feeling pretty faint once the adrenaline wears off from this round of questioning."

"You're crazy!"

Rowan shook her head. "No, I'm *determined.* Now that you understand just how determined I am you need to start answering my questions. Playtime is over. I have stuff to do."

"I won't use magic."

Which wasn't that much of a promise, but it was enough for the moment. Rowan nodded at Donna, who took the other towels David had provided and used one to press down on Ernesto's side to halt the flow of blood.

"She can use her magic to help block the pain," the prisoner said.

Rowan shrugged. "She could. But she's not going to. You're in the hole when it comes to your credit with me. Do you understand that saying?"

He nodded, pale but a little calmer.

"Who from Hunter Corp. hired you? Feel free to add details you know I'm going to ask you. If you make me work too hard for this I'm going to conclude you need some more lessons. I have more than one knife with me."

"I don't know his name. He got in touch with some others who refused to do what he wanted, but they gave him my information."

Rowan waited, looking at him expectantly. When it was clear he was still going to make her work for it, she stabbed him near his shoulder joint. Slicing through tendons.

He howled in pain and then went very white. Rowan wiped the blade on his shirt and stepped back.

"We didn't always talk to the same guy. It was two different men and one woman. At first they wanted us to watch you. We couldn't get to you inside the Keep. But when you left for Las Vegas and then when you headed off to Prague someone would contact us to let us know where you were headed."

"First they wanted you to watch me and then?"

"She had to leave Prague. We knew where you were. In the house belonging to the Nation. Can I have some water? Something for the pain?"

"I find pain is a really good motivator. You have to get along to go along, Ernesto. Keep talking. You knew where we were in Prague how?"

"The Blood Front had someone in place at the Keep. He's been giving us information for several years. He showed up a few days ago. Said he'd left the Keep for good. Had some stuff with him. She was pretty excited about that. Then the orders from the people from

Hunter Corp. changed. We were supposed to take you from the villa here in Venice. Kill everyone else. The shutters were rigged to open at full day and flood the room with light."

And totally violating the Treaty because Hunter Corp. had given them safe harbor and it had been violated. That, so close to the attack on Rowan that had been a violation of the same kind, only from the Vampires and Theo's shaky constitution and things would descend into full-on war soon enough.

TWENTY-FOUR

ROWAN WAS ALREADY up when Clive surfaced at sundown. But she hadn't gone far. He found her sitting in the adjoining room, wearing the robe he'd given her, a phone pressed to her ear, her fingers flying over the keys of the laptop at the desk.

He paused to kiss the top of her head then checked his voicemail and in with his human secretary back in Las Vegas. And what he heard had him waiting not so very patiently for her to end that call.

"The Lacoste family has a smaller offshoot, the Berns. The Berns have been in service to The First for four generations. One of them, Giancarlo, was a house guard at the Keep. I often trained with him when I was young. His cousin is on Theo's staff. His mother was actually born at the Keep, as was his grandfather. He's been giving the Blood Front information for the last four years. It may have gone on longer, but that's what we've been able to verify for sure so far," Rowan said as soon as she hung up.

Clive knelt in front of her, taking her hands, kissing her fingertips. "Is your father all right?"

Rowan nodded and told him the story of how she'd walked into that room and recognized Giancarlo immediately. "I called right before sunrise and caught Nadir. The human staff took everyone Giancarlo is related to into custody and they'll be questioned shortly. I spoke with Nadir's human chief of staff earlier. I expect she'll check in with me in a few hours depending on what she's learned."

She closed her laptop and rose. "We're going to need a meal for the telling of the rest of this."

He stopped her, needing some private words. She looked tired and sad. The tired was one thing, but the sad broke his heart. "Last night you did what you needed to do. And you were remarkable. I have no doubt that you've spent all day out at that estate, ordering people around, gathering information. When did you come to bed?"

"I got three hours' sleep. That's not bad. I need less sleep now. When this is over—" She halted mid sentence. "I used to say that and think I meant after I'd killed Enyo but now that I've killed her it's still not over."

"No it isn't. But we're all better off with her gone."

"Come on. I'm starved and I need coffee. I heard David out on the landing about ten minutes ago so he'll have left us some."

Relief settled in. He'd thought she meant to go downstairs and be with everyone. He wanted her to himself for a while longer. Wanted to talk with her privately about all that'd happened.

He opened the door and indeed, David had left a tray with a carafe of coffee and one of citrus juice of some type. Under a dome there were several sandwiches and Rowan wasted no time making herself a plate and going back into the bedroom with it and her cup of coffee.

"You knew I eat in bed before you bound yourself to me. Too late to cry now," she called over her shoulder.

"You have other qualities to make up for it."

"You're talking about my ass, huh? That's better," she said with a happy sigh after her first drink of coffee. He settled in bed with her, both on top of the duvet with food between them.

"Before you fill me in on what you found out today, I wanted to talk about this entire mess with Hunter Corporation and the recent developments with Roth."

She sighed hard, taking a few bites of her sandwich while he had some melon.

Clive knew she'd found shelter in Hunter Corporation when she'd run from the Keep when she'd been sixteen. They trained her and she'd bonded with them in a way he was quite certain she had no idea she had.

"Roth betrayed you. He betrayed the Hunter Corp. He betrayed the oath he took to uphold the Treaty. That's untenable and it won't continue. He tried to harm David, also untenable. The move to table this issue while you're out in the field risking yourself on their behalf—again—that's different. That's betrayal on a wholly different level."

Her breath had gone shaky for a moment. He took her hand, running the pad of his thumb over her ring. "You understand my fealty to your father. To the Vampire Nation and my people. You have your own loyalties and allegiances. Despite all that, you and I belong to one another. I wish to be your safe harbor. It hurts to see you so devastated over this."

She frowned, her brows knitted. "If you know I'm devastated why are you making me talk about it?"

"You don't always have to be strong. You don't always have to pretend you're impervious to getting your feelings hurt."

"It hit me as I was getting ready to kill Enyo just how much pain and near deathing I've been dealing with and how it could have been avoided, at least most of it, if Hunter Corp. had truly had my back. I have been loyal to them from the moment they opened their door to me in Paris all those years ago. I lost count of how many bones have been broken. How many times I've been bruised and battered to do my job. And I accepted that because it was part of the deal." She held her coffee cup close enough to breathe in the steam to comfort herself.

He got a little closer, close enough to brush his thigh against hers.

"I never could have imagined this. Not then. Not even before the Joint Tribunal. It's just sad because I'm going to London when I'm done mopping up the mess here and I'm going to throw down with these assholes once and for all. And I don't know if I'm staying either way."

"Because you shouldn't have to go to London. They should stand up for you as you deserve."

She rolled her eyes, but he was right.

"You'd leave Hunter Corp. then? And go out on your own?"

"I just know that Hunter Corp. made me feel like *nothing*. Like my life wasn't worth it to make someone else on the staff uncomfortable. 'Oh that Rowan, she'll make due. We'll just ask her to not force us to face this horrible problem at her expense. She always does that.'"

He kissed her shoulder.

"I sound like such a petty whiner. Ugh."

"Darling, you're not a whiner. You can be petty, I won't lie to you about that. But you're not being petty with this situation in any way. That you're still here despite this situation speaks volumes about you."

She harrumphed.

"Being on my own would work. I don't much like taking orders or having to run my activities by other people. I have training. I have the contacts. I might lose my staff like Carey and David, who are both paid by Hunter Corp. That would be…they'll have to make that choice. But this is all just talk until I get there so I can look them in the face when I present all my evidence."

Clive just wondered if anything Hunter Corp. could do or say would make this enough for her to stay. "I'm just waiting for you to realize they need you a lot more than you need them. And I doubt very much that Carey or David would leave your employ. You have the resources to pay them yourself."

She polished off one of the sandwiches, not saying more about it for another five minutes or so. "I need to brief the Vampires on everything we've learned today." One corner of her mouth tipped up as she put her plate and empty coffee cup on her bedside table. "I need to shower first. You should come with me."

"Are you trying to avoid the discussion?"

She got up and let the robe drop to her elbows as she stood at the doorway to the bath. She gave him a look back over her shoulder. "I'm quite capable of telling you I'm done with a topic. I just wanted you inside me before we then have to spend time dealing with more politics, betrayal, death threats and other assorted bullshit." She let the robe drop, bent to pick it up but he was there, handing it to her, ushering her inside.

It took a bit but by the time he'd gotten undressed and she'd retrieved towels and made sure they had toiletries, the water was hot.

"I'm not sure if you noticed, but the water tank here is very large."

"The reasons I love you are myriad."

She ducked her head under the water and he joined her, the heat of the spray loosening his muscles. "The first time I had you was in the shower."

She put shampoo in her palm and slid up the front of his body to massage it into his hair. He closed his eyes as his soap-slick palms gripped her ass and held her close.

"I remember. You were so mad that you wanted to fuck me. Which made you even more irresistible. I'm a terrible person."

He laughed, getting close enough to kiss her. "It is uniquely Rowan to get aroused when I'm annoyed. I was mad because I knew once I gave in and tasted you everything would change." He switched so that he massaged her scalp, her head tipped back, exposing her neck to him.

She smiled, her eyes closed. "And did it?"

"Indeed. To coin one of your phrases, you rocked my world. You continue to do so every day. My greatest challenge and my finest possession."

THE WARMTH HIS words left behind seemed to soak into her skin as his fingertips dug into her scalp. He stood so close he blocked out the lights in the ceiling behind him.

Avarice was sensual to Vampires. They surrounded themselves with beautiful things, beautiful people, lived in beautiful places. Their clothing tended to be of incredibly high quality. A delight to wear against the skin.

Rowan hadn't fooled herself into believing part of her appeal wasn't related to that. She was unusual. In Vampire terms, she was desirable. Vicious. Powerful. Connected to the most influential being in their world.

But it was more. In Clive's tone she heard pride. Tenderness. Concern. That possessiveness was acceptable. It neither harnessed nor silenced. Rather it was nice to belong to him. In the very real way he belonged to her.

He backed her to the tile, the water hitting them from both showerheads. He poured soap into his palms and then drizzled it over her breasts and belly.

"Oops, I suppose I shouldn't waste that," he murmured and began to lather her up.

She hummed her delight. "My nipples must be really dirty."

"My thoughts about them are."

He made her laugh and then that laugh strangled into a moan as he tugged and rolled her nipples between his thumb and forefingers. She gasped, disappointed when he let go. Until he repositioned his hands at her waist and lifted her, rinsing her off and then licking to make sure she was extra clean. He kept her pinned here, his mouth on her breasts and her legs wrapped around his torso, hands on his shoulders as she writhed.

He let her slide down the wall, his cock entering her as he thrust up. She hadn't expected it to happen so fast but she was coming hard around him as he snarled a curse but kept his pace slow.

"Warn a girl next time," Rowan gasped, licking up his neck as he continued those long, delicious strokes up into her body.

"I fail to see the fun in that," he said, nuzzling her neck, drawing his incisors down her veins, driving them both to distraction.

She laughed, moaning when he changed her angle so the stream from one of the showerheads hit her pelvic bone. A few adjustments and her moan deepened when he got it directly on her clit.

He was so good at that stuff.

She slid her fingers into his hair, pulling to get purchase as she met his thrusts. Her inner muscles tightened as another climax began to build.

"You first, darling."

"I already did."

"You're aware you're arguing with me about coming. Just be quiet and have an orgasm, Rowan."

Fine, then.

She concentrated and let it happen, the pleasure building at her toes, slowly taking over until she nearly shouted his name when she came. He wasn't too far behind her, groaning as he slammed hard and deep.

"I'm going to remind you this is what you have to look forward to if we live together."

"Rousing fucks in the evening or constant danger?"

He laughed, turning off the water.

"Both, I have a feeling." He kissed her again, pleased with himself.

"There's no way I'm living at *Die Mitte.*" The pretentious opulence of that entire Vampire Nation owned hotel casino would drive her to something drastic before the end of the first week there.

He got out, handing her a towel before getting himself one.

"I won't always be in Las Vegas. The capital city the Scion of North America holds court in rotates every five years. In any case, we don't have to live at the hotel. I suppose your penthouse is fine."

She toweled her hair dry, got dressed and then braided it back. "If I leave Hunter Corp. I'll have to give the penthouse back. And I don't know if I trust them enough to keep living there even if I did stay. Though, as I say that, I feel like that's the answer to the should I stay at all question."

TWENTY-FIVE

EVERYONE ELSE WAITED for them in the salon. "About time," Warren grumbled.

"We were having sex. It takes time to do that right." Rowan sat. "Let me tell you all about the day I had." She explained to the Vampires about Giancarlo and how he'd been hooking the Blood Front Vampires up with lodging in Vampire Nation properties worldwide.

"Nadir tells me the human staff was able to halt outside access to many accounts but it's hard to know just how much he had the chance to get into." Over the coming months they'd need to go through all their properties to see if things had been taken. Look through all finances and the like. "I brought the things from his room at the estate so you can look through it. We should get over there so you can talk to him, Recht."

"As soon as you tell us what the sorcerer said."

"He was reticent to share at first. But we came to an understanding. Enyo made one of their number into a Vampire about thirty years ago. He was taught the soul stealing stuff by Enyo personally as he was growing up but until recently they only did it once a year. She travels around with three or four of them and about a year ago, the frequency of their working increased and sorcerers he'd never seen before started showing up. She was working with other people he never met. And I believe that."

"Do you think it's Roth?"

"I don't know. Maybe. But I don't think so. He wants to destroy all Vampires. I can't see him working with them. There's something more than stealing souls to keep young or whatever going on here. This isn't about Enyo and Theo. The addition of magic into this particular situation is most distressing. Carey has been working on some of the computer data we found on various flash drives. Plans for buildings. Financial data though we don't know for who."

"Curious," Warren said.

She told them the rest of what she'd learned before Recht and Warren headed to Giudecca to question Giancarlo, leaving her alone with Clive, David and Alice.

"I sent Carey pictures of the men who were waiting for me at the Hunter Corp. villa last night, along with shots of the sorcerer. One of the humans was a contract killer. One of the Vampire crime families has used him in the past, though goddess knows why. These guys were so inept.

"He ran their pictures, along with some of Roth and Hilary through his facial recognition stuff and there's nothing we found with them together. However, my source found some financial transactions that match up with the payments that were made to the humans and sorcerers to take me out. And I found a picture of David on the phone of one of the guys we killed at the estate yesterday."

David's face hardened for a moment. "We're going

to London when we're done here? They want you to present evidence, we'll present it."

"Yes that's what they want. And I will give them all the evidence. Because Roth and his friends are going down. But after that I don't know."

"Whatever we decide—"

Rowan interrupted David. "We?"

David's resolve firmed up and he stood taller. "Yes. We. I'm your valet. Where you go, I go."

"Even if it's out of Hunter Corp.?"

"Yes. Do you think I want to be in a place that put so little weight on my life and safety? On your life and safety? I serve you, Rowan. Not Hunter Corp."

Panicked but strangely satisfied, Rowan stood, pretending she had something she needed to brush off the front of her pants. "Ugh. Let's go already. I am all done with this sharing my feelings stuff and we have prisoners to interrogate. David, when you get the chance, please make travel arrangements to London. I won't be staying at the usual hotel, but don't tell them that. Then get us a flat or a house and arrange for a car. We have a lot more things on the list to finish up."

"I have a home in London," Clive said to David. "Get with Alice to make those arrangements. I'll be coming too."

"You have a continent to run, Clive," Rowan said as people began to mill around and get working. "I'll come back to Vegas when I'm finished in London. Though I'm staying at your flat. Mayfair?"

"Our townhouse. Belgravia. Would you like me to buy you a flat in Mayfair?"

He totally would because he was that way.

"I'm sure Belgravia will suit me just fine."

"Excellent. I quite like the neighborhood. I'll show you around while we're there. Don't argue with me, Rowan. I may not be staying the whole time depending on how ridiculous this situation is with Hunter Corp. But I will be accompanying you. I want you to meet my family, I want you to be in our townhouse." He stepped closer and she allowed it, even smiling up at him briefly before she remembered to frown.

He grinned then.

"Let me show you the London I love. I want to be there with my wife. My mate."

"Ooh, you're so good at this. I don't stand a chance, do I?"

He laughed, grabbing that bit of joy she gave him with both hands. "I'm not sure which one of us stands a chance, but I think perhaps, it's both."

She hugged him for a brief moment. "That works. Get cracking, Scion. We have stuff to do."

"I do adore you." He kissed her nose and she narrowed her eyes at him but didn't try to punch anything so he stepped neatly away and got to it before she changed her mind. What a truly lucky Vampire he was.

* * * * *

For more information on Lauren Dane's upcoming releases from Carina Press and Harlequin HQN, including the next Rowan book and a new paranormal romance series starting in late 2015, please visit www.LaurenDane.com.

ABOUT THE AUTHOR

THE STORY GOES like this: While on pregnancy bed rest, Lauren Dane had plenty of down time so her husband took her comments about "giving that writing thing a serious go" to heart and brought home a secondhand laptop. She wrote her first book on it before it gave up the ghost. Even better, she sold that book and never looked back.

Today Lauren is a *New York Times* and *USA TODAY* bestselling author of over fifty novels and novellas across several genres. Though she no longer has to deal with Polly Pocket and getting those tiny outfits on and off, you may catch her in a nostalgic moment when the house is silent because the kids are all in school and she can get work done. Just a moment though.

Visit Lauren on the web at www.laurendane.com
E-mail: laurendane@laurendane.com
Twitter: @laurendane
Blog: laurendane.com/blog
You can write to her at: PO Box 45175, Seattle, WA 98145